THEIR HEALING HEARTS

CARDINAL CREEK
BOOK THREE

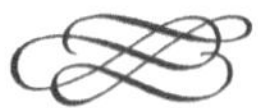

ANGIE COLE

Content Warning

This novel contains themes of domestic violence and emotional abuse. While these elements are not depicted gratuitously, they are central to the protagonist's past and her journey toward healing. Some scenes reference manipulation, control, and psychological trauma within a marriage.

Reader discretion is advised.

If you or someone you know is experiencing abuse, confidential support is available through the National Domestic Violence Hotline (U.S.) at 1-800-799-SAFE (7233) or thehotline.org.

*For those who had to start over
and needed a place to heal.*

CHAPTER 1

Deborah's foot settled on the brake pedal with a soft hiss. The farmhouse waited at the end of the drive, its white clapboard faded to the color of old bone, paint hanging like a peeling sunburn. From here, it looked like it held more memory than she was ready to face. It hadn't budged in seventy years, a stark contrast to changes she had endured.

Two years ago, she left her abusive husband, Chad, but the divorce wasn't finalized until six months ago. She couldn't have imagined this moment. Yet here she was, her heart pounding as she shifted the car into park. Tucking her phone into her pocket, she gripped the cold brass key, its uneven teeth nicking her thumb—a stark reminder that this was real and that it was her chance for a new beginning.

It would take permits, money, labor, and faith. But perhaps this time, she could muster at least two of those.

By June, the Texas Hill Country heat pressed down, wrapping itself around everything it touched. It settled on her arms and face. Warmth rose from the sunbaked earth. Even the breeze was thick, burdened by the relentless sun. Cicadas droned in the oak tree. The yard lay baked to a golden crisp, except for a stubborn patch of green that clung to the shade beneath the oak tree near the porch.

Deborah exhaled, palms flat against the steering wheel longer than necessary before stepping out. The heat settled heavily on her shoulders. Sixty wasn't old; she was too young to quit. Yet Chad's voice whispered in her mind: *Too late to start over.* The car door slammed behind her, sealing her decision. *There was no going back now.*

Gravel crunched under her shoes as she approached the steps. The porch groaned beneath her weight, but she didn't retreat. Strips of curled paint clung to the door. She turned the key in the lock. It resisted before snapping open. The door exhaled stale heat and the faint sweetness of forgotten flowers. She stepped inside.

The entryway was narrower than she remembered. Light filtered through rippled glass, casting columns of dust. She stood half in, half out, and whispered, "One fresh start, ready for pickup," mimicking the Realtor's voice. Her fingertips brushed a quilt scrap in her pocket—one Liz had sewn when Deborah left the Rockin' D Ranch. *May this keep you warmer than Chad ever could.* The snug stitches held, unwavering where she once felt herself unravel. Her throat tightened as she stepped fully inside; the creak of the floorboard sent her heart racing. She froze, her shoulders hunched, waiting for the sharp bark of her name. Therapy had helped, yes; her therapist, Xavier, was exceptional. Still, certain triggers cracked her wide open, the memories slipping through before she could catch them, crowding with the dust and ache of the past. Inside, the mantel still held a toppled ceramic cat, and cold ash settled in the hearth. Her own footprints trailed behind her—proof she was trespassing in her own life.

"Not bad, old girl," she murmured. "You held up better than I did."

She climbed the stairs to the second floor. In the first bedroom, two sparrows perched on a wire outside a sagging window, one pecking the other's head.

Even the birds found someone.

She moved further, letting the ache settle too deeply. The second bedroom blinked awake under a flickering bulb. Deborah closed her eyes and pictured beds lined with patchwork quilts, women stepping inside with suitcases full of fear. Her chest tightened.

The silence felt strange, yet Chad's voice filled it anyway — barking orders and reciting everything she'd failed to do for the kids. She clenched her fists, wanting to scream back at the ghost in her head, but her throat closed. This shelter could be her redemption or her final humiliation. After all her struggles, she finally reached this point yet doubt gnawed at her. Was freedom merely an illusion, a gilded cage that left her feeling trapped? This shelter would leave women depending on her, and the fear of being too broken loomed over her, whispering that she might not be strong enough to protect them, even if stubbornness urged her to keep pushing forward.

She shook her head. *Not today.*

The bathroom took her straight back to 1976, with the avocado-green sink and cartoon ducks marching across peeling wallpaper. Laughter escaped her before she could stop it.

"Well," she muttered, "I hope y'all like ducks." The Quiltin' Bees would cackle for days over this.

She braced her hands on the sink and caught her reflection in the cracked medicine cabinet—fragmented pieces of her face. Chad once said she was too shattered to bother fixing.

"You're doing fine," she whispered to every broken shard. "You're the boss now."

Her chest tightened, threatening to fold inward, but something clicked.

She wasn't here to survive.

She was here to rebuild. As she started down the stairs, she drew in a steady breath, each step firmer than the last.

Back in the living room, dust danced in the sunlight like gold flecks. She smiled. She used to catch ladybugs and rescue earthworms from the sidewalk. She still liked to collect overlooked things, like the old farmhouse she was walking through

The house isn't mocking me. It's waiting. Like a quilt top with crooked seams, it was rough, but salvageable. She lifted her chin.

"One day at a time."

From the kitchen window, everything was overgrown and unattended—dead flies on the sill, leaves strewn across the lawn, and blackberry canes crowding the fence.

She turned the faucet, and rusty water coughed, then cleared. A small mercy. She'd spent years shrinking herself to fit into Chad's world. This place was too big, too wild, and maybe that was the point.

Deborah reached for the upper cabinet, bracing herself for a rodent to scurry out, or at least some droppings, maybe a cloud of dust.

Instead, a sudden thud from inside the cabinet jolted Deborah into action. Her heart raced; she stumbled back, her breathing quickening as shadows danced across the walls. When she realized it wasn't Chad, in one of his 'moods', she inched closer, her pulse pounding in her ears, drawn by an unspoken promise to uncover whatever secrets were hidden within.

She froze, standing on her tiptoes. A small compartment opened, revealing a small black three-ring binder, the kind sold in drugstores in the 1940s. It was plain and scuffed with no label except a cracked strip of masking tape on the spine that read:

Hughes Family Recipes–1945

Her finger traced the faded handwriting. A recipe card slipped free and drifted to the counter.

Grandma Mae's Sunday Biscuits–For when words aren't enough

Deborah went still. She opened the binder.

Inside were recipes on yellowed lined pages, typed and handwritten, preserved together.

King Ranch Chicken–1958

Pecan Praline Pie –1969

Texas Sheet Cake–1972

Chili Con Carne–Serves 15 ranch hands

A small handwritten note peeked from beneath a recipe for Sour Cream Cornbread. Deborah pulled at it until it was free. It wasn't a recipe. It appeared to be a diary entry. The handwriting was slanted, careful, and a little smudged.

June 1947

Today I cooked a full supper with a smile. A woman can die from smiling too hard. Jeb slammed the screen so hard my knees shook. The baby startled but didn't cry. I'm grateful for small miracles.

Halfway through the entry, a cold weight settled low in her gut. She stopped, her eyes fixed on the sentence.

A woman can die from smiling too hard.

The words lodged somewhere in her throat. She used to smile like that.

Back when Chad's temper showed itself in spurts after their wedding. It hadn't looked like anger. Not really. Closing a cabinet too hard. A fork flung into the sink because the roast was dry. A plate dropped with a sharp crack against the tile.

"Deb," he'd say, voice low, almost charming. "If you'd just listen the first time, we wouldn't keep having these problems."

He'd step close. Too close.

His hands firm at her waist. No bruising. Not yet.

"Don't make me the bad guy."

And she'd smile.

Smiled because that's what obedient wives did. Smiled because it was easier than arguing. Smile because the apology always came after.

He'd kiss her temple. "Don't push me."

She squeezed her eyes shut, the memory rolling in like a storm she couldn't hold back. The film was running on a loop behind her eyelids. In that instant, it was real again; her chest pulled tight as her rib cage ached, and she almost didn't need to read the rest of the entry to know what it would say. The words were waiting for her just on the other side.

One of these days, this house will fall from the force of his anger. I kneaded the bread dough until my hands stopped shaking. I don't know if the secret to good bread is love, but I'm pretty sure fear ruins it. I'm whispering prayers into the rising dough now. I believe God hears them, even if He doesn't answer yet.
MH

By the time she reached the end of kneading the dough to stop trembling, her chest was so tight she wasn't sure she could breathe.

She flipped the page, another date, another entry. She couldn't read it yet.

Deborah dropped the paper on the counter. Bile rose in her throat. She flipped another page—more recipes. But tucked between the ingredient lists were slips of handwriting. Different ink. Different pressure. Different stories. As she turned the pages, she realized the recipes weren't the only things preserved in the binder. There were tales of women written in the margins, confessions folded between pie crusts, and instructions for pot roast.

Her breath caught.

She stopped and closed the binder, as if the words might rise up and spill into the room. Her hands trembled as she grabbed the piece of paper and slid it inside. She couldn't read anymore, not now...not today.

Her thumb brushed the cracked masking tape again, a tactile reminder of the mysteries sealed within the binder. What secrets lie in those pages? Something terrible lived in those pages, alongside something brave. She dropped the binder on the counter and turned to leave, but an invisible pull stopped her. *Why am I so drawn to it?* It was like a magnet, yet the weight of the past hung heavy on her shoulders.

Not ready to dive into the memories of the Hughes women, but equally unwilling to walk away. She tucked it under her arm, holding it close as if it contained answers she desperately needed. What if the words inside echoed her own struggles? The thought sent shivers down her spine.

She'd come a long way since leaving Chad, yet trauma didn't vanish simply because she escaped. The binder was like a key to understanding the past of others who survived someone like Chad. Women who had fought their own battles in silence.

With a shaky breath, she recalled how the binder fell from an obscure compartment, as if fate had conspired to bring them together. Was it meant to be? Buying the farmhouse and transforming it into a shelter felt like a second chance and an opportunity to create a safe haven for women seeking new beginnings.

Before leaving the kitchen, Deborah looked around and imagined laughter filling these walls, coffee brewing, and women finding peace in rocking chairs on the porch. The house bore the imprint of what had happened here, and she knew it needed to become a refuge for women who would come after.

Her hand drifted back to her pocket, brushing the quilt block that Liz had given her. "It was left over from the quilt I made for you. Keep it close when you feel lost. Let it remind you that you aren't alone. May this keep you warmer than Chad ever could."

A warmth spread through her chest—relief or longing, she couldn't tell.

By dusk, she sat on the stairs with the quilt block across her knee. She traced the careful piecing. The house wasn't mocking her.

It was waiting.

She pressed the fabric to her cheek, the lavender scent grounding her. The house creaked around her—old but not defeated.

She rose, walked outside, and stood on the weathered porch. Honeysuckles scented the evening. She pictured the house six months from now with lights glowing, quilts on beds, the craft barn full of laughter, and quilts drying on the porch railing.

It would never be flawless, just like her. She glanced around the clutter, a sigh escaping her lips. "This place is a mess," she murmured, shaking her head. "And I feel like I am too."

For the first time in years, she didn't feel like running.

Thoughts of Luke surfaced, strong and steady. She could call him. She could let him see where her armor had cracked. She could risk needing someone and maybe find something stronger than fear.

She squared her shoulders, clutching the quilt block like a promise. Tonight, she would start making plans and let hope take root. Maybe— if she was brave—she'd let someone else in.

Her phone buzzed against her palm. Her stomach tightened as Chad's name flashed across the screen.

> Chad: One more chance, Deborah. Before
> things get ugly.

Her thumb hovered over the screen. For years, she'd chosen quiet. She'd chosen peace. She'd chosen survival. Each choice seemed right at the time, but looking back, she realized she'd chosen wrong.

Deborah's gaze fell onto the binder in her hands. Her breath caught in her chest. She swallowed the tremor rising in her throat. The porch light clicked off, and the house surrendered to darkness. For a moment, the stillness pressed in, thick and absolute.

"Not this time," she whispered. The words barely left her lips, a shaky promise to the night.

But even as the vow escaped her, she realized she had no idea which man she meant.

CHAPTER 2

$\mathcal{E}$very morning, the Cardinal Creek firehouse came alive with a symphony of hoses hissing, clattering, and slapping against concrete. Luke breathed it in like coffee. There was comfort in the clockwork of his crew, each member revealing their character in small, telling ways: the precision of folded canvas, the tight spiral of cord looped just so. On his worst days, when that hollow ache settled in his chest, these rituals anchored him against drifting away.

He stepped through the main bay, his boots echoing on the damp concrete as he nodded at the blur of activity around him. Jon Clemmons, sleeves rolled up, guided a rookie in the fine art of folding turnout gear. Will hunched over the engine, grease staining his hands as he wrestled with a stubborn repair. In the kitchen, two other firefighters bickered over who was the better cook.

He clipped the sheet to the wall, straightened, and smoothed a wrinkle from his uniform. A glance in the steel-framed mirror on the closet door confirmed what the guys had been telling him for years: he looked more like a high school wrestling coach than a fire chief. It was the result of too many years of lifting weights, not enough time for a proper haircut, and a brow that hadn't figured out how to relax since 2002.

He returned to the bay just as Jon dismissed the rookie, who jogged off toward the kitchen, and Jon arched his back until something popped. "Got a live one there," Jon said with a nod in her direction. "Eager as hell, but I watched her battle a helmet for five minutes. With her bun the size of Texas, I thought she might knock herself out cold trying to cram it in the helmet."

Luke's mouth quirked up at one corner, the smile that came from years of leadership rather than genuine amusement. "Rookies," he said, the word carrying the weight of similar moments, each stacked in his memory as neatly as the station's hoses.

"Yeah, weren't you sporting that much hair when you were a rookie? You know the late eighties, early nineties Blake Shelton mullet?" Jon shot back, running his hand over his own cropped hair.

Luke smiled at the familiar jab. Jon stood before him, now forty-one, with crow's feet framing the icy blue eyes he had inherited from his father. His uniform stretched tight across shoulders burdened by too much—the weight of a beam that had collapsed during a warehouse fire two years ago, his sister's casket, and the fragile newborn he had cradled a year ago with trembling hands. He was not like his father, who'd stood at Jon's bedside, reeking of bourbon and hurling accusations at the son who'd nearly died saving a man from a fire.

"How's your mom?" Luke asked, the question slipping out before he could stop it.

Jon's eyes narrowed slightly. "Why do you ask?"

Luke shrugged, trying to appear casual. "I just realized I haven't seen her around for a while. Everything okay?" He stared at the ground, kicking at nothing to avoid eye contact. They were the same age, yet Deborah—Jon's mother, for God's sake—had been on his mind since the first time he'd seen her at the hospital. He remembered the fading yellow bruises on her wrist and told himself it was only a concern. Professional courtesy. Nothing more.

They both carried the ache of losing a child—her daughter, his son —both gone too soon. Since moving to Rockin' D Ranch, a family compound for Will Deluca and Jon, who lived there with Kati's mom, he'd noticed a subtle yet undeniable change in her. She held herself straighter and spoke without looking down. He looked for her at the grocery store, making excuses to visit Will and Jon. Yet a voice in his head kept warning - *She's Jon's mother. She's still healing; she doesn't need your complications.*

Will lifted his head from the engine, grinning like a coyote. "Chief, are you sweet on Jon's mom? You're gonna tank the betting pool. I put in ten bucks, saying you're married to this job until they force you to retire."

Luke drew in a deep breath through his nose. The denial never made it past his tongue. "That's crossing the line, Will."

"Just saying…" Will gripped the dirty rag and worked to remove the grease from his hands. "Haven't seen you look twice at anyone since that disaster—"

"You mean Justine?" Jon asked, making a face. "She moved to Montana with a paramedic."

Luke shook his head and walked past them toward his office. Jon and Will trailed behind him, already winding up for another round.

Jon snorted. "Unless Montana's closer than I remember, that ship's sailed."

Luke kept walking to his office, his jaw clenched, feeling overwhelmed by the noise in the station.

They followed him, needling. "When was the last time you even had dinner with someone, Chief?" Will asked.

At his office door, Luke turned, knuckles white as he gripped the handle. He caught Jon's worried expression, and something twisted inside him. Guilt? He couldn't tell anymore. "Anything else?"

"Nah, we're looking out for you," Jon said.

Luke nodded, his throat tight. "Thanks." He nearly escaped when Will called after him.

"I've been meaning to tell you about the old farmhouse that belonged to the Hughes family," Will said. "Tammy Kaye, the Realtor, told Peggy Sue at the Diamond Saddle Boutique that it finally sold."

Luke froze. The place—rotting wood, sagging floors, and broken windows—was uncomfortably familiar. He wasn't sure the house was sound enough to save, but tearing it down felt like surrender. "Who'd be crazy enough to take that on?"

Will shrugged. "Confidential. Didn't you go inspect the property recently?"

"Yeah," Luke said as he pictured Deborah there, rebuilding something broken like they had discussed the last time they had dinner together. His chest ached. "Hope they know what they're in for."

"One more thing," Will said as he looked at Jon. "I don't think you answered the Chief's question. How's your mom?"

Luke's jaw locked. These two were up to something, and he was afraid to hope for what it might be.

Jon shifted, flustered. "She's fine. Working with Sissy. Staying out of trouble." He shot Will a warning look. "Unlike some people."

Something about the exchange made Luke's stomach knot. He willed his face to stay neutral. "All right, you two. Get the tools loaded for inspection and try not to scare off all the rookies."

Will saluted with mock seriousness, and Jon offered a small, knowing smile. "Will do, Chief."

Luke watched them go, then retreated to the sanctuary of his office and shut the door behind him. The voices in the firehouse faded to a dull murmur. He braced himself against the desk's edge, exhaled slowly, and closed his eyes. The Hughes farmhouse materialized in his mind. The sagging porch, the cracking foundation, and the old electrical panel. His fingers drummed against the wood. Deborah's face replaced the farmhouse, her determined eyes when she mentioned the shelter. He pushed away from the desk, paced three steps, and stopped at the window. A photo of his children, Caleb and Sammy, sat on the filing cabinet, his son's eyes seeming to follow him. Luke turned away, picked up his phone, scrolled to the county permit office, and then set it back down without making a call. Not his business. Not his place.

He hadn't let himself think about her in a while—at least, not consciously. But there she was, slipping into his thoughts more often than he cared to admit. He missed her. The night he and Will helped Deborah escape—when Chad had brought her to Jon's bedside, only to turn on her—it still haunted him. He'd seen the finger-shaped bruises on her wrist, and Will had stepped between them before Chad could do more. Later, in the waiting room, Luke watched her while they waited for news of Jon's condition. She sat wringing her hands, timid, barely able to look anyone in the eyes. He wanted to go to her and hold her, something he knew he couldn't do.

In the first few weeks, Luke stopped by Liz's cabin to check on her, inviting her for coffee and dinner. He knew he was crossing a line, but he couldn't help returning, drawn to the way grief made her voice catch when she spoke of her daughter—just as his did when he talked about his son.

Soon after Jon's son was born, she squeezed Luke's hand once before letting go. "Jon needs me now," she whispered, but her eyes darted to the window, scanning for Chad's truck.

He nodded, relief and disappointment tangled in his chest. Had she pulled away to protect him from Chad's threats, or had she seen his damage and decided it was too much to bear? It was easier to think it was better this way; his cracks ran too deep to support anyone. He couldn't shake the feeling that she had left to protect herself from him and the weight of his burdens.

Luke opened his desk drawer and pulled out the day's reports. He tried to focus on the paperwork—maintenance logs, training schedules, requisition forms—but his attention kept sliding off the page, circling back to Deborah's name. He pictured her standing at the threshold of the old farmhouse, her chestnut hair pulled into a ponytail. Her face bore the lines of a life well-lived, gently etched crow's feet from smiles that had endured storms, and a thoughtful crease between her brows from years of caring too much. He remembered the jokes she shared with him as their trust grew. He recalled the way she would laugh when he joked about her antique sewing machine—not the measured chuckle she gave her ex-husband, but a full, unguarded laugh that lit up her face, revealing her perfect teeth.

He was still sitting at his desk, papers untouched, when Jon poked his head in. "Chief, they just delivered a pallet of bottled water, and it's blocking the bay door."

Luke glanced at the clock. Only ten minutes had passed, but it felt like it had been an hour. "I'll help," he said, setting the reports aside.

As they walked toward the bay, Jon said, "My mom's divorce is final. It was about six months ago. She just got the settlement."

Luke kept his face blank, the same expression he used when assessing damage at the scene of a fire. Eyes steady, jaw set, lips pressed into a line that revealed nothing. "Oh, hadn't heard," he said, even though he had heard it from the town gossip. The lie tasted metallic on his tongue, like the residue after a fire.

"She's doing okay," Jon added, eyes darting toward him. "Better than I expected. She even moved out of Momma D's cabin."

"That's good," Luke said, swallowing hard as a knot rose in his chest. His collar was like a vice around his neck.

"Look, Chief, I know people talk. There was gossip about you and her." Jon's tone was not accusatory; it was more resigned than anything. "But I want her to be happy, not..." He trailed off, shrugged, then tried again. "Just don't let Will get to you. He means well, even if he's an ass about it. He seems to forget how mad he got at everyone matchmaking after Shelly passed."

Luke nodded, slipping his hands into his pockets. "Thanks, Jon."

As Jon turned to help Will, Luke's gaze fell on a black canvas bag with a white duck stitched on the side. Jon had started carrying it some time ago, and it always had more than a change of clothes. Today, the zipper gaped, revealing the yellow blanket Deborah had made for Jon and Kati—and the top of a baby bottle.

The sight tugged at something in Luke. He remembered the hospital—the raw pride on Jon's face when he named his son Bobby after Kati's father, and the exhausted joy in Will's eyes as he cradled his daughter, Shelly, named for his late wife. The feeling settled in Luke's chest, familiar now: longing, threaded with warmth.

Luke shouldered his way between the stacked cases, grabbing one with both hands and hauling it to the storage area with enough force that his biceps burned. Will dragged a bandanna across his forehead and collapsed into a metal folding chair after they moved all the water. "Not sure why that delivery guy thought it was okay to block the bay and leave."

Jon tossed each of them a bottle of water and sat in the chair next to Will. "Well, that was a workout," Jon said as he wiped the sweat from his brow.

"Chief?" Will said, shooting Luke a sly look. "You're quiet today. You planning to run for mayor or something?"

Luke ignored the bait and started stacking bottles on the storage rack. Jon joined him, the two working in quiet sync. After a moment, Jon broke the silence.

"You ever think about retiring? Leaving all of this?" He gestured around the firehouse, then toward the town beyond it. "Starting over somewhere new?"

Luke had considered moving to Austin when Sammy applied to college there. He even applied for a job, but he loved Cardinal Creek and enjoyed being a firefighter there. "I like it here, even when it's a pain in the butt."

Jon laughed. "Yeah, me too."

When they finished stacking the water, Will wandered off to the kitchen in search of a snack and a moment to call his wife. Jon lingered for a moment, eyes on the far wall.

"Seriously, Chief," he said at last. "If you're thinking about Mom, please...don't rush it. She needs to learn how to breathe again, you know? Not just jump into something."

Luke wanted to argue, to say he had no such plans, but it would be a lie. Instead, he nodded and accepted the advice for what it was. "I hear you."

Jon nodded, gave Luke's shoulder a quick squeeze, then headed for the kitchen, his boots echoing against the cement floor.

Luke let out a slow breath, tension draining from his arms but gathering somewhere deeper. He went back to his office, glancing at the clock—his shift was crawling at a snail's pace. He squared his shoulders and dropped into his chair, but the words on the paperwork swam and shifted, refusing to settle. The pen in his hand hovered over the requisition form, leaving a blue dot where the ink pooled from sitting too long in one spot. The letters blurred, refocused, then blurred again as he blinked. His leg bounced under the desk. Even surrounded by order in an office he'd memorized, some part of him was bracing for the next fire.

Luke wondered if that feeling would ever go away.

Out in the bay, the sounds of work resumed: Jon's running commentary, the rookie's laughter, and his footsteps echoing off the walls–like someone counting seconds. The air conditioner wheezed above the window, rattling as it spat lukewarm air that stirred dust into lazy spirals. The office walls were closing in on him as the noise echoed in his head—a fifteen-by-twelve-foot beige box that had never changed. The same desk he'd had for thirty years, its surface scarred by coffee and cigarette burns. The drawer that jammed unless you jimmied it just right. Chairs across from him that creaked and shifted, as if they might collapse if anyone leaned too hard.

Luke sat, elbows braced on the desk, studying his open palms as if they held answers he'd lost. His broad hands and thick fingers bore calluses like armor, remnants of a life of service. The half-moons of soot beneath each nail refused to come clean, no matter how hard he scrubbed. These hands had dragged unconscious bodies through smoke and found live wires by touch alone in blackout conditions. Yet lately, when they weren't saving someone or fixing something, they betrayed him—a faint tremor he couldn't quite still.

He pulled open the top desk drawer and pushed aside the papers, pens, and training schedules until his finger found the edge of the photo frame. It was simple black plastic, the kind you get at the local dollar store. Fingerprints streaked the glass, and the corners were chipped from multiple moves. He lifted it out slowly and set it in the single rectangle of sunlight coming through the window.

The young man in the frame was twenty-one, wearing his college football uniform and holding a football. Frozen in time. That stubborn glint in his eyes, unmistakably Luke, was paired with a smile that tilted slightly to the left. He carefully touched the edge of the frame as something hollow and familiar expanded inside him.

He never planned on keeping the photo here. He'd brought it in after the funeral to have something to look at when the silence got too loud. Within the walls of the firehouse, he was Chief Erikson—the man who knew what to do, who people turned to. He was not the hollow-chested father who still paused at Caleb's bedroom door before remembering he was gone. With Sammy off at college in Austin now, too, the house had become nothing but corners of quiet, waiting for him each night. The picture somehow stayed. It weathered two promotions, a dozen new hires, and more structure fires than he could count. Some days, he forgot it was there, buried under forms and inspection lists, and on other days, he took it out three or four times, to prove his memory hadn't vanished.

Jon's words from earlier hung in the air. *If you're thinking about Mom, please...don't rush it. She needs to breathe again; you know?*

Luke tried to remember the last time he'd done that himself—just breathed, without waiting for the next alarm. He let his gaze drift to the window, over the gravel lot and along the strip of road leading into town. For a moment, he imagined Deborah visiting the Hughes farmhouse, making plans for her dream shelter. He pictured her shoulders set against whatever came next, stubborn and maybe a little scared, and something deep inside him shifted.

He traced the photo's cracked corner, then pressed his thumb over Caleb's smile. In his mind, the stories tangled together—what he'd had, what he'd lost. His son had been gone long enough that the sharp edges of grief had dulled, but the ache stayed.

Deborah stood at the edge of her own beginning, maybe as raw and lost as he'd been. Luke admired her courage; she'd taken control of her life and left he own personal "war" behind. It takes strength to leave an abusive marriage, to seek help, especially when you are in your fifties. He couldn't fathom how she endured the abuse for so long. She was truly a remarkable woman—brave, loving, and compassionate. She felt things deeply, to the core, and had a wonderful outlook for the future.

A smile crept onto his face. He thought of her, hoping to run into her soon. He rehearsed conversations in his head, wondering what he would say if they were alone again. What words could convey his understanding? I see you. I know what it's like to feel hollow and haunted, to wake up not knowing who you're supposed to be anymore. I can help you if you'll let me. But he was haunted by the thought of Jon, and a town full of people would never forgive him if he hurt her.

After a while, the sun shifted, and the room grew darker. Luke gently slid the photo back into the drawer, closing it with a quiet click. It felt like locking away the past and all the things he longed to say.

He sat there for a long time, hands folded, head bowed, shoulders slumped against the silence. He didn't realize he was holding his breath until his lungs burned for air.

As he finally exhaled, a thought struck him with sudden clarity. What if this was the moment to stop hiding? What if he could be the one to help her find her way?

CHAPTER 3

Deborah woke to the pale ceiling of her apartment, her chest tight and the weight of what she'd taken on pressing down before she even sat up. She'd bought a crumbling farmhouse and promised herself she would turn it into a women's shelter. Something she needed to do not just for other women but for herself. She lay for a moment, her fingers drumming a rapid, anxious rhythm on the sheets, a physical manifestation of the turmoil swirling in her mind. The soft fabric couldn't absorb the restless energy. What had she gotten herself into by buying the old Hughes place? Was she truly capable of doing this? She hadn't told anyone she'd bought it. Had she been reckless? A dog-eared page of the shelter plans on her nightstand caught her eye, each scribbled note like a whisper of encouragement and a reminder of the task ahead.

She grabbed the notebook from the nightstand and pressed it tightly to her chest, her heart beating furiously against the pages full of plans and wishes that were equally terrifying and exhilarating at the same time. She was actually building something on her own, and she wanted to believe she could take on this project, but there was a twinge of doubt. She'd never planned anything on her own. She'd always done what she was told, but this was hers, all hers. The thought made her lips turn upward as she tapped her fingernail three times, meant to calm her anxiety. She shot upright, flinging the covers aside, and her bare feet slapped against the cold floor. She'd taken the leap, but doubts shadowed her every step. Could she truly forge a future for herself and others when the weight of the past still closed in around her? The thought lingered, leaving her second-guessing everything.

"The Quiltin' Bees," she whispered, her voice rough with sleep, half prayer, half panic. Their laughter and encouragement flashed in her mind. Toothpaste foamed at the corners of her mouth as she brushed quickly. Then she yanked on faded jeans and a wrinkled T-shirt. She grabbed the quilt block that had become her lucky charm, a reminder of the strength she found in the group of friends she'd made since leaving Chad. She stepped out the door and slammed it behind her, as if to shut out her doubts.

Deborah entered Cardinal Creek Quilting with the small quilt block tucked into her pocket, her notebook heavy in her hands with ideas for the shelter. Light spilled across the colorful bolts of fabric and the soft pastel walls, and the familiar hum of sewing machines told her she was in the right place. Deborah's heart raced as she scanned the classroom. This mattered. Sissy's silver-streaked hair was near the back wall as she arranged fabric squares on the table. Deborah weaved between the chairs, bumping one with her hip. The clatter made Sissy look up.

"The old Hughes place—it's mine. I bought it with the settlement." Deborah's words tumbled out before she even reached the table, her voice pitched higher than usual.

Sissy's hands went to her face. "Oh, Deborah, that's wonderful."

Deborah set her notebook down, flipped it open, and spread the sketches across the table. Her finger hovered over the fabric swatches of cornflower blues and soft cream. Her hands moved quickly as she explained her vision—sketches of quilts and curtains for each room of the farmhouse, paired with paint chips for the wall colors she had in mind.

Sissy examined the drawings, then looked back at Deborah. "Oh, I can't wait to help you with this. We need to put out a mass text to the rest of the ladies," she said as she pulled out her phone and began tapping the letters on the keyboard.

She placed her phone back in her pocket. "Okay, dear, let's get to work on some preliminary planning," she said, rubbing her hands together. "You know, Deb, old houses hold secrets, especially those that have been empty for a while. There's been talk about the Hughes family, but you know how that goes."

Deborah wanted to ask about the rumors surrounding the Hughes family. *What had they endured?* She had thumbed through the pages of the book, which were filled with handwritten notes whispering secrets of the past. Raising her eyebrows, she realized the book was keeping their secrets, and for now, she'd keep them to herself.

The diary-cookbook sat on her kitchen table, a tangible reminder of the truths she wasn't ready to share with the ladies. She feared that revealing it would mean exposing her own vulnerabilities. The thought sent a shiver down her spine. Trusting anyone but Jon with the darkness of her marriage was frightening.

Renovating the farmhouse felt like a way to purge the bad energy left by the women who had lived there before her. It was a way to reclaim the space for herself and those who would come after. Perhaps it was fate, a chance to start over.

As she browsed through fabrics, her initial enthusiasm began to fade. Before her lay a mountain of daunting tasks–permits to secure, construction to navigate, and decisions she felt ill-equipped to make. Uncertainty gnawed at her; the complexity of permits and the intricacies of building felt like a mountain to climb.

Running her fingers over a floral pattern, her hand snagged on the frayed edge of the swatch, a small reminder of her own fraying confidence. The lengthy list of tasks ahead is unfamiliar and overwhelming. She forced herself to breathe deeply, feeling the cool fabric beneath her fingertips as she sought to ground herself in the present moment.

"Deborah?" Sissy said.

She looked at Sissy. "Yes?"

"You looked a million miles away, and your posture tensed all of a sudden. What's going on?"

Deborah let out a mirthless laugh. "I keep wondering if I'm biting off more than I can chew with this shelter," she murmured.

The thought wasn't entirely her own. It sounded like him.

You can't even keep the laundry straight.

You start things you never finish.

You're too sensitive.

Who's going to take you seriously?

Her jaw tightened. He never yelled those things. That would've been easier to dismiss. He'd said them gently, like facts. When he wasn't drinking, his words were gently degrading.

You're a good mom, but...

Big decisions overwhelm you. Let me handle the big decisions.

Why would you want to work? You'll embarrass yourself!

She'd believed him once. Believed she wasn't cut out for more. Believed the world outside their house required sharper edges than she had. Even craft classes- She swallowed.

"Those women are just going to fill your head," he said when she mentioned signing up. "You don't need hobbies. You need to focus on the kids and me."

Sissy put her hand on her shoulder, startling her back to reality. "Okay, let's start with the first worry." Her voice had that easy, slow Texas drawl that always anchored Deborah, allowing her to breathe again. "Luke Erikson—you know that tall drink of water with those chestnut-brown eyes—he owns a small construction company. You could ask him." She squeezed Deborah's shoulder. "Second, you are definitely enough for the women who need your help—we need to work on that confidence—and third," she said, her silver bangs jiggling as she counted on her fingers, "you won't fail, because before us Quiltin' Bees are done, you'll have the whole town behind you, right down to old Mr. Henley, who hasn't left his porch since '98."

Sissy inhaled deeply, her floral perfume mingling with the fabric softener clinging to her coral tunic. "You remember the quilting rule, don't you. The one my momma taught me?" Her eyes crinkled at the corners. "It doesn't matter if the seams are crooked; they still hold together."

Deborah nodded, her lips tipping upward, as Sissy's words mended something inside her. For the first time in months, hope felt safe. It was like discovering the perfect pattern piece that completed a design she'd been struggling with. The wisdom of Sissy's words resonated deeply, stitching together the frayed edges of her life. The shelter project was the invisible thread that created connections, holding her world together and offering her the stability she longed for.

Encouraged by Sissy's words, Deborah made a list of people to call for the items she needed for the construction project. Luke's name was at the top of the list. She hoped she'd have the courage to call him, but for now, she pushed those thoughts away. She and Sissy went to work selecting fabrics for different rooms. As they set aside options for each one, she ran her fingers over a purple piece. "I have an idea," she murmured, looking down at the fabric.

"Deborah, look up at me," Sissy said. "Speak to me about your idea. I want to hear it."

She slowly raised her head and turned to Sissy. "I want to give each room a theme and make quilts to match. I'll call the living room the Heart Room, since it's going to be the heart of the shelter family."

Sissy put her hand over her mouth with tears brimming in her eyes. "That's beautiful. So, our goal right now is to pick fabrics and colors. We'll make a pile for each room."

Deborah clapped. "I'm so glad you like it. I can almost envision it."

Sissy squeezed her hand. "Good. We can work on this, so when we meet with the Bees, we can start making plans."

As they continued selecting fabrics, Deborah fingered a soft blue cotton and set it aside. Her mind drifted back to Chad's familiar words. "You don't need friends, hobbies, or a job; you need to focus."

Focus on what? She wanted to ask. Sissy's encouragement tried to rise like a gentle breeze, but it was faint compared to the heavy weight of Chad's voice. It wasn't the farmhouse that overwhelmed her. It was the old question clawing back into her life. *What if he's right?* Her shoulder rounded as she sank deeper into her chair, a familiar heaviness pulling her down.

What if I was never meant to build anything on my own? Deborah thought, her fingers trembling as she picked up the floral print and examined it like a detective searching for hidden flaws. She exhaled sharply, shaking her head as if she was trying to dislodge the toxic thoughts. She needed to remain rooted in the present and keep the past from creeping back in.

A truck rumbled past the shop windows, its engine growling like a distant storm. The noise pulled her from her reverie, jolting her back to reality. She found herself momentarily paralyzed, fingers clutching the fabric like a lifeline. A wave of unease washed over her, tightening her chest, as the truck lumbered down the street, dragging her thoughts back to the chaos she was trying to escape.

It moved slowly enough that Deborah froze, her fingers tightening around the fabric. Her breath hitched as the truck continued down the street.

Sissy's eyes softened. "Deb, you're safe here."

She nodded, but her shoulders had already climbed toward her ears at the sound of a truck's engine coming to a stop. Her breath caught, and the fabric in her hand creased as she squeezed it tighter. The truck passed. Still, her lungs burned as she held her breath, waiting for the familiar slam of Chad's door, the particular rhythm of his boots on the walkway: three quick steps and a pause, the key scraping in the lock. Even now, her stomach clenched, anticipating the way his eyes would sweep the room, looking for something out of place, something to comment on, his voice soft but edged like a knife sliding between her ribs unless he was drunk. She shivered at the memory.

Their hands moved together across the table, selecting burgundy for the living room curtains and yellow gingham for the kitchen towels. Deborah tried to concentrate on the fabrics instead of the external noise.

Sissy's weathered hand covered hers, stilling it against the fabric. "This one is perfect for the upstairs curtains," she said, then added quietly, "You just went somewhere, didn't you?"

Deborah nodded as she bit her bottom lip in contemplation. She pictured women she hadn't met yet, standing in the doorway with the same wary hope she carried right now.

Sissy placed a square of steel-gray denim in Deborah's palm. "Everyone talks about courage like it's loud," she said. "But most of the time, it's quiet. It shows up anyway." She placed an arm around Deborah. "Like this." Sissy squeezed her hand, the kind that left no room for argument.

Deborah closed her fingers around the fabric instead of handing it back.

As they finished, Deborah ran her fingers over the separate piles of fabric: soft cotton florals for the bedrooms, sturdy denims for the common areas, cheerful yellows for the kitchen. She held paint swatches to the light, squinting as if already seeing them on walls that didn't yet exist.

Deborah took a deep breath and cleared her throat. "Let's start with the children's quilts. I want them to have something when they come," she said, surprised by the steadiness of her voice.

When she left the quilt shop, the summer afternoon sun warmed her neck as she walked to her car. Deborah's notebook bulged with fabric swatches peeking out in bright, colorful strips. The blue calico for the children's room had slipped halfway out, tangled with the burgundy stripe meant for the living room. The notebook settled on the passenger seat beside her. The small quilt block Liz had given her was still in her pocket—nine perfect squares, broken pieces arranged into something whole. The pieces of fabric were large yet manageable, much like her project. A realization came to Deborah that her life was like a quilt; it was coming together piece by piece, creating something beautiful and strong from the fragments of her past. Three women waved from the window of Cowgirl Sweets and Treats as she drove past, and she lifted a hand in return, no longer startled by the gesture. For the first time, Cardinal Creek didn't feel like a place she passed through—it felt like somewhere she might finally belong.

CHAPTER 4

The smell of bacon hit Deborah before the bell over the Cattle Trail Café door finished jingling. Today wasn't just breakfast—it felt like the moment everything could shift for the shelter. Normally, the café was a place for bonding with the Quiltin' Bees. This morning, she needed to make sure every word counted.

Liz, Sissy, and Peggy Sue were huddled around the corner table, steam rising from their ceramic mugs of coffee. The rich aroma of fresh-brewed dark roast mingled with the scent of cinnamon rolls, causing Deborah's stomach to growl so loudly that she pressed a hand against it. She sank into the vinyl chair opposite Liz, setting her bulging notebook on the red gingham tablecloth, as if it might steady her.

Liz's hand covered Deborah's, her turquoise ring catching the light. "Those circles under your eyes are getting darker. Are you sleeping, okay? Do you need a couple of days at the ranch? Your old room is still made up for you."

Deborah forced her lips into what she hoped resembled a smile. "No, stayed up until two in the morning trying to organize everything." The words slipped out quicker than she intended, revealing the tension coiled within her.

The stress of buying the property loomed over her like a thundercloud, casting shadows on her thoughts. Extensive construction loomed ahead, the search for a contractor was daunting, and the forms piled up like a mountain she had to scale. Anxiety swelled in her chest, coiling tight, reminding her of past battles she thought she had left behind.

As memories threatened to resurface, fear, control, and suffocating doubt loomed. She clenched her fists under the table, determined to push the doubt into the recesses of her mind. Some memories refused to stay buried, surfacing at the most inconvenient times, whispering truths she wasn't ready to confront. She leaned on the coping skills she learned in therapy, taking deep breaths and focusing on the moment, yet it was often an uphill struggle to remain grounded.

Deborah knew the harsh reality. Unless someone had walked the same path of abuse, they could never truly comprehend the complexities of her experiences—before, during, and after. The thought ignited a familiar ache in her heart, a reminder of the isolation that lingered even in the company of well-meaning friends.

Margie, the server, approached their table with her flaming hair twisted into a messy bun, a yellow pencil jabbed through it like a makeshift hairpin. The familiar sight of her lively presence snapped Deborah back to the moment, breaking the spell swirling in her head. She pulled out her coffee-stained order pad. "Ready, ladies?"

Deborah ordered her usual—coffee with two creamers and a bowl of steel-cut oatmeal topped with sliced strawberries and blueberries. It was as dull and uninspiring as beige wallpaper, but sufficient for her these days. While they waited, Deborah flipped open her notebook and walked them through the immediate hurdles—paperwork, permits, and finding someone she could trust to do the work right, without cutting corners.

"Luke Erikson would be perfect for that job," Liz said, twirling her toffee-blonde streaked hair, which was once cut into a chic bob but was now long and layered. It looked lovely on her. She appeared and acted much younger than her sixty-three years. Deborah had seen her work with kids at the equine center, riding horses and swinging up into the saddle with more ease than people half her age. "He's a wiz with construction and knows all the fire, zoning, and building codes better than anyone I know. Danny seems pretty knowledgeable about that stuff, too."

Three pairs of eyes—blue, hazel, and brown—shot toward Liz. "What?"

Peggy Sue's eyebrows nearly disappeared into her bangs.

"Danny?" Sissy leaned forward, her chunky turquoise beads around her neck swinging dangerously close to her coffee.

Liz rolled her eyes heavenward. "We're not here for my love life or lack thereof. We are here for Deborah."

Just as Liz finished her sentence, Margie appeared, balancing a tray loaded with steaming plates. Sissy pointed a French-manicured finger at Liz, "Lucky you. Saved by breakfast."

"Who says we have to stop the interrogation while we eat?" Peggy Sue grinned, stabbing a home fry with her fork.

The corners of Deborah's mouth lifted into a genuine smile, amused by their playful banter around her. Yet she couldn't shake her curiosity about how exactly Liz knew her ex-brother-in-law, Danny, outside the brief encounters in the waiting room when Will's and Jon's babies were born, as well as Jon's wedding.

Her mind drifted back to a conversation with Jon, when he had teased Danny about how Liz seemed closer to his age. Jon had jokingly pointed out that Deborah had a soft spot for Luke, who had quietly found his way into her heart. It had been unexpected when Danny revealed his feelings for her, but they decided it wasn't right because he was Chad's brother. But now, with Liz and Danny spending more time together, Deborah couldn't help but wonder if there was a spark between them.

As laughter filled the air, a warmth spread through Deborah. Maybe there was room for love and new beginnings for everyone—even for her.

A smile broke across her face, and she seized the moment to have fun. "So, Liz, how do you know so much about Danny?"

Liz set her fork down and wiped her mouth. "Well, if you must know, your ex-brother-in-law asked me out to dinner. I said yes. We've gone out...a few times."

"Elizabeth Deluca," Sissy gasped, eyebrows shooting up. "I've known you since we were five, and you're only telling me this now?" A smile lingered at the corners of her mouth, undercutting the mock indignation of her voice.

Peggy Sue shoved a strand of hair behind her ear and gave a slow nod of shock.

Liz leaned forward, steepling her fingers. "We're just friends," she said, tapping the notepad with one finger and already moving on. "Now, let's talk about the shelter."

Deborah took a hearty mouthful of oatmeal, the sweet aroma of cinnamon rising to her nose. She swallowed and said, "Danny's a good guy. He deserves someone—" She cut herself off as everyone turned to stare at her, silent. Her mouth went dry. She cleared her mind with a shake of her head. "So, on the construction team, do you know anyone besides Luke?" Her voice wavered. It wasn't that she disliked Luke—quite the opposite—but starting something now felt like navigating a minefield.

"I'll ask around," Sissy promised, jotting a note on her phone.

They sketched out ideas for turning the old red barn into a communal craft space—workstations where the ladies could create together and sell what they made at the farmers' market, building something of their own. Deborah's heart swelled at the vision, even as a cold tremor of doubt trickled through her.

Suddenly, she threw her hands up, the quilt block sliding off her lap and fluttering to the floor. Her breath hitched, sharp and uneven, as if something inside her had finally slipped its grip. She bent to retrieve the block, fingers trembling.

The three women exchanged glances—concerned, steady, waiting.

Deborah reached into her tote bag, pulled out the small weathered three-ring binder, and set it on the table. "I found this at the farmhouse," she said. "Hidden in a compartment inside a kitchen cabinet. I didn't know what it was at first."

Sissy's brows lifted. "What is it, honey?" She gave a faint smile. "Family secrets?"

Deborah opened the binder carefully. She ran her fingers over the yellowed pages, which held a mix of typed entries and neat, looping handwriting. "It's a diary from the Hughes women that dates back to the 1940s." Her voice caught. "It looks like they were abused. I only read one entry; I had to put it down. She left her husband eventually based on the peach cobbler recipe."

Liz leaned close, breath catching. "Oh, honey."

"Secrets," Sissy whispered.

Peggy Sue slid her coffee aside. "Read us something."

Deborah swallowed and flipped to a page with a dried tearstain. Her voice shook as she read.

November 15, 1989

Moved into Momma and Daddy's house. Feels like I'm walking in her shadow. If I could leave, I would. But he checks the doors at night. He says I wouldn't make it two miles. Maybe he's right. I wish there were someplace for women like me in this area. I want to breathe again without fear. I hide my babies when he comes home drunk and beats me. What kind of mother does that? What if he beats them? Momma escaped Daddy, but I married someone just like him.

RH

A shiver rippled through everyone at the table.

Deborah pressed the diary to her chest. "A scared mother," she said, tears falling down her cheeks. "I did that to Jon and Shelly."

Liz covered her hand. "A good mother protects her babies, and you did that."

Sissy's face was red, her eyes filled with anger. "What kind of man does this to someone they love?"

"Full circle, honey. What you're doing brings all that pain full circle for all the women who didn't get help. You will be there to help them now," Peggy Sue said as she wiped her eyes.

"She was trapped in the same house I'm turning into a shelter," she said. "That's the irony. She needed that shelter...they all did."

Sissy covered Deborah's hand, firm and warm. "I know you're afraid that you'll fail, and those thoughts may come and go, but you are finishing what she prayed for."

Liz squeezed Deborah's other hand. "I know you're scared," she said softly, her thumb stroking Deborah's knuckles. "But healing doesn't happen in isolation. We rely on one another, just like the patches in a quilt depend on each other. A torn quilt can be mended, and you can be too."

Her phone buzzed. She picked it up and looked at the screen.

> Chad: Deb, things are fixin' to get really
> messy. And it won't be pretty.

Her stomach plummeted. *I'll ignore the threats. What can he do?*

She picked up her phone, but before Deborah could respond, the bell over the door jingled. She looked up and froze. Luke walked in, tall and easy. He paused by the counter, scanning the room, and then his gaze landed on her. She dabbed at her eyes. Her pulse slammed against her ribs. His warm smile made her heart flutter. It had been too long. She'd forgotten how easily he could undo her—her body reacted before she could stop it. He ordered coffee, then crossed to their table with a smile that made Deborah's stomach drop. *He's coming this way. Not now, I look a fright after reading that diary.*

She tried to smile back as a flush crept up her neck. When his attention settled on her, she shifted without meaning to, suddenly aware of her breathing, her posture, and the space between them.

"Good morning, ladies," he said, his voice low, calm, and friendly with his eyes fixed on Deborah, who was anything but calm. For her, the room tilted.

"Good morning, Luke," Liz, Peggy Sue, and Sissy sang in perfect unison.

Deborah stayed silent, her throat traitorously empty while the rest of the room practically gushed with approval. Luke winked, and she nearly fell out of her chair. What on earth was happening?

He turned to Deborah. "How are you? Jon told me your divorce is final. Are you holding up, okay?" His voice was gentle and genuine.

She managed to nod, cheeks hot, words stuck in her throat. The café's chatter buzzed around her, but all she heard was the pounding of her heart. The moment stretched, awkward and intimate, until Luke cleared his throat.

He glanced at his watch. "Did you hear about the town hall meeting? Someone is opposing a new development on a property at the edge of town."

Sissy leaned forward. "What kind of development?"

"They're not saying," he admitted. "It's at City Hall, but I'm not sure when. Thought you might want to know. It could affect the small businesses." He looked at each of them, then back at Deborah. "It was really great seeing you all, especially you, Deb. I miss our dinners."

Deborah's breath hitched. "It was great...for me too." Heat flushed her cheeks and she could only watch as he turned to leave. When the door jingled shut, she realized she'd been holding her breath. Deborah put her face in her hands, trying to recover from possibly the most embarrassing moment ever. She lifted her gaze to six sympathetic eyes looking back at her.

"That was intense," Liz finally said.

"Yep," Sissy agreed with a crooked grin.

Deborah cleared her throat, trying to steady her racing heart. "So, back to the town hall meeting. Do you think it's about the shelter?" she asked, fidgeting with the quilt block she'd been carrying everywhere. She pressed her palms against her cheeks. "City Hall isn't exactly known for playing fair."

"First off," Sissy said, "you don't know that it's about you."

Liz gave Deborah a steady look. "Second, courage isn't the absence of fear. It's showing up anyway." She smiled. "And you've got us, Jon, Kati, Will, Anna..."

Sissy smirked. "And Luke."

Deborah drew in a shaky breath. Their faith bolstered her; the warmth of their friendship steadied her. Nodding, she lifted her chin while her heart still thundered.

"All right. Let's do this," she said.

Her phone buzzed under the table.

Unknown number.

CHAPTER 5

*D*eborah's hands trembled as she stuffed the permit paperwork into her leather portfolio. The kitchen table had vanished beneath the stacks of forms--nonprofit applications with yellow sticky notes, supporting documents paper-clipped in triplicate. She gulped the last of her coffee, grimacing at how cold it had gone, and swept her palm across the chaos.

"There they are," she mumbled, fingers closing around her keys.

Her stomach clenched as she recalled Luke's hushed warning at the Cattle Trail Café. *Someone's opposing a new development on a property at the edge of town.*

No details. No names. Just enough information to spread gossip.

It had gnawed at her all night. In Cardinal Creek, rumors didn't start without reason—and they never stayed contained for long. She wondered if there was a subdivision or other development on the edge of town. If it were the shelter, would they oppose a safe haven? Why?

The walk to her car seemed longer this morning. She'd been away from Chad for two years, but his voice still echoed in her head. *You'll never manage without me.* She clicked the key fob to unlock her SUV's doors, then climbed in. Bile rose in her throat, coffee-bitter and acidic. Her knuckles were white as she gripped the wheel. *I can do this.*

When she climbed the stairs at City Hall, her leather portfolio felt heavier with each step. Filing divorce papers had been simpler than this. At least she knew exactly what she wanted. Now, the glass doors reflected her clenched expression. She pushed through them, and goosebumps formed on her arms from the cool air inside. What if they laughed at her plans?

For years, Chad had reduced her world to what he approved. Signatures, meetings, and decisions, with her standing beside him, silent as he spoke for them both. Today, she found herself without anyone to hide behind.

The stack of forms unsettled her, but she no longer confused discomfort with incompetence. She could learn this. She could ask questions. She would write things down rather than nodding mindlessly. Her friends hadn't offered to rescue her. They'd reminded her she didn't need it.

She smoothed the papers in her portfolio. If she didn't understand something, she would say so. If she needed clarification, she would ask. She bit her bottom lip. That was new.

Behind the front desk, a young woman with a tidy ponytail glanced up. Deborah's throat tightened. The speech she practiced vanished into thin air. *Okay, don't chicken out now. You've faced worse than the permit clerk.* "I— I'm here about renovation permits," she managed, hating how her voice wavered.

The receptionist's lipstick cracked as she smiled. "That's down the hall in suite 114."

"Thank you."

Deborah's heels clicked against the worn linoleum as she walked down the hall. She'd always thought it would smell like old paper and disappointment. Instead, it carried a faint scent of waxy floor polish and citrus, mixed with burnt coffee that turned her stomach. Her fingers tightened around the leather portfolio as she approached the office door with its peeling gold lettering. She took another steadying breath, squared her shoulders—a habit from years of bracing herself—and opened the door with a trembling hand that betrayed her.

Behind the counter, a woman in her mid-fifties squinted at the computer, brow creased, unaware Deborah had entered the office. She wore her hair in a tight ponytail, and her reading glasses were perched on top of her head. She didn't look up until Deborah was standing directly across from her.

"Permit application?" the woman asked, not kindly.

"Yes, ma'am." Deborah's voice wavered at the end. She slid the application forward, hands trembling just enough for the clerk to notice.

The clerk took the application and began flipping through the forms, her lips moving as she read silently. Her nails were short and cherry red. Deborah found herself fixated on them as the woman scanned each page, occasionally pausing to make a note or highlight a section.

"This is for the old Hughes place?" the clerk asked, glancing up for the briefest moment.

Deborah nodded. "It's going to be a woman's shelter," she said, careful to keep her tone matter of fact, the way Liz had told her. "It's temporary housing for people who need a place to land."

The clerk's eyes lingered on her for a moment, then went back to the paperwork. "I see." Her pen hovered over a signature block. "This one is missing a signature." Deborah's shoulders tensed.

"Oh," Deborah said. She leaned in, trying to read upside down. "I thought—I mean, I asked the Realtor—"

"Needs to be initialed by both parties and notarized."

She flipped to the next page.

"These accessibility plans are outdated—the code changed in 2007."

Another page.

"You'll need the contractor listed."

Another pause

Deborah's throat tightened. *Luke.* The thought startled her as much as the problem itself.

"And the zoning form is an older version."

Deborah tried to moisten her lips, but her mouth was dry. "The website showed 11-A when I printed them."

"I know." The clerk offered a sympathetic smile. "Happens constantly. They're all simple fixes."

Simple. Deborah's pulse thudded anyway. "Sorry, I'm new to this."

"No need to apologize," the clerk said, kindness reaching her eyes. "No one gets it right the first time. That's what I'm here for." She turned to the printer. "Let me grab the new forms. You can fill them out and bring everything back when you're ready."

The printer came to life behind the counter, spitting out crisp white pages into the tray. Deborah spread her fingers against the cool laminate countertop and drew in a deep breath. *Ten, nine, eight...* She could almost hear Liz's voice in her ear: *Remember, stumbling isn't the same as falling.*

"A public hearing is required," the clerk said. "It's mostly a formality; you will be notified and must attend."

Deborah blinked. "I thought the next town meeting was scheduled?"

"It is." The clerk handed her a bright green flyer. "There's an agenda item about the Hughes property—someone sent a letter of concern. It'll come up then."

A letter of concern. The air left the room. Who even knew she bought the property? She's only told a handful of people: Liz, Sissy, Peggy Sue, Luke, and the real estate agent.

"Who—" Deborah's voice cracked.

The clerk shrugged. "They don't say. It could be anyone. They keep it anonymous to avoid...well, issues." She gave a thin smile that did nothing for the pressure building behind Deborah's ribs.

Of course, in Cardinal Creek, privacy was a rumor. One conversation at church could travel throughout half the county by lunchtime.

Maybe Sissy shared her plans with someone at church. Maybe Liz mentioned it to Will or Kati.

Her hands shook as she tried to gather the scattered forms. The crisp pages slipped through her fingers like her confidence. One caught the edge of the counter, sending the papers scattering across the tile floor with a sharp slap that echoed through the quiet office.

Heat rushed up her neck.

As she knelt to retrieve them, Chad's voice flooded her mind. You'll never get this right. You've always messed everything up. The memories pressed in, tightening her chest. With trembling hands, she fought to quiet the echo of his sharp words. She pressed her lips together and gathered the papers, one by one. He wasn't standing here. She was. And that would have to be enough.

"Bless your heart," the clerk said softly, helping gather the forms.

She clipped them together and handed them to her in a folder. Heat rushed up her neck and settled in her cheeks. From the waiting area, two women leaned toward each other, whispering.

"I'm sorry," Deborah mumbled. She clutched the quilt block inside her tote, rubbing the stitches with her thumb.

"No harm done," the clerk said. There was kindness threaded in her words. "Don't let this process bring you down. If everyone waited for the rules to make sense, nothing would ever get done in this town."

Deborah's mouth twitched upward, a gesture that almost looked like a smile. "Thank you for your help."

She stuffed the flyer deep into her bag and turned toward the door, certain she was being watched. Deborah collapsed onto a bench in the lobby, papers sliding from the folder into her lap. The new forms blurred in her vision. The quilt square, soft and faded, pressed into her palm, grounding her. She blinked hard, refusing to cry. But all the care she'd sutured together with Sissy, Liz, and Peggy Sue seemed fragile now, as if one hard tug could undo it. The town hall meeting loomed over her, and a cold suspicion began to spread. She couldn't shake the feeling that someone was working against her. Deborah closed her eyes and counted backward, not from ten, but from the number of years she had spent waiting for a place to belong. It was bigger than she cared to admit. She sat until her breathing steadied, anchoring her in the present. Then she stood, her shoulders squared, facing the invisible burden of the town's curiosity and suspicion. She gripped the applications tighter, then relaxed her hold and let them rest on her lap. Taking a deep breath, she got up and headed toward the exit. The automatic doors slid open with a soft, muted swish, and she walked into a world that suddenly seemed too bright.

Deborah squinted as she stepped out of City Hall, the sunlight hitting her face causing her to squint. The world outside seemed so normal, with everyone going about their business—drivers idling at the intersections, kids playing in the park across the street, a delivery driver wrestling with a dolly stacked with packages. Deborah tried to steady herself, but her limbs felt loose, and her mind felt disconnected as she slowly took the steps, counting each one to calm her pounding pulse.

The folder of rejected paperwork dug into her chest like a bad omen.

She clutched it tighter as she walked to the car, not looking up, but not slowing down either. She would fix all the problems the clerk had pointed out and return tomorrow, the next day, and for as many days as it would take.

At the curb, she fished in her bag for the keys, connecting with everything but her key fob. The moment she found them, they slipped from her trembling grasp and struck the pavement with a thud.

"Darn it," she whispered, the sidewalk scorching her fingertips as she picked them up. A shadow blocked the light. Deborah's senses sharpened at the familiar cologne. Nausea racked her body. Every inch of her skin was suddenly on alert. She straightened, bracing herself, and standing in front of her was Chad.

"Busy day at City Hall?" he asked. The words came out too low, almost polite, but Deborah knew the danger in his tone; she'd heard it many times. His smile flickered, not reaching his eyes.

Except for the lines of age, he looked the same as he did the day they met —his charm overshadowed by what lurked beneath it. When he was angry or on the verge of losing his temper, his eyes shifted unmistakably, the blue deepening, hardening to steel. He stepped toward her, slow and deliberate, like a predator that knew it had the advantage. His silver hair gleamed in the sun, every strand precisely placed, like the stitches in his expensive suit.

She hugged the folder closer, stepping back. "I—I don't want trouble."

"You could have fooled me." Chad's voice was smooth, almost warm. The kind of tone that would fool anyone who didn't know him.

Deborah's pulse thundered in her ears. "Chad…please don't."

He raised his hands, palms out, as if she were the unreasonable one.

"Honey—Deborah," he corrected himself quickly. "I'm just asking a question. You always jump to conclusions."

She took a step back, and he stepped forward, closing the distance between them. His gaze dropped to the portfolio in her arms.

"That's a lot of paperwork." His smile widened. "Let me buy you lunch. You look stressed, and you always feel better after you eat."

She hugged her folder tighter. Not sure what he wanted or why he was being so nice. "No, I-I'm fine."

He breathed out a laugh. "You never did know how to take care of yourself."

His hand drifted out, settling on her arm—light, almost gentle—practiced.

She stilled, her body rigid. Not because it hurt, but because he knew she couldn't pull away without looking dramatic. This was a classic Chad tactic; one he used when starting an argument in public. Gentle touch. Soft voice. Steel underneath.

"Please, let go." Her voice thinned to a whisper.

He continued to rest his hand on her arm and leaned in just enough that their shadows touched.

"Deborah...why are you doing this to yourself?" He gave her arm a slow pat, as if comforting her. "You don't understand how these things work. A woman's shelter. In this town?" He made a low, irritated sound. "Let me help you. I know people."

Her mouth was dry, her head spinning. "I don't want your help."

He smiled, dragging his finger down her cheek in a gesture that might have looked affectionate to anyone watching, but made her skin crawl. "I'll drive you to lunch. We can talk about Jon and the grandkids—"

"No, Chad, I—I need to go."

Chad exhaled sharply through his nose, something Deborah recognized as annoyance.

"You're being emotional," he murmured. "People make mistakes when they're emotional."

She stepped away, straightening and lifting her chin. "Excuse me, I need to go," she said, attempting to step around him.

"Just remember," Chad said, straightening his collar. "This town doesn't take kindly to mistakes."

He let out a menacing laugh. "You always did underestimate how quickly things unravel."

He walked away at an easy pace, hands in his pockets, as if they were two friends visiting. Deborah stayed where she was, staring at the cracks in the concrete, breath shuddering, vision blurring as the shame crept in behind the tears.

For a moment, the world felt overexposed. Too sharp. Too loud. Cars rolled past. A door slammed somewhere down the block.

Chad's words echoed in her mind. *"You're not strong enough for this."* Her jaw tightened. That voice followed her into kitchens, parking lots, and grocery aisles. It didn't need walls.

The City Hall door swung open behind her, and the sound echoed across the square.

~

Luke stood inside the glass doors of City Hall, a shoulder pressed to the wall, and his arms crossed tight to keep from chewing on the skin around his thumb. The corridor echoed with the steady hum of the copier and the faint clicking of someone's dress shoes on the marble floor. The air always smelled of citrus and civic disappointment, the kind that made Luke grind his molars until his jaw twitched. The mayor, in her crisp cream-colored suit, stood across from Luke, fanning herself with the town hall agenda. He'd worked with her for years on council projects but still couldn't bring himself to call her by her first name.

"You know the rules, Luke," she said. "If a citizen files a complaint, I have to respond. That's the law."

He nodded, his gaze skimming the hallway as she talked.

"There's going to be issues with the zoning permit," she continued. "People are already complaining." She snapped her agenda shut. "Your friend needs to prepare. The opposition isn't going to be subtle. There's talk of a protest."

"How bad?"

"Bad enough, I wish you were back on the city council," she said with a half-smile. "People listen to you."

"People listen to the uniform," he muttered.

"It still counts." She leaned closer. "Between us? Someone submitted a safety and morality complaint about the shelter. It's been forwarded to the state. If they dig up anything, it'll stall her project for months."

"She could still get the building permits, right?" Luke asked.

"Yes, once the paperwork is complete. It's the zoning that'll be the problem."

Luke's jaw flexed. "Any idea who filed it?"

"Anonymous," she said. "But the return address was on Miller Road."

Anger ignited in his chest. Miller Road–Chad had lived there. "I'll tell her," he said, the words clipped.

"Luke? Keep things civil. We can't afford a spectacle."

He nodded, turned, and froze.

Through the glass doors, he saw another shape slide into view—tall, broad-shouldered, moving with a lazy swagger Luke remembered too well. *Chad.* He'd stepped into Deborah's path just outside the entrance, touching her elbow lightly and leaning in as if they were sharing something private.

For a split second, Luke stalled, and a sour thought hit him. *Are they...getting back together? Why is she letting him touch her?*

But when Deborah's posture changed, her spine locked straight, her shoulders tightened, and her hand jerked back a fraction. The color drained from her face. That shift punched the breath out of Luke's lungs.

Chad ran his fingers down Deborah's cheek, and her body went rigid.

That was all it took.

Luke shoved through the door before he'd even registered he was moving. It slammed open with a crack like a gunshot, snapping both of their heads toward him.

Deborah flinched where she stood. Chad stepped back, sliding his hands in his pockets as if he'd done nothing at all.

"Busy mornin', Chief," Chad drawled. "Small town. You see everyone."

Luke ignored the jab, keeping his eyes on Deborah. "You, okay?" he asked.

She nodded, but her throat bobbed as her trembling fingers clutched the folder tight against her chest.

Chad smirked. "Just catching up with my ex-wife. No harm in

talking, right? She knows I'm only looking out for her." He let out a long breath. "I wanted to talk about Jon. I miss my son."

Deborah stiffened.

Luke stepped closer, not touching her but positioning himself squarely between her and Chad. "Deborah, do you want to go inside?"

She let out a slow, uneven breath. "Yes."

Chad chuckled under his breath. "I didn't realize she had a bodyguard. Or is it something more, Chief?"

Keep it civil, Luke. "Have a good day, Chad," Luke said between his teeth.

Chad let out a low, humorless chuckle but didn't bother replying. He flicked open his lighter, lit a cigarette, and walked away.

Deborah leaned her weight against the wall just inside the door. Luke positioned himself between Deborah and the door, giving her space while shielding her in case Chad tried to come inside.

"You're safe," he whispered.

She shut her eyes for a second. "I hate when he touches me like that. He always did it in public. I guess to make me look like the difficult one."

Luke's jaw flexed. "He had no right."

She shook her head. "He found out about the shelter. He said he could help me and we could go to lunch." She let out a mirthless laugh. "He even said he wanted to talk about Jon and our grandkids."

Luke steadied his voice. "He knows you are slipping out of his control."

Deborah's breath trembled again. "It feels like he's always one move ahead of me."

"No. He wants you to think that."

For the first time since he stepped outside, she looked at him directly, her eyes full of fear and something else he couldn't name. "Thank you," she whispered.

He dipped his head. "It's what I do."

They stood in a quiet pocket of the vestibule as the building buzzed with activity around them. He wanted to draw her close, offer her the protection of an embrace.

After a moment, Luke cleared his throat. "Deborah...didn't you use to live on Miller Road? When you and Chad were still...?"

Her face drained of color. "Yes."

"So, he was the one who filed the complaint."

She nodded once. "Yeah, it probably was."

Luke wanted to punch the wall. Instead, he softened his tone. "You don't have to do this alone."

Deborah's head shot up, and she looked at him. "I—I know. It's just a lot."

He smiled at her. "Maybe you're stronger than you think."

A quiet laugh escaped her lips. "Or too stubborn to quit." Deborah exhaled. "I always thought courage wasn't feeling fear. Turns out it's showing up even when your hands won't stop trembling."

Luke nodded. "That's what makes you brave."

She straightened her little shoulders. "I need to fix the paperwork... and find a contractor."

Luke swallowed a dozen things he wanted to say and said, "You can call me anytime."

Her expression warmed. "I know."

They stepped into the sunlight together, the cicadas screaming overhead like the world was spinning too fast.

"Thank you, Luke," she said softly. "For everything."

He smiled back. "We're just getting started, Deb."

They walked to her car together, their shoulders nearly brushing with each step. The space between them was not defined by distance but by restraint.

Deborah sat in her car and watched Luke walk away, his broad shoulders tight with worry he hadn't said out loud. She lifted her hand to her cheek, to the place where Chad's fingers had brushed her skin. A chill ran through her—nothing to do with the temperature. Muscle memory. Humiliation. He'd done it for years. That gentle, possessive touch in public that looked affectionate to anyone watching…and it always meant she'd pay for it later. She hated that it still had power to reach inside her.

Her fingers curled around the quilt block in her lap, pressing it to her palm until the fabric creased. So many things were stacked against her now—the permits, the zoning, the whispers, and Chad circling back into her life like he'd never really left. He would do everything he could to destroy the shelter.

What she needed was a hero, and she hated herself for even thinking it.

But for now, all she could do was breathe and allow herself to fall apart for one minute before she had to stand up again.

She shifted into reverse and pulled away from City Hall.

On the drive home, she mentally listed everything she needed to fix on the permit application, contractor information, and the updated form. Luke's offer echoed in her chest like an answer to an unspoken prayer. *You can call anytime.*

Inside her apartment, Deborah dropped her bag, kicked off her shoes, and walked straight to the shower. Steam curled around her as she lathered lavender and vanilla soap across her skin. Every drop of water that slid down her body loosened the day's tension—not gone, just quieter. By the time she wrapped herself in her robe, her heartbeat slowed, no longer rattling, but still alert.

The copper kettle clattered against the burner. Chamomile. Honey. Familiar motions. Her hands steadied when she wrapped them around the warm ceramic mug and inhaled the scent.

It worked briefly, but then Chad's voice played again. *You can't do this alone. We need to talk about Jon.*

Xavier's therapy voice followed. *In through your nose, out through your mouth.*

Then came Luke's voice—quiet, steady, and infuriatingly kind. *You don't have to do this alone.*

Deborah sipped her tea, her thoughts drifting to Luke. The way his eyes watched her when she talked. How his voice settled something restless inside of her. She wondered how his calloused hands would feel against her skin. "No, that's not going to happen," she muttered.

Deborah reached for her phone. Her thumb hovered over the screen before she typed,

> Deborah: Your father showed up at City Hall today when I was there about building permits.

Three seconds later, Jon's face filled the screen.

"Mom? What happened? Are you okay?"

"I'm fine," she said automatically. Then, before she could overthink it, she added, "I bought the old Hughes place. I'm turning it into a women's shelter."

Jon's eyebrows shot up, his face freezing in an expression she knew too well, the one he'd worn as a teenager when she'd done something unexpected. He opened his mouth to say something, then closed it again. The silence stretched between them. Her fingers found the table's edge and she gripped it, waiting for him to speak.

"That's incredible, Mom." His voice softened. "Is Dad giving you trouble?"

"You know how he is."

She wanted to change the subject, so she began describing the wraparound porch, the sewing room, and the soap-making studio. Jon's expression shifted from surprised to proud to something that almost looked like awe.

When the call ended, she leaned back until her spine touched the chair, reached for the leather-bound notebook, opened it to a blank page, and wrote four words.

Shelter. Permits. Quilts. Community.

They looked small, too fragile, but she traced them anyway.

What if Chad was right?

The charity gala had been her idea. Her guest list. Her carefully typed timeline. She confirmed the band twice. The band never showed. Chad had taken the microphone while she stood frozen beside him.

"Seems like someone forgot to secure the contract," he'd announced with a smile. "I'll handle it."

He didn't look at her afterward. Not until they were alone. "I tried to warn you," he'd said. "You rush. You miss details. And I have to clean it up."

Later, she found the contract on his desk in the envelope she'd asked him to mail.

She shut the notebook, then opened it again. Luke came to mind, and with him the danger of how easily she could fall. She reminded herself she was too bruised to risk it.

Back then, she believed the failure proved something about her. Now she wasn't so sure. She sipped her now-cold tea and let the quiet settle. Tomorrow wasn't about hope–it was about showing up.

And this time she wouldn't stand alone.

CHAPTER 6

*D*eborah's phone buzzed before she could finish her first cup of coffee. She picked it up, turned it over, and saw the text.

Chad: We need to talk. It's about Jon.

Her heart thundered in her chest. After yesterday, what could he possibly want?

A second text followed before she could breathe.

Chad: I'm worried about him. Please meet me.

Deborah's stomach flipped. She stared at the message until the screen dimmed. Her thumb trembled over the delete button, then dropped away. She set the phone face down on the counter, walked to the sink, and splashed cold water on her face. When she returned and picked it up, the screen was dark. She pressed the button, and there it was again—the message with Jon's name glowing at her.

This could be manipulation, but what if something is wrong with Jon? I'll tell him to meet me at the Cattle Trail Café...it's safe...it's public.

Her shoulders slumped as she stared at her phone, swiping to unlock it. Chad knew Jon was one subject he could still wield like a knife.

Deborah: What about Jon?

Three dots blinked.

> Chad: He won't answer my calls. I'm worried. Thought you might know something.

Liar! She should have closed the phone right then, but her instinct to protect Jon was woven into her like threads in a quilt block. One mention of his name and everything else—logic, self-preservation, even her hard-won independence—unraveled like a loose strand.

> Deborah: He's fine. I talked to him the other day.

> Chad: Then why hasn't he spoken to me? I want to fix things. Can we meet? Noon? Please.

Please. He always used please like a choke chain.

She typed *no*, deleted it...typed "*I'm busy*," deleted it... Then, finally, I responded.

> Deborah: Cattle Trail Café. Noon.

~

At 11:59, Deborah hesitated at the entrance to the Cattle Trail Café, then pushed the wooden door open. The overhead bell made her flinch, even though she'd braced herself. Burnt coffee mingled with the greasy scent of bacon, igniting a wave of nausea that twisted her stomach and dragged her back to breakfasts that had become nightmares.

Those smells were once a morning greeting. Now they are a bitter reminder of Chad's rage and of the life she was still trying to escape, physically and mentally. She scanned the bustling room, her heart pounding. Chad was already seated, facing the door. His gaze locked onto her, cool and deliberate. A dazzling smile settled across his face, the kind that convinced strangers and warned her. The mask was firmly in place. Deborah recognized it instantly. A rush of panic fluttered in her chest. Her stomach was tied in knots. This was a mistake. I should leave, she thought, as her feet stayed planted where she stood.

She froze as he rose and crossed the room. His fingers closed around her arm. Her body reacted before she could stop it. A recoil she couldn't hide. Then anger came, sharp and humiliating. Still, she stepped when he guided her.

The movement came too easily, as if some part of her had already decided that fighting would cost more than compliance.

That realization stung.

Chad smiled, satisfied, and adjusted his grip, signaling her forward without a word.

"You look good, Deb," he said as he led her to the table and pulled out a chair for her.

Deborah glanced at him with a tight smile. "Just tell me what's wrong with Jon," she said, taking a seat opposite him in sharp contrast to when they were married, and he'd force her to sit next to him.

He gave her a soft smile, his eyes flickering over her face the way they used to when he scanned for any weakness. "You look tired."

She folded her hands in her lap. "You said this was about Jon."

Chad sighed, leaning back like a martyr. "I know you think I'm the villain, Deborah..." He leaned forward, resting his elbows on the table. "Maybe I deserve that. But he's still my son, and I deserve to know my grandson."

The thought of Bobby being anywhere near Chad made her clench her jaw. "You had years to act like his father."

Chad's face crumpled in a way that would have looked wounded if Deborah hadn't spent years watching him rehearse that expression in the mirror.

"Deb, I know I've made mistakes. I want a chance to make things right." He paused and softened his tone. "With both of you."

There it was—the hook. She said nothing. Silence worked better than arguing with Chad.

The server dropped off the coffee, smiling at Chad, then at Deborah. Chad poured half-and-half into her coffee without asking her preference—just like always—and pushed the mug toward her.

"Just the way you like it, babe."

Deborah ground her molars as she stared at the milky coffee, then at Chad's expectant face. The mug remained where he'd pushed it, cooling between them like everything else.

"So, what are you working on? You always had some sort of little project. What is it now, the quilting group? Redecorating that farmhouse you bought?"

Deborah swallowed hard, the movement tight in her neck.

"I heard rumors," he continued while stirring his coffee. "Something about renovations."

Deborah cleared her throat. "It's nothing you need to worry about."

"But I do worry," he said, softening his voice. "I think it's admirable. Helping other women."

She blinked but didn't respond.

He chuckled. "You always wanted to make people feel safe." His gaze sharpened in a way that was barely perceptible unless you knew him. "So how big is this place? Bedrooms? Staff?"

She didn't want to answer, but old habits tugged at her. Explaining. Justifying.

"Six bedrooms," she said slowly. "A barn that will be converted for workshops. I'm applying for nonprofit status."

His eyes warmed with approval.

She relaxed just enough before he swooped in like a vulture.

He leaned in, reached for her hand, and spoke in a low voice. "Baby, it doesn't have to be like this. You're trying to carry this all by yourself. You and me—" He tapped the table between them. "We were good together once."

"No," she whispered. "We weren't."

He ignored her and continued. "Baby, if you come back, we could fix things. Jon would come around. We could have our grandson over. You wouldn't have to worry about money, permits, or people attacking your...little project."

Her fingernails bit into her palm.

"You remember the gala," he continued. "How that turned out." He tilted his head. "You've always needed a little help steering. That's all."

Deborah held his gaze. A hundred responses crowded her throat, sharp, deserved, and overdue. But they stayed there.

From the outside, she looked composed. Her hand rested on the table, her nails digging into her palm.

A surge of adrenaline coursed through her as she yanked her hands away and folded them beneath the table, out of his reach. "Chad, I appreciate the apology, but we're not getting back together. That part of my life is over."

Her cheeks burned as she stood up to him, a mix of defiance and vulnerability swirling through her. She hoped no one could hear their conversation. The thought of being part of the town's rumors sent a fresh wave of humiliation over her.

She was already mortified for even agreeing to meet him, knowing all too well how he could turn charm into manipulation. Anger simmered inside her, urging her to reclaim the power that had been stripped away for so long.

The warmth evaporated from his face, and his smile no longer reached his eyes. His mask was beginning to slip. Deborah shifted in her seat, knowing he was having trouble controlling himself.

"It kills me," he said quietly, "to watch you throw away everything I built for you."

She flinched at the wording. *"I built?" That's not how I see it.*

He leaned back, his voice like ice. "And if you think I'm going to let you turn my town into a shelter for broken women, you're more naive than I thought."

Deborah shook her head and drew in a breath, but he cut her off with a laugh before she could respond.

"You either come back to what's familiar..." He paused, leaned in, and stared straight into her eyes. "Or I tear down everything you're trying to build."

Anger simmered inside Deborah as Chad lifted his coffee, smiling as if they'd just discussed the weather.

She leaned in and whispered, "I would think you'd be happy to replace me in your bed. You never loved me anyway."

Chad slammed his hands on the table so hard that it rattled the silverware. Everyone turned to look at them. He froze, then he smoothed his shirt and planted a smile on his face. Bile rose to Deborah's throat as she watched him slip his mask back on with ease.

He scooted his chair closer to hers and leaned in. "Deb, what you don't understand is that you're *mine*. And if you don't come back to me, I will take everything from you." Chad reached out, touched her face, and whispered, "I will ruin you."

He stood, left money on the table, and walked out as if nothing had happened.

Dead silence filled the restaurant. All eyes were on Deborah.

She sat frozen, her pulse pounding in her ears as she gripped the coffee mug tightly, then lifted it to her lips and whispered into it, "The threats have only begun. He won't stop until he destroys me." Her gaze remained fixed on the dark liquid, unwilling to meet the eyes of those around her. The weight of the stares was suffocating, a reminder of her past shame.

Deborah sucked in a deep breath, forcing herself to calm the storm brewing within. Inhale. Exhale. The mug was warm against her hands, but she gripped it so tight her knuckles turned white, afraid it might shatter under the pressure.

Tears threatened to spill, gathering at the corners of her eyes, yet she refused to let them fall in public. Chad had humiliated and belittled her too many times. There was no way she would give him that power again. Determination flooded her veins. No more. She would learn to stand tall, despite the echoes of his cruelty.

～

Deborah entered her apartment, her body heavy with exhaustion from her meeting with Chad. *What was I thinking, meeting with him? Jon would have told me if something was wrong. Now I have a target on my back.*

She leaned against the door frame, massaging the knots in her neck. As she made her way to the kitchen, she stumbled slightly. Paperwork covered the kitchen table, a mountain of tasks that felt insurmountable. She filled her kettle and placed it on the stove. As she waited for the water to heat, Chad's threat echoed in her mind.

I'll ruin you.

The kettle's whistle startled her. Steam rose as she poured water over the tea bag, added honey, and stirred. A wave of nausea washed over her as she recalled his fingers grazing her cheek outside City Hall as he wore that calculated smile he reserved for audiences.

The spoon clinked rhythmically against the mug, and suddenly it wasn't tea she was stirring but a memory—Jon's tiny sleeping form in her arms, the nursery door opened, Chad's shadow stretched across the floor.

"Put him in the crib now," his voice echoed from years ago. The words still made her flinch.

Deborah laid the baby in the crib, his warmth leaving her arms. Then Chad dug his fingers into her arm, dragging her from Jon's room to their bedroom, and slammed the door so hard the hinges rattled. The rage in his eyes—and what followed—made Deborah drop the spoon with a clatter. She picked it up with a trembling hand and started stirring faster. She blinked rapidly, shaking her head.

She knew Chad hadn't wanted to marry her when their parents forced them to, but she had never imagined he would be so cruel to her.

The apartment's silence pressed in around her, broken only by the sound of her stirring. She shook her head, trying to dislodge the memory, but it clung in a blur—right alongside the image of Luke.

Deborah sank into the kitchen chair, letting the steam from the tea warm her face as she surveyed the explosion of paperwork scattered across the table. Her gaze drifted to her phone. With hesitant fingers, she picked it up and began typing a message to Luke. She typed, *Can we talk?* Then she deleted it.

What she really wanted was to speak with him, but she didn't want him to hear the tremble in her voice.

His words echoed in her mind: *You don't have to do this alone.* He sounded sincere—unmistakably so—but Chad had taught her that sincerity didn't always mean safety. She set her phone on the table.

Her fingertips traced the worn edge of her notebook. She flipped through the pages filled with her handwriting, stopping at the fabric swatches of yellow flannel she had imagined in the sunshine room at the shelter, the same color as Jon's nursery when he was a baby. She wondered if any of this would ever become real or if she was playing pretend, like when Jon was small, and she'd imagined running away.

Deborah opened a fresh page. She clicked the blue ink into place with a decisive snap and pressed it onto the paper. She wrote "Attend town hall meeting." She underlined it twice. Beneath it, she added, "Show up and speak up." Her hand moved faster as she sketched the floor plan, designating spaces—a kitchen, counseling room, and childcare area. In the margin, she jotted a note to ask Kati about hospital stats and circled it three times in red ink. She started listing ways the shelter could serve the community, but halfway through a sentence about crisis intervention, she crossed it out so hard that the pen tore through the paper. Who was she kidding? The town would listen to Chad, not her.

Then Liz and the Quiltin' Bees' words flooded her mind. Deborah closed her eyes, took a deep breath, and bit her bottom lip for a moment. "Show up and speak up," she murmured as she reached for her tea. Her hand was steady for the first time all day.

She closed the notebook, running her palm over the cover as if sealing a promise. Her shoulders straightened as she stood. Walking to her bedroom, she caught her reflection in the hallway mirror.

For the first time in years, her shoulders weren't bowed. She held herself upright.

CHAPTER 7

Deborah stopped her SUV in front of the old farmhouse and sat for a moment, her hands gripping the steering wheel. The wraparound porch sagged like a weary spine. She gripped the splintered railing as she climbed the stairs, each creak echoing the ache in her chest. The railing's rough texture grounded her amid a flood of memories that overwhelmed her.

With her free hand, she reached into her pocket and closed her fingers around the quilt block—her anchor in this storm of uncertainty. Paint curled from the weatherboards. Three steps were broken, and a shutter hung by a single hinge. Beyond it, waist-high weeds swallowed what had once been a garden.

Just like me. Damaged yet still standing.

She tried to do the math in her head, adding up the lumber, paint, and labor, but she stopped before she got too far. It was going to cost much more than she had. Chad's voice crept into her mind, quiet and certain. *You'll never get this right.*

To clear her mind, she exhaled slowly. This wasn't about proving him wrong. It was about proving herself right. She pictured the porch swept clean, rocking chairs lined up, and women laughing in the evening light, their lives calm and safe. This was her dream, and she had to fight for it. Chad's threats twisted in her gut, but a spark of rebellion flared hotter than fear.

The tires rolling over loose gravel jolted her back to reality. Luke's red truck emerged from a cloud of dust, and her heart leaped traitorously even as her brain screamed, *STOP!* She tucked the quilt block away and straightened her posture, half-wishing he'd leave and half-hoping he'd stay.

Luke's smile reached his eyes as he approached. "Thought you might want some company." He gestured toward the farmhouse. "We could go on a tour of the property and try to break down what needs to be done into a digestible list."

Deborah nodded. They circled the farmhouse together, their footsteps crunching on gravel. Luke paused at a broken fence, running his fingers along the splintered wood. "Some two-by-fours will fix these fences," he said.

At the barn, he squinted up at the loose shingles flapping in the breeze and said, "Rodriguez at the firehouse does roofing on his days off. I'll talk to him."

Deborah's throat tightened. Accepting help meant being judged, but refusing it meant failure.

Luke pulled out his phone, thumbs moving quickly across the screen. "I'm logging everything. We could start this weekend." His shoulder brushed against hers as he leaned in to show her the screen. Deborah drew back, her breath catching as her pulse quickened.

"I was thinking about you last night," he said, his voice low. "Did you try to call me?"

Did I? Her chest tightened. "No...I don't think I did."

"I saw a missed call from your number."

He went back to talking about materials and timelines—steady, calm, hands moving in sure gestures. Nothing about him hinted at danger. When they reached the wild, overgrown garden, she looked over the tangled weeds and broken fences—formidable work and potential beauty.

"It's a lot," she whispered. She wasn't sure if she meant the garden or him.

As they left the garden, Luke mentioned the town hall meeting. "I could help you prepare if you want."

Deborah reached into her pocket and pressed her thumb against the quilt block, grounding herself. A nod was all she managed, until barely above a whisper, she said, "Let me think about it."

When they finished walking the property and returned to the porch, Deborah couldn't keep her fingers still. She twisted them together, staring at the peeling paint instead of Luke. Ten seconds passed...then twenty. The cicadas droned in the distance.

Luke waited. Silent, patient, gentle.

That made it worse.

Deborah finally looked up as Luke continued waiting. He was calm and steady, not demanding what she wasn't ready to give.

For one suspended moment, she almost said yes to the help, yes to him, yes to believing she could do this. But her throat tightened, and the words scraped out of her before she could stop them.

"I appreciate your offer," she said, her voice cracking, "but I'm thinking about selling the farmhouse instead." The sentence tasted like betrayal on her tongue. It hung between them like a surrender flag, and she braced herself for him to argue. Luke's jaw flexed, and he looked toward the barn like he needed a second.

"I appreciate everything you're doing," she said, her voice raw. "But every time someone has helped me, I've ended up owing them. I can't do that anymore."

Luke's brows knit together. "Deborah, receiving help isn't the same thing as owing."

"Chad used to say the same thing."

"Don't let Chad ruin this," he said, his voice low.

Deborah wrapped her arms around herself and stared out at the field. Luke's boots range down the stairs, then his truck door slammed. A moment later, the engine roared to life. She stayed on the porch, unmoving, watching his red taillights disappear down the gravel drive and around the bend by the wild blackberry bushes. When his truck was out of sight, she paused to consider what she wanted. Half of her wanted to reach out, grab Luke's hand, and tell him she'd fight for the shelter; the other half imagined Chad's sneering face and the whispers that would follow her. Deborah reached into her pocket for her phone to call the Realtor, then stopped, curling her fingers into a fist against her thigh. She climbed into her SUV and drove toward town.

∾

Deborah parked her car outside Cardinal Creek Quilting and gripped the steering wheel until her knuckles lost their color. She told herself three times that she would go inside. Three times, she faltered. The fourth time, she stayed.

The engine ticked as it cooled down. Through the driver's side window, Deborah stared at the painted sign swinging in the breeze, her pulse pounding in her throat as she rubbed her thumb over the quilt block in her hand like prayer beads, slow and rhythmic.

She grasped the handle. *Just open the door.*

Across the lot, a woman carried a bolt of fabric inside, laughter trailing behind when she opened the door.

Deborah inhaled, closed her eyes, and exhaled—one breath—then another.

She grabbed her purse, climbed out of the car, and walked to the door before she could change her mind. Her hand trembled on the handle as her body remembered what her mind tried to ignore. Walking through a door had never been safe with Chad. Today, she shook off the thought, lifted her chin, and pushed it open anyway.

When she walked into the shop, the hum of the sewing machines filtered through the classroom door. The cheerful buzz made her want to both run toward it and retreat at the same time. Sissy and Liz looked up when she entered, eyebrows raised as they set down their work. Deborah stood frozen at the doorway, unable to still her fingers. Tears burned her eyes as her mind pulled her in opposite directions—the shelter seemed both impossible to abandon and impossible to continue. Luke's steady hands appeared in her mind and morphed into Chad's grip. What if his kindness was just a mask all men wore before revealing themselves? What if Luke were different, and she were sacrificing her once-in-a-lifetime opportunity for happiness? The shelter plans, Luke's smile, and Chad's threats swirled together until she couldn't separate them.

Sissy's eyes widened when she saw Deborah's disheveled state and red-rimmed eyes. She whispered, "Lord, have mercy," reaching out to brush a strand of hair from Deborah's face, where it had escaped her usually neat ponytail. Deborah stilled, as if the small touch startled her, then looked down, fidgeting with her hands, her shoulders hunched toward her ears.

"Come sit by me," Liz said, patting the empty chair. "Tell us what's going on."

"I saw Chad yesterday," Deborah whispered, sinking into the chair. "He texted me about Jon...that something was wrong." Her voice cracked. "He lied. We met at the Cattle Trail Café...and when I told him I wouldn't come back to him, he slammed his hands on the table and said he'd ruin me." Tears fell as her shoulders trembled.

Liz put her arm around Deborah and pulled her close. "Honey, he's trying to break you because he can't control you."

Sissy leaned in, her voice low. "Bless his little heart, he thinks he's the only one who knows how to play dirty." She shook her head and set down her rotary cutter. "Give me five minutes and a church directory; we can spread gossip that would ruin his reputation." She leaned on the table. "I love playing dirty with jerks like him."

Liz covered Deborah's trembling hands with hers. "The day you walked away, you became his worst fear," she said, her voice quiet but firm. Her hand made a sweeping gesture that included the circle of women. "And if he comes for you again, he won't face just you; he'll face all of us."

Deborah's eyes moved from Sissy to Liz, whose expression carried the same compassion she'd shown her during the year and a half they'd lived together.

Mable, who rarely spoke while working, looked up from her sewing machine. "My Harold talked to me like that once." She looked down at her machine. "Notice, I said once." She shrugged and smiled.

Deborah's eyes widened.

"Mable, don't scare the girl," Peggy Sue said. "She made Harold sleep on the couch for a month."

Mable looked over her glasses. "What? I didn't imply anything. A cast-iron skillet full of hot food works too. I learned about that in a movie."

"Not sure why I never thought of that," Deborah mumbled.

Liz nudged a stack of quilt blocks toward Deborah. "You want armor? Build it one square at a time. Just like we'll build this shelter."

Brenda looked up from the fabric she was cutting. "Sissy, are we still making quilts for hospice?"

Everyone looked at her, perplexed. Sissy responded. "Yes, why?"

"I was thinking we could make one with Chad's name on it."

A startled laugh burst from Deborah, tears still in her eyes. She looked around the circle at the determined faces of these women who'd become her shield. "Lord, help anyone who crosses y'all," she whispered, as she dabbed her eyes with her sleeve. Her voice was steadier than it had been in months.

Sissy said, "Honey, murder isn't part of what we do, but if Chad wants to start something, he picked the wrong women to mess with."

Peggy Sue lowered her ruler and looked up. "We will fix this the same way we fix a quilt. One piece at a time. You won't do this alone."

"We need to come up with a plan. I'll call my cousin at the newspaper to get public support," Sissy said.

Liz put an arm around Deborah. "If Chad decides to go to war with the Quiltin' Bees, we'll snip him down to size."

"There are three quilts ready to donate to the shelter or to raise money," added Sissy.

Deborah traced the half-finished pattern on the table. "What if I can't do this?"

Sissy set down her rotary cutter with a snap. "Girl, you lived with that man for over thirty years. You think a bunch of folks at a meeting should create fear after him? Don't give him one more day inside your head. He doesn't pay rent to live there."

Liz squeezed Deborah's hand. "Honey...have you talked to Jon?"

Deborah shook her head.

"Do you want me to call him?"

She opened her mouth to say something, but instead, tears spilled down her cheeks, and she whispered, "Yes."

As their hands covered hers—weathered, smooth, ringed, plain—all reaching across the fabric, something shifted within Deborah.

"Okay, I'll make that call," Liz said as she excused herself.

"When it's time for the town hall meeting, we'll be there," Peggy Sue said.

With her fingers no longer trembling, Deborah folded her quilt block carefully and placed it into her pocket. She took a deep breath that reached all the way to her toes. The corners of her mouth, which had turned downward for so long they'd left a crease, twitched upward. Hope flickered in her eyes, small but unmistakable.

For over thirty years, she'd stood between her children and Chad's rage. Now, surrounded by these fierce women with scissors and determination, Deborah wondered if she could step outside from behind the shield and let others stand in front. The thought unsettled her, yet left room for what might be.

The firehouse smelled like the coffee that had burned two hours ago. Luke stood at the sink rinsing his mug when Jon walked in—too stiff, too controlled. One look told him something was wrong.

Jon approached Luke in the kitchen and said three short sentences that sparked a war. "Chad threatened my mom. He's going after her. We're going to need help."

Luke's pulse thundered in his ears, drowning out everything else. "Where is she? Is she safe?" The words tumbled out as his hands curled into fists at his sides.

"Yeah, she was with Liz earlier," he said as he shoved his hands into his pockets. "He told her if she didn't go back to him, he'd make sure the shelter never opened."

"That would explain why she said she was thinking about selling the farmhouse." Luke narrowed his eyes. "When was this?"

"The day before yesterday. She went to the diner to meet him."

Luke raised an eyebrow. *Why would she meet him? Why didn't she tell me yesterday?* "Why?"

"He told her he was worried about me."

Luke wanted to leave work and drive to Chad's house, but he forced himself to stay glued to where he stood because that wouldn't help anything. "How can we help her?"

Jon shrugged. "I don't know, I thought you'd have an idea. The

Hens, on the other hand, have a plan that includes the Town Council meeting."

"Did he put his hands on her?"

"I don't think so. She met him at the Cattle Trail Café."

Luke exhaled, his shoulders dropping with momentary relief, but beneath his composed exterior, his rage still smoldered like embers waiting to ignite. "You know, I had a missed call from her that day, but she said she didn't try to call." *She must not trust me.*

He paced across the floor and looked at Jon. "This is war. But she decides how we fight it." He always knew Chad was a problem. Now he was a threat.

The alarm blared through the firehouse. Jon sprinted toward his locker as Luke grabbed his keys and radio. Their conversation was shelved by duty. Sliding behind the wheel of his truck, Luke tightened his jaw. "You picked the wrong woman to threaten, Chad," he muttered. "And the wrong man to challenge."

CHAPTER 8

*W*eeks of planning collapsed into one terrifying realization: the town hall presentation was quickly approaching. Deborah stared at the unfinished paperwork, her pen hovering over the signature line. Part of her wanted to sign in bold strokes, while another whispered that she was fooling herself. Meanwhile, Chad was plotting ways to sabotage her dream, and there was something almost comforting in the familiarity of his opposition. At least if she failed because of him, she wouldn't have to blame herself.

The horizon shifted from pale peach to molten gold as Deborah wrapped her hands around her coffee cup, savoring the warmth. Dew clung to the porch rail, and the gentle buzz of birds filled the air. She stared across the field, envisioning women in rocking chairs watching the same sunrise one day—safe, healing, real.

She could almost hear their laughter echoing against the old red barn, a peace she craved since her marriage to Chad. She needed that peace now more than ever.

The cool morning air carried the scent of damp earth, grounding her as she turned toward the future she was racing to build.

Deborah closed her eyes against the sun's glare, imagining Luke's easy grin in the firehouse bay and the steady confidence in his voice as he offered to supervise the renovations. *Volunteers. Free labor. A lifeline.*

She'd only nodded then—a small, guarded gesture born of fear.

Too close. Too dangerous.

She struggled to breathe as tension gripped her chest. She needed a contractor, but letting Luke in meant giving him access to more than just the farmhouse. He'd be close enough to make her walls crumble.

Every time she looked at him, her heart lurched with a mix of excitement, fear, and hope. She hadn't realized how dangerous hope could be until now. Fighting Chad felt manageable, but facing Luke—facing what she truly wanted—felt foreign. The memory of his steady gaze made her chest tighten further. With other contractors, it was easy to keep things strictly business, but not with Luke; his gaze unraveled her defenses. The thought of working beside him made her breath catch. Opening her heart felt riskier than standing before the city council while Chad plotted against her in the shadows.

Liz, Sissy, Peggy Sue, and Jon were willing to rally for her. Their encouraging faces were etched in her mind, and their words echoed like a faint drumbeat, transforming into her mantra: *Show up, speak up.*

Deborah exhaled as she pulled out her phone and opened the Notes app, creating a page titled "Pros and Cons: Luke as Contractor."

She typed the word "hope". Then deleted it.

Her gaze drifted to her forearm. Though her skin was unmarked, she could feel the ghost of Chad's touch—a practiced, possessive stroke meant to appear tender in public and keep her silent in private. There were no visible marks, no pain. Yet she flinched inside. Flexing her fingers, she willed the memory of his dark eyes and clenched jaw to fade, but they remained burned into her mind. Chad held power, money, and connections in high places. Could she really stand against him? He could undermine her plans by convincing someone to withhold a signature or by manipulating a zoning hearing against her. He bought loyalty and crushed opposition. Did she have the strength to resist him?

As doubt flooded her mind, she instinctively reached for the quilt square in her pocket. A wave of comfort washed over her as she curled her fingers around it, as if it could steady her. An awareness hit her deeper than fear: community. Rather than being overwhelmed by isolation or doubt, Deborah felt the quiet strength of those who stood behind her. The presence of Liz, Sissy, Peggy Sue, and Jon lingered in her mind, and their faith in her served as a grounding force. In this moment, their encouragement and solidarity became tangible, reminding her that she was not alone in her struggle. The sense of belonging, of being supported by a group that genuinely cared, filled her with resilience that fear could not shake.

Maybe a united circle of women could outmatch one man's money.

The low rumble of an engine pulled her attention from the sunlit field. She lifted a hand to shield her eyes as a truck eased to a stop in the driveway. Her heart fluttered beneath her ribs. The dusty red pickup's engine cut off, and the door opened as a man stepped out casually.

"Luke," she whispered.

Why was he here so early? As her pulse thundered in her throat, she realized the question held two answers, each pulling her in a different direction.

After he offered to help, Luke gave Deborah some time to think. He'd given her the space, but he hadn't walked away. As he drove down the gravel driveway, Deborah sat on the porch, her thumbs tapping away at her phone. A strand of hair fell across her face, one she didn't brush away. He tightened his grip on the steering wheel as his pulse quickened. The gold band that had circled his finger for over twenty years was gone now, leaving a pale strip on his skin —a painful reminder of how many summers had passed since his divorce. He watched her tuck the loose strand of hair behind her ear, a gentle movement he remembered from their past outings. She looked up, squinting in the sunshine, shielding her eyes with her hand. Luke's stomach churned with uncertainty. Why had he driven out here? An unseen force had pulled him from his restless sleep.

As he stepped out of the truck, Deborah watched with a nervous smile that made his heart race. He paused, taking in the farmhouse porch, where flakes of paint curled away from the gray wood. The sagging steps had been weathered by decades of footfalls. The farmhouse stood in the morning light—broken yet beautiful, much like her. His gaze swept over the split railings, loose boards, and a gutter hanging askew. Wildflowers pushed through the cracked soil, surviving despite everything. It was the perfect project for a man with a toolbox and something to prove. He should offer to fix it, but would she see that as help or control? He shifted his weight, grounding himself against the rising tide of emotion. The morning sun caught in Deborah's hair, turning stray wisps to gold as the fields nodded in the breeze. Luke tested the railing, the first step groaning under his weight. She turned toward him—light and warmth meeting caution halfway.

"Hey," she said softly.

"Hey," he replied, shifting nervously. He could command twenty firefighters through burning buildings, but standing before Deborah, the words in his throat felt like kindling that wouldn't catch.

"What brings you out here today?"

Luke shrugged, thumbs hooked in his jeans pockets. "Thought you might want to go over the list of repairs. This place...it's got real potential."

Her lips curved into a slow smile, reaching the corners of her brown eyes, a flicker of warmth that felt like a latch finally opening within him.

"I agree," she said, sweeping her arm toward the farmhouse and sagging barn.

"Let's have a seat on the steps. No chairs yet, just possibilities."

Deborah set a leather-bound notebook beside him and eased onto the worn boards. When her elbow brushed against his arm, his breath caught. She flipped open the notebook, revealing neat sketches of the farmhouse with fresh white siding, a widened porch, and the barn transformed into a workshop. Her enthusiasm was contagious, and his heart thudded as she traced each line, sharing her vision.

"Do you need help with the building permits?" he asked, trying to keep his voice steady despite the worry that it might sound too pushy.

Her pencil stilled, and she bit her lip, twisting the page between nimble fingers. "Maybe. I've got a few loose ends to tie up before I can file."

He caught her gaze. "Like what?" She shifted, and the air between them thickened. Had he made her uneasy? "You don't have to tell me," He blurted, regret flooding in.

She slowly turned her head and laid a hand on his shoulder. "It's not you," she whispered. "I'm just scared it'll all fall apart before it gets started."

Her confession struck him like a bolt of lightning. "All right," he said, "open your notebook to a blank page."

She flipped to a blank sheet, pen ready. "Okay..."

"Let's list every task that needs to be done."

She scratched her pen across the paper, words and arrows crowding the page until she paused and looked up. "That's it for now."

He nodded. "Good. Now, on the next page, let's make columns: Do Now, Plan/Schedule, Delegate, and Park."

Her brow furrowed in concentration as she drew the columns with precision. A flicker of pride rose in Luke as she sorted her tasks into categories. The first task in the do-now column was "Building Permit: Town Hall."

He cleared his throat. "What do you need to file the permit?"

She exhaled slowly. "A contractor," she admitted, eyes downcast.

Silence stretched between them. He glanced at her, and she swallowed hard, opening her mouth to speak, then closing it again.

"Chad knows about the shelter," Deborah blurted.

Luke's jaw tightened. He knew, but it was her story to tell. "How?"

She hung her head. "I met him at the diner. He pretended to be worried about Jon, but that was a lie." She traced the notebook binding with her thumb. "He said if I didn't come back to him...he'd ruin me."

"Are you okay?"

"He didn't hurt me physically, but he reminded me of what he could take away if I don't do what he wants."

His thumb brushed the spine of her notebook. "I figured something happened the day I stopped by, and Jon confirmed it, but I wanted it to be your story to tell."

She smiled and touched his hand. "Thanks, Luke."

"I'm not here to drag answers out of you. I'm here to help you and to stand between you and whatever he tries next, but you get to steer this thing. Not me. Not him."

Her mouth twitched into a grin. "I appreciate your kindness."

His pulse thundered. "I'm a contractor," he murmured. "A few of the guys at the fire station volunteered to help."

Sweat beaded on his neck as Deborah toyed with the notebook's ribbon marker. He fought the urge to look away and let the moment pass. Instead, he tucked a loose strand of hair behind her ear, gently lifted her chin so their eyes met. Her breath hitched. She bit her lip, searching his face. Luke's hand trembled, uncertain if he'd crossed an invisible line or if they stood on common ground. As the breeze stirred the porch boards beneath them, neither moved to break the charged quiet.

~

A tight knot formed in Deborah's stomach as she held Luke's gaze—desire threading dangerously close to fear. When he slid his hand away, relief came first—confusion followed close behind. He turned his head, jaw tight, as if guarding a thought he didn't want her to see. Should she let him in? He had shown up twice now, steady and real—but the idea of needing anyone made her chest constrict.

"Penny for your thoughts?" she nudged him playfully, trying to ease the tension.

A half-smile curved his mouth. He shifted and met her eyes again. "I'm giving you space to think." He tilted his head. "Quiet support."

Warmth crept in, but she fought the instinct to pull away. "That's why I like you, Luke. You give quiet support."

He chuckled. "This isn't just about permits."

Her heart skipped. Was he...attracted to her? Leaning closer, she searched his eyes.

Luke drew one hand down his jaw, his eyes flickering toward the fields. "I want to help you because I believe in what you are doing. You light up when you talk about turning the old farmhouse into a sanctuary for women," he said, pausing to gather his thoughts. "I believe in you."

Tears pricked Deborah's eyes. "I don't know how to..." Her voice wavered.

Luke turned, fully facing her. "So many people believe in you. Believe in yourself."

Memories of Chad's threats flooded back in, and she swallowed hard. "I'm not sure I know how. One phone call, and I'm that scared woman you and Will rescued from the hospital after Jon got hurt." Images of terror, bruises, and her trembling flooded her mind. What would have happened if she hadn't left with Luke and Will that night? The thought made her shudder. Since she was nineteen, she thought she'd never escape. Yet here she sat—trembling but free—the owner of an old farmhouse in shambles that could become a sanctuary for women just like her.

Luke sat beside her, his presence steady and strong, an anchor in her turbulent thoughts.

"Luke," she said, her voice low.

He tilted his head. "Hmm?"

She closed her fingers around his forearm, feeling the warmth radiating from beneath his shirt. "You have no idea how much your words mean to me. Will you be my contractor and help me with the permits?"

His smile bloomed as sunlight caught the flecks of amber in his eyes. "Yes, what's first on the agenda, boss lady?" He nudged her shoulder.

She flipped open the page marked *Building Permit Application*. "Let's tackle the building permits first. When can you come by next?"

"I can swing by tomorrow afternoon," he said, stepping off the porch.

"Perfect."

Luke squared his shoulders, his hands in his pockets. He looked at her with earnest intensity. "We'll make this work," he said.

Deborah's throat tightened. She laid a hand on his arm; the warmth was both a promise and a flicker of dread. "I have faith in you, too."

He brushed his finger along her jaw, searching her face. "See you tomorrow."

Deborah watched him walk to his truck, the sun casting long shadows across the porch. Hope tugged at her chest, warring with fear. She wasn't alone anymore—and that was the part that terrified her the most.

CHAPTER 9

Deborah's knuckles whitened against the edge of the farmhouse sink as water trickled down the rusted joint where metal met porcelain. Drip. Drip. Each splash echoed through the kitchen like an accusation. A shaft of sunlight streamed through the dusty window, illuminating the water droplets. She blew a strand of hair from her face and squared her shoulders. "Thirty years of Chad's temper and I'm supposed to be afraid of a leaking sink." Her fingers traced the smooth plastic of the pink toolbox, still glossy with the price tag barely removed, before flipping the metal clasps with a click.

Peering inside, she rummaged through the tools until she wrapped her fingers around a wrench. Deborah slid beneath the sink and stared at the maze of corroded pipes. On her first attempt, the wrench slipped, metal scraping against rust. Biting her lip, she tried again, gripping tighter. The pipe gave way with a groan, releasing a gush of rusty water that soaked her shirt. She jerked upward and cracked her head against the underside of the basin.

"Dammit," she said as she wiggled forward. She emerged from the cabinet and stood, water pouring from her hair and clothes. Her soaked T-shirt clung to her, jeans heavy with moisture. A laugh bubbled up as tears pricked her eyes. Maybe Chad was right. She couldn't even fix one simple pipe.

A knock at the back door came just as she wiped her face. The hinges creaked as the door swung open, followed by the sound of footsteps.

"Deb, are you here?"

Oh, Lord, my shirt is practically see-through. She quickly crossed her arms. "Oh, hey Luke," she said casually.

A grin spread across his face. "What happened here?"

Does he think I'm a joke? She cleared her throat. "Well, the faucet had a leak, and I wanted to fix it…" Her voice trailed off.

His grin faded, replaced by a focus that grew as he unbuttoned his shirt, one button after the other. He removed his button-down, revealing a plain white T-shirt stretched across his broad chest. Deborah blinked quickly, her gaze drawn to the way the fabric clung to his biceps, pulled taut over his muscles. It was hard not to look, not to notice things about Luke that she'd never let herself consider.

He walked across the room and put the shirt around her shoulders. "Hold tight, I have a shirt in the truck you can wear."

She watched as he exited through the back door. *Is it hot in here?* She thought as she waved a hand in front of her face. *Deborah, you need to stop this insanity. He's here to help you.* She groaned as she pulled the shirt tight around her. She took a deep breath to inhale the woodsy scent that clung to it. "Oh, this isn't a good idea," she muttered.

Her eyes followed Luke as he walked to the back porch carrying a T-shirt in one hand and a toolbox in the other. When he walked in the door, Deborah's heart skipped a beat. How could one man look so good in just a plain cotton shirt and Wranglers?

Luke smiled. "I hope this helps," he said as he handed her the shirt.

Deborah nodded as she accepted it. "Thanks," she murmured.

He set the toolbox on the counter. "I can work on the sink while you go change."

Deborah headed toward the bathroom just off the kitchen. Before she exited, she looked back at Luke, who was already going through his toolbox, searching for a tool. What was happening here? Why did her heart flutter and her skin burn at his touch?

When Deborah returned to the kitchen, she found Luke's lower body stretched out beneath the sink, working on the pipe. The soft cotton of his shirt brushed against her skin as she watched him. She moved closer and watched his muscles flex as he tightened a fitting. But something about his position hit her wrong, striking the same nerve Chad had bruised for years.

Her breath became rapid and shallow, and a cold sweat spread across her body. She curled her fingers into her palms as the room tilted.

Luke slid out from under the sink. "I think these pipes need to be replaced, but I can at least stop water from leaking for now."

He stepped toward her.

"Deb, are you okay?"

Too close...he was too close.

The room spun. She couldn't breathe. Her eyes darted around the room. She flinched when she saw him move a step closer. There was a loud, sharp ringing in her ears.

Luke froze, his face softening. He lowered his hands and angled his body sideways, giving her space.

"Deborah," he said, his voice low and warm like a blanket around her shoulders. "Tell me what you need."

She broke. A tear slipped down her cheek before she could stop it. She swiftly brushed her cheek. "I'm sorry. I'm fine. I don't know what, why..." Her voice trailed off as she shook her head.

"It's okay. I'm right here. You're okay. Take your time," he said, taking a step backward. "Just breathe with me."

Luke took in a long breath and exhaled slowly. Deborah mirrored him until her breathing was back to normal.

"I-I'm sorry...I—" Her voice cracked.

"You didn't do anything wrong," he said as he guided her to a chair. "Just take your time."

She sat for a moment, orienting herself to the present the way she'd learned in therapy. She turned to see Luke leaning against the sink, waiting. His face was riddled with worry—or was it pity? She couldn't tell.

She whispered, "I'm fine. Just a moment of...weakness." She pushed herself up from the chair and smoothed down the top Luke had lent her with trembling fingers, desperate to keep her hands occupied as she tried to calm herself. She turned to him and smiled as if nothing had happened. "What were you saying about the sink?"

"Don't worry about the sink, we'll get it taken care of," he said. "Do you feel up to talking about the building permits?"

Deborah's stomach dropped. "I left them at home," she said, her voice catching. She'd been so distracted thinking about Luke coming over that the permits had completely slipped her mind. She nervously twisted the hem of her borrowed top and watched his face, waiting for the flash of anger Chad would get when she forgot to buy something at the grocery store or pick up his dry cleaning.

"I can handle it myself," she added, then hesitated. "But...maybe I could call you? If I need help? Or not. It's fine either way." The air in the room dissipated as she spoke; she needed to escape. *What is happening? He doesn't look mad, but I feel like something bad is gonna happen.*

He smiled. "Of course, you can call me anytime. I think if the building permit is in place and renovations have started before the town hall meeting, it could make a difference."

Deborah nodded. "I'll work on the permits this afternoon," she said. "Luke, it wasn't you earlier."

"I know," he said, his voice low. "I need you to know I'm not him. I never will be."

A silence settled between them. Luke reached out slowly with a gentle touch and brushed a tear from her cheek with the back of his knuckle. Her breath hitched, not from fear, but from the tenderness of his touch.

Luke retrieved his shirt from the chair and slipped it on, his fingers working each button with practiced ease. "I'm off today." His eyes lingered on her a beat too long. "If you need anything, just call me." He gave her an encouraging pat on the arm, and his fingertips brushed over her skin, sending a shiver of sensation in their wake. Goosebumps rose wherever he touched, delicate and immediate, betraying her heightened anticipation.

Deborah forced a smile. "Thanks, Luke."

"Walk me out?"

She nodded.

They moved together, neither of them speaking, as they crossed the yard to his truck. The sound of their footsteps filled the quiet between them. Deborah stole a glance at his profile, wondering if his calm exterior was a facade, hiding the same unsettling thoughts she couldn't seem to quiet.

When they got to his truck, he turned to face her. "Deb, if anything feels off when I'm not here, anything at all, call me. No hesitation."

Deborah frowned.

Luke didn't elaborate. He just stood there with his gaze locked on hers, the intensity in his eyes conveying a promise that ran deeper than any verbal reassurance could.

In that silent exchange, she understood exactly what he meant.

He climbed into his truck; the engine caught with a full-throated roar. Deborah stepped back as he eased onto the road, his tires crunching over the loose gravel. Just before he disappeared around the bend, he leaned out and lifted his hand in a last wave.

Deborah pressed her palm to her chest. "Thanks, Luke," she whispered, pulling in a slow, deep breath. His scent on the borrowed shirt embraced her, and for a moment, she settled into it. But then, reality crashed back in. *Stop, Deborah. Focus. We have work to do, and fawning over the contractor isn't part of it.*

Her phone buzzed in her pocket, jolting her from her thoughts. She smiled as she took it out, but her heart sank when she saw the message.

> Chad: The place is starting to come together. I hope the repairs hold.

Her lungs tightened at the sight of his name. Of course, he'd phrase it that way. It wasn't a threat; it was his doubt wrapped in feigned concern.

Repairs hold. The familiar words pressed down on her, heavy and suffocating.

As she walked to her SUV, the world felt too bright, too loud. The porch boards creaked behind her, and for a fleeting moment, she wanted to run away. Hide from the weight of her past. She needed to breathe, yet each inhale came shallow and tight. Her pulse thudded in her head, a relentless reminder of her anxiety.

By the time she reached the driver's seat, her hands were shaking so hard she dropped her keys, the metallic clatter matching her racing heart. She reached into her pocket and brushed her fingers across the quilt square. It was solid. It was real. Her breathing steadied as she reminded herself that she wasn't alone in this. Chad didn't get to decide how this ended.

With renewed determination, she turned the key and drove home.

CHAPTER 10

*D*eborah's heart raced as she guided her SUV up the drive. As the farmhouse came into view, its worn facade bathed in warm morning light, excitement surged through her. She reflected on how swiftly the building permits were approved. Just a week after she hired Luke as the contractor, a moment that felt exhilarating. It felt like standing at the brink of something new. As she parked, a cautious swell of pride surprised her. She let it pass before it could take root. Experience had taught her how fragile hope could be. Was she really willing to risk believing this might work?

Preparations began as soon as Deborah got the permit. While Luke assembled his construction crew—most of whom were volunteers from the fire department—she enlisted the Quiltin' Bees to handle meals and grounds cleanup. As she stepped out of the car, she couldn't help but smile. Determined to showcase substantial progress on the house, barn, and grounds, she poured her energy into every detail of the project. From the porch, she surveyed the garden and yard with a critical eye before unlocking the front door. In the kitchen, she began drafting detailed cleaning schedules, mentally checking off tasks that would transform the neglected property into her dream.

Warm hues of pink, gold, and peach filled the sky above the pale blue horizon as Deborah stepped outside. A convoy of trucks rumbled up the driveway, kicking up a cloud of dust. Luke's truck rolled to a stop first—like it always did. He climbed out, calm and unhurried, already focused on work—so different from Chad's unpredictable flare-ups. Deborah smiled as he looked over and gave her a quick grin and a wink. Then he turned, gathered the crew, and started giving instructions.

As the crews dispersed, a blue SUV kicked up dust at the end of the drive. Jon stepped out with a tool belt slung over his shoulder and a box of casserole dishes in hand. Kati emerged in paint-spattered overalls, Anna carried a bag of chips and bread, and Will wrestled with a cooler.

Liz's car rolled up behind them, Peggy Sue's smiling face visible through the passenger window. Sissy leaned out the back, waving and calling out something lost in the morning breeze.

The last two out of the SUV were Deborah's grandkids, Eva and Caden. She blinked away tears as Caden sprinted toward her, the spitting image of Will down to the shape of his grin. Eva was all Shelly, and for a moment, Deborah thought her heart might give out. *Not today, it's not the day for that.* She closed her eyes, trying to forget the funeral she couldn't attend and the years she'd missed with her grandkids.

Caden crashed into her, enveloping her in a bear hug. His warmth and energy chased away every lingering regret. "Grandma, I'm ready to help," he said, bright and eager. Deborah hugged him back with a desperate relief.

She ruffled his hair. "Well, Chief is by the barn. Maybe you could help the crew," she said, looking at Will. "As long as it's okay with your dad."

Caden looked up at Will with puppy-dog eyes. "Please, Daaad! I promise I'll listen."

Will gave a nod. "Listen to Chief, okay."

Caden ran toward the barn. As she watched, Luke tousled his hair and stooped to talk to him. Deborah smiled, then Eva stepped forward and hugged her.

"Hey, Grandma, I miss having you at the ranch."

"I miss you too. You can always come spend the weekend with me if it's okay with your dad."

Eva hugged her again. "I would love that."

After waving, Anna, Kati, and the Quiltin' Bees entered the house, with Eva trailing behind. A lump caught in Deborah's throat. It wasn't the blue of her mother's eyes or the gold of her hair that pierced Deborah's heart; it was the tilt of Eva's head, the way she moved, the shadow of Shelly in every gesture.

"Hey, Mom," Jon said, making her jump. "She looks like Shelly and acts a lot like her. Makes my heart miss her."

With tears stinging her eyes, Deborah nodded in response. She cleared her throat, forced a smile through her tears, then hugged Jon. "It hurts some days more than others, but if one blessing occurred, it's that she gave us Eva."

He whispered, "It's like she's here sometimes."

After pulling back, she wiped her eyes.

Putting his arm around her, Jon said, "Okay, Momma, let's get to work," as they went toward the house.

When Deborah entered through the back door, Kati and Anna greeted her with hugs. Liz stood with her hands on her hips. "Okay, lady, tell us what to do. We're at your disposal."

Deborah glanced at her watch and bit her bottom lip. It would be about four hours until they needed to worry about getting food ready. She looked at her list of things they could paint and clean. Luke had told her the walls were stable, so they could start painting and cleaning the rooms. In fact, except for a few plumbing issues, the bones of the house were good. It just needed cleaning and cosmetic repairs.

"Okay, in the living room there's paint, and each can is labeled with the room it goes in," she said. "There are buckets and a list of things that need to be cleaned. The only rooms we aren't going to paint or clean are the kitchen and bathrooms."

From there, the ladies grabbed their supplies and scattered throughout the house. Deborah kept her hands busy painting, moving methodically from wall to trim and back again, but it was impossible not to notice Luke. Whenever he came through the door with an armload of lumber, conversing with Jon or joking with Will, Deborah's attention was drawn to him like a moth to light. Although she kept her head down, she felt his eyes on her as if he were watching for her reaction. Heat and unrest churned inside her, and she couldn't ignore it, no matter how hard she tried.

The hours blurred past. Paint dried, laughter echoed up the stairwell, and lunch snuck up on them. Deborah put aside her paintbrush and headed to the kitchen. She laid out bread and cheese, then lined up the plates, determined not to think about anything but the sandwiches in front of her. The plan was to have sandwiches for lunch and a potluck for dinner before they called it quits for the day. She continued layering turkey and ham when Jon strolled in, sweat darkening his collar, an open bottle of water dangling from his hand. He leaned against the counter and took a long drink. Deborah felt the weight of his gaze before she even turned.

She shot him a sideways look. "What, Jon?" Her tone sounded sharper than she'd intended, but she didn't take it back.

"Is there something going on between you and Chief?"

Deborah rolled her eyes. "Besides working together to get this place fixed up?"

"Mom, come on. I've known him for a long time, and since his divorce, I haven't seen him look at a woman the way he looks at you."

Her heart raced, and she bit her bottom lip. "Even if I liked him, isn't that my business?"

He turned to face her fully, straightening his posture with quiet resolve. "Mom, I'm just worried. I know what you went through with Dad, and you haven't well…"

Deborah put her hand up. "Jon, I don't want to talk about this." She wiped her hands with a towel.

"I'm just worried. I don't want you to get hurt."

She pivoted toward him. "Does he hit or assault women?" Her voice rose an octave.

Jon furrowed his brows. "Noooo! My God, I was talking about your heart."

She exhaled slowly, and when she glanced up, her eyes met three silhouettes framed in the doorway—Anna, Kati, and Liz—watching her with expressions she couldn't quite read.

Kati raised an eyebrow when she looked at Jon. "Everything okay?"

Deborah put a hand on Jon's arm. "Yes, fine. I'm sorry," she said, looking at Jon.

Jon kissed her temple. "No, I'm sorry. I'm still learning."

"We both are," she said, forcing a smile before she turned to Kati. "He did nothing wrong. He just asked a question."

Liz chimed in. "Well, let me know. I know where a broom is, and I'll use it."

They all burst into laughter.

"I'm going outside before Momma D hits me," he said. Before heading for the door, he leaned in and whispered, "I'm okay if you like Luke. I never saw you look at Dad the way you look at Luke. I was just worried about you."

The ladies joined her to help prepare the crew's food. They set up tables inside with sandwiches, chips, and cookies for dessert. When the crew took a break, they filled their plates and went to the porch, the tables, or the tailgates of their trucks.

Deborah sat at a table with Liz, Sissy, and Peggy Sue, picking at her sandwich and thinking about what Jon had said. The only man she had ever been with was Chad. Her chest ached at the thought that she'd never had a man truly show her intimacy or touch her with tenderness or love except for Luke. She liked it when he tucked her hair behind her ear or touched her arm.

Warm fingers brushed across her arm, pulling her thoughts back to the crowded table. Luke had slipped into the empty chair beside her, his eyes crinkling at the corners. "Penny for your thoughts?"

"Just sitting here enjoying checking out all the work y'all have completed today," she said, placing her hand over his. Butterflies fluttered in her stomach. *What is this man doing to me?* "Thank you for all of your hard work," she said.

"We're gonna get through this together," he said.

As they ate, the clink of forks against plates filled the space between them. Deborah matched her breathing to Luke's without meaning to, their shoulders occasionally brushing as they reached for napkins. She kept her eyes on her plate, torn between wanting to lean closer and needing to pull away.

Luke set a bottle of water in front of her. "You didn't eat much," he murmured. "You, okay?"

"I'm fine," she said, pasting on a smile. "Really."

"You say that when you are exhausted," he said with his eyebrow raised. "At least hydrate."

He noticed. No man has ever watched out for me like that before.

She wasn't sure if she wanted to run away or lean closer.

Every time their elbows brushed, she flinched slightly, then immediately missed the contact. When their plates were empty, Luke's calloused fingers grazed hers as he collected her dish with his own. She hesitated for only a moment before standing, aware of how close he was as they moved into the hall. He led her through the half-finished rooms, his palm hovering near the small of her back without quite touching it, pointing to new drywall and repaired floorboards. Deborah couldn't help but notice his capable hands, the kind that could build things...or break them. Her throat tightened.

"I'll catch up with you all later to check the list," Luke said, stepping toward the crew. He turned once more. "See ya at dinner."

His smile and wink continued to warm her after he left.

She took a deep breath, inhaling the scent of old pine and new lumber. She pressed her hand against the doorframe as her fingers grazed the grooves left by decades of Hughes women who had suffered. Now she was making this a sanctuary for women who needed it.

As the sun dipped toward the horizon, painting the Texas sky in soft pinks and oranges, the color stirred a memory of the pink dress she'd worn on her wedding day—and the way Chad had said it made her look pale. She had believed him. Sweat trickled down her neck as she snapped the final tablecloths over the picnic tables, the plastic clinging to her damp fingers like the doubt that wouldn't let go. The mesquites and live oaks cast long, slanting shadows across the yard where Luke stood directing the last of the day's work, his silhouette strong and unfamiliar in ways that both beckoned and terrified her. Jon flipped burgers on the grill; they sizzled and smoke rose with each turn of the spatula.

Every few minutes, Jon glanced her way, his smile mirroring hers. Deborah paused to watch Luke laughing with the crew. The moment was real enough to make her nervous. Chad's text lingered at the edge of her thoughts—not loud, just present. She let the unease sit beside the hope and kept breathing. The smell of hamburgers and hot dogs sizzling mixed with dust and sun-warmed grass, homey scents that felt borrowed rather than permanent.

From inside the house, serving spoons clattered against ceramic as Liz, Anna, and Kati arranged potato salad in a bowl. Their laughter drifted through the screen door, punctuated by the persistent rhythm of hammers and saws from the barn. As they started carrying food out to the table, Deborah's hands trembled. She heard Luke tell everyone to break for the day and head over to eat. Gratitude washed through her, quickly followed by nerves as the group began to gather. She wasn't used to being the focus or to finding the right words when people were watching.

Deborah took a deep breath. "I want to thank everyone for being here today," she managed, her voice catching. She paused and swallowed hard. "This project…" Her words faltered as she looked into the crowd of faces around her of everyone who'd come to help her make this project—her dream—come true. She smiled through her tears. "This project means the world to me. I can't thank you enough." She pointed toward the food. "Okay, let's eat."

Jon put his arm around her shoulders and pressed a kiss on her temple. "I'm so proud of you, Mom. I love you," he whispered before joining Kati in the line forming at the buffet table.

Deborah sat with Liz, Sissy, and Peggy Sue as laughter rippled up and down the tables. Her shoulders tightened with each burst of laughter. Support had never been free. The old reflex flared—count the cost, settle the debt. She recognized it for what it was, even if it hadn't loosened its grip. Care always came with a price, and she never learned how to stop keeping score.

Deborah twisted her napkin into a rope as Liz, Sissy, and Peggy Sue shifted down to make room. Luke slid beside her, his shoulder brushing hers.

He leaned close and whispered, "We made so much progress today." His breath was warm against her ear, making her shudder.

Although she smiled, her eyes darted away as she turned. "We did, didn't we?"

When his fingers grazed her ear, she leaned in, then immediately straightened her spine. "Luke, thank you for all you have done."

"We're just getting started," he whispered.

His words carried a promise that sent something wild fluttering beneath her ribs. Hope and panic tangled together until she couldn't tell them apart. The sensation thawed something long frozen inside her, and fear rose—something she'd learn never to ignore. Panic surged through her, betraying the man who'd offered her nothing but kindness. She sat frozen. She couldn't draw away from him, but she couldn't move closer either. Her body felt like a battleground—thirty years of fear colliding with this brand-new fragile hope. It was all she could do to hold on, stuck in the middle as her warring instincts threatened to tear her apart.

A week into the renovations, the farmhouse no longer looked abandoned. The sound of hammers and laughter filled the air as Luke's crew worked diligently—even when he wasn't around. Deborah picked up her mug of coffee; she'd forgotten its warmth, long gone. She cradled it as she watched the men move in sync, transforming the house piece by piece.

Each swing of the hammer echoed her hopes. The unease that followed wasn't about the work—it was about him. Luke never slowed down, never complained, and an old instinct stirred, warning her of the cost.

Soon, she'd need to leave for her meeting with the Quiltin' Bees, but for now, she savored this quiet moment of observation—a brief escape from the chaos of her thoughts.

The farmhouse walls, once gray and neglected, now stood bright with fresh paint. Luke had purchased premium paint that wouldn't yellow with time and could withstand wear and tear. Yesterday, she'd watched him on his hands and knees with a level, muttering about the uneven floorboards while his crew moved around him like a well-choreographed dance. Her chest tightened at the memory of Chad's sneering face at City Hall. She gripped the counter. *Stop the negative thoughts. Move forward. Show up, speak up.* These words were her mantra. Even when it felt hollow, she said them anyway, hoping she'd believe them.

Deborah traced her finger across a swatch of cornflower fabric that peeked out from her overstuffed notebook as she walked out the farmhouse door. Luke looked up from his work on the porch when she stepped outside. She surveyed the fresh paint on the porch's wooden railing and smiled.

"Looks nice."

"Thanks, Deb. On your way to town?"

Deborah nodded.

"Be safe," he said. "See ya soon."

"Thanks for everything, Luke."

He just smiled and winked.

Deborah slid into her car and headed toward Cardinal Creek Quilting. Warmth lingered from Luke's generosity, but her grip tightened on the steering wheel all the same. Experience had taught her to watch for the fine print.

Her thoughts swayed like a pendulum. One moment, Luke's generosity warmed her; the next, she wondered what the farmhouse's beauty would cost. What would he expect in return?

Outside, standing in the quilt shop lot, she clutched her notebook against her chest as she exited the car, feeling the flutter of fabric samples against her fingers. Approaching the entrance, she caught her smiling reflection in the glass door. The expression surprised her. She'd worn a tight, careful smile for years, but now, something genuine reached her eyes. Something that had appeared more frequently lately. Maybe someone was the reason. Luke.

When Deborah entered the classroom of the quilt shop, the ladies looked up, and Sissy greeted her with a hug. "How are the renovations going?"

"Good, Luke and his crew have almost all the big renovations done. He got a crew out there to finish clearing the garden and build a chicken coop," she smiled. "He's amazing."

Sissy raised an eyebrow. "That was kind of dreamy when you said that."

Deborah waved her hands. "Luke is just helping me, but there's nothing more."

Liz stood, grabbed a bolt of yellow fabric, and set it on the table with others grouped by color. "Girl, the way he looks at you says he has more in his heart than helping you."

Peggy Sue moved a fire-engine-red fabric to the same table. "This matches the fire in Luke's eyes when he looks at you."

The room burst into laughter.

Warmth crept up Deborah's neck, leaving her skin tingling beneath her hairline. She tried to keep her eyes on her work, to focus on the bolts of fabric she, Liz, and Sissy were sorting, but beneath her composure a silent current hummed. She was sure that if they looked closely, they'd see the way her thoughts circled back to Luke again and again. Did they notice their unspoken chemistry, too? It was clear to her, but she wondered if the spark was hers alone or something they both felt that lived quietly between them. Perhaps Luke's kindness was genuine, but it also felt like a trick she'd fallen for in the past, one that could easily turn dark, just as it had with Chad.

Peggy Sue joined in. "Didn't he fix the faucet for you? That's like a marriage proposal in this town."

Deborah's face burned hotter as she fumbled with the bolts of fabric. The air was thick as her mind swirled with images of Luke—the way his T-shirt pulled across his chest, how the curve of his biceps filled the sleeves. She fanned her face with a fabric swatch, trying to cool the flush in her cheeks.

The ladies sat around the table, stacks of patterns and color samples spread out, their playful teasing winding through the conversation as they debated which designs belonged in which rooms and which quilt or curtains would work best. But the laughter and talk of Luke, so bright and lively, faded as the conversation shifted, and the spotlight of their teasing swiveled away from Deborah and landed on Liz.

"So, Liz, tell us about the dinner dates you've been going on with Danny?"

Deborah's head jerked up, a smile spreading across her face. "Really, Liz?"

Liz rolled her eyes. "It's just been a few dinners and a movie or two."

"Has he kissed you?" Peggy Sue asked.

"Heavens, no, he's a gentleman," Liz said with laughter.

"A gentleman is not what I want. I'm old, not dead. I want romance, and well, you know," Sissy said.

"Oh, for heaven's sake, Sissy, that kind of stuff is personal," Liz said.

Deborah nodded in agreement, hoping everyone would get the hint that these kinds of conversations were very uncomfortable for the person on the receiving end.

"Well, some of us have to live vicariously through others," Sissy said, laughing.

Deborah smiled at the teasing, truly hoping that Danny would find someone to love. A few years ago, he'd told her he once had feelings for her. Quiet ones. The kind he'd never acted on, never burdened her with. Time had finished what kindness and restraint had started, allowing them to fade.

"Do you like Danny, Liz?" she asked in almost a whisper.

Liz looked at her. "I do."

"Good, he deserves someone like you." She smiled at Liz.

"Thanks, honey."

The bell over the door jingled, and every voice froze mid-sentence. A blonde woman in her thirties stepped inside, her heels clicking decisively against the floor. She adjusted the strap of her designer purse with a manicured left hand without a wedding ring. Her makeup was flawless, and her jeans hugged an hourglass figure beneath a loose, draped tunic. When she smiled, her lipstick didn't bleed into the fine lines around her mouth. Confidence radiated from her as she crossed the room with effortless grace.

Deborah watched, unable to look away. There was something steady and self-assured about her, and Deborah longed to be that confident.

Lowering her gaze, the woman began, "Hey, y'all, I heard that someone is trying to open a shelter for women."

Sissy stepped forward. "Yes, I'm Sissy," she said, tipping her head as she gestured to Deborah. "She's working on renovating an old farmhouse for the shelter."

Deborah stepped forward, extending her hand. The woman's confident demeanor barely concealed the familiar shadow in her sapphire eyes—one that Deborah recognized all too well. "I'm Deborah. And you?"

"Oh," she said with a nervous laugh. "I'm Tiffany. I wanted to know if you needed help with anything." She looked down again. "I recently divorced my husband of fifteen years, who was abusive. I just moved here for a fresh start. I'm a teacher at the elementary school."

The ladies greeted her in unison, smiling.

Liz's eyes crinkled at the corners as she stepped forward. "Teachers are always welcome in our little circle," she said, offering her hand. "I spent thirty years in the classroom myself before trading my lesson plans for quilt patterns and loving on my grandkids."

Tiffany took a seat beside Deborah and shared the story of her abusive marriage and divorce. Her husband was her high school sweetheart. She got pregnant during her senior year but lost the baby after they got married. Losing the baby led her to overeat and gain a lot of weight, and he blamed her when she didn't conceive. The more she couldn't get pregnant, the more he drank, and the more he drank, the more he hit her. The vicious cycle of his drinking and hitting led her to even more overeating.

Tiffany waved her hands over her body. "So, it all led to this. I went from cheerleader to this. Even though I get treated differently, I'm still the same person inside."

"Darlin', you're beautiful. I love the way you do your makeup," Liz said. "People get hung up on outer beauty, based on what the media tells us, but real beauty is on the inside. The outside is just packaging."

"Men are mean no matter what," Deborah blurted out. Then, she placed a hand over her mouth.

All the ladies stared at her, and the words that tumbled out surprised her. "Don't they all want something? When they do something for you, they think they have a reason to control you." Anger constricted her chest, and heat crawled up her neck. "It doesn't matter what they do—especially if they have money. They can imprison you, and nobody helps...at all."

She stood abruptly, almost knocking over her chair. Tears burned her eyes, and her chest heaved. "I don't want a man looking at me or wanting anything. I want to be free."

Liz, Sissy, and Peggy Sue inched closer with caution, like she was going to explode.

"Deborah, are you okay?"

Deborah closed her eyes and nodded as the tears cascaded down her cheeks. She placed her hand over her heart and released a long breath. "God, that felt good," she said as she opened her eyes. "I don't know where that came from."

She turned to Tiffany. "Never let a man define who you are. If he does, he'll have them to deal with," she said, pointing at Liz, Sissy, and Peggy Sue. The room erupted in laughter.

Liz put a hand on Deborah's shoulder. "Honey, you aren't the same timid woman who showed up at my house two years ago. Let it out; you're among friends."

"Listen, Deb, if us teasing you about Luke is getting out of hand, let us know," Sissy said.

"Well, the teasing about Danny bothers me," Liz said.

Sissy waved a hand at her. "Who asked you?"

Deborah loved these women because they always offered her unconditional love.

"Okay, ladies, I need to know about this Luke and Danny," Tiffany said with a huge smile.

"Well, here's the short version. Luke is the fire chief who works with Liz's son Will and Deborah's son Jon. He's quite smitten with Deborah. And Danny is Deborah's ex-brother-in-law, who has taken quite a liking to Liz," Sissy said.

Liz raised an eyebrow at Tiffany. "Danny is off-limits to talk about," she said in her stern teacher's voice.

Tiffany blinked quickly. "Yes, ma'am." Then she quickly turned to Deborah.

"About the fire chief," she said. "His name is Luke?"

Deborah waved a hand at her dismissively. "He's helping with the shelter renovations. That's it." But as the words left her mouth, her heart quickened, betraying the wall she'd carefully built around her feelings for Luke.

Tiffany placed a hand on her shoulder. "You know, I found the best way to move on is to find someone new."

"You should see how Luke looks at her," Peggy Sue said.

"Will said the Chief has been in a better mood ever since he started helping with the shelter," Liz said.

"Girl, if I had a man looking at me that way, I would go for it,"

Tiffany said. "I have my eye on this sexy cowboy who tends bar at the Saddle Up. I love his copper hair and goatee."

The ladies giggled and murmured, "JW."

"Oh, y'all know him?" she asked.

"Yes, he's friends with our sons," Liz said. "He's a good man."

Tiffany bit her bottom lip. "Y'all, I'm not here for match makin', but I wanted to let you know the gossip mill in town is churning about the shelter."

Deborah's heart began to pound so hard it was in her ears. "What are they saying?"

"The lady at the library—the one who talks nonstop about everyone —said there's a guy named Chad running his mouth. Saying the shelter would be trouble and whoever's opening it is unstable."

Tiffany exhaled sharply, and her hands flew up. "I knew right then I needed to meet you," she said, squeezing Deborah's hand.

Deborah's mind raced. What was Chad doing? Why did he care about stopping the shelter? It didn't make sense. She took a slow, deep breath to regain control, forcing a smile as she looked at Tiffany. "Thanks for letting me know."

Should I tell Jon? No...let's see what he does.

"Do you know this guy?" Tiffany asked.

"She does," Sissy said. "It's her crazy ex-husband."

"If it's okay with y'all, I'd like to join in and help."

"Welcome," they all said in unison.

"Tiffany, are you ready to hear about some decorating for the shelter?" Deborah asked.

Tiffany nodded.

Deborah stood. "Okay, ladies, we have four themed rooms: Hope, Courage, Grace, and Renewal. In this pile, we have the colors for Hope —sky blue, pale yellow, and white linen. We are using the Bear Paw quilt block and five-inch squares to make patchwork curtains."

As she talked about each room, she could hear Tiffany's voice playing in her mind, an echo that kept repeating, filling her with doubt. Was the shelter the right idea, or would it just draw unwanted attention from Chad? The anxiety coiled in her stomach as she contemplated the risk of stepping into the light only to be shadowed by his presence.

"Patchwork curtains just warm up a room. That reminds me of grandma's house," Liz said.

"Alright, we have our assignments," Sissy said. "Let's get to work."

Everyone dispersed and went to work at their sewing machines, the hum of the radio playing George Strait in the background.

As everyone settled in, Deborah scanned the room. Tiffany sat at the table with Liz and Sissy, chatting as if she'd always been part of things. Her hands moved as she measured and cut through cotton prints while her words tumbled out between spontaneous, contagious giggles, as comfortable as if she'd been attending these gatherings for years. As Deborah cut the fabric and began sewing, she realized her dream shelter was finally taking shape and becoming a community movement.

Tiffany's words about Luke lingered in Deborah's mind like a persistent echo. *If I had a man looking at me that way, I would go for it.*

Deborah's stomach tightened. She had once smiled at a man at a business dinner. It was just a polite smile.

Chad's fingers had closed around her arm beneath the tablecloth, tight enough that she kept smiling through it. He'd laughed at the table, made a joke, and excused them early. The ride home had been silent. She remembered the abrupt stop of the car that pushed her forward. The way the headlights cut across the yard. The way the front door slammed so hard, the window shook. After that, the memory blurred into fragments–the wall, the taste of blood, the sound of her breath trying not to sob.

For two weeks, the bedroom door stayed locked. He told the neighbors she was ill. She heard him screaming at Jon when he frantically asked where she was. He commanded them not to go near their bedroom.

She learned how small she could make herself.

How quiet.

How invisible.

That was the night she stopped smiling at other men. That night, she learned how dangerous it was to be seen.

And Luke saw her.

CHAPTER 12

Deborah pulled into a parking spot facing Cardinal Creek's square and wondered whether she was ready to be seen. The morning light illuminated the weathered brick storefronts, catching on the windowpanes and the metal frames of the café chairs. Stepping out of her car, keys jingling in her hand, she inhaled the scent of ripe peaches from Henderson's Orchard mingling with the cilantro and chorizo from the taco truck on the corner. Her stomach growled at the smell of breakfast tacos, even as anxiety knotted it.

The farmers' market bustled with voices, laughter, and the scrape of tables being dragged into place. Life had kept moving while she'd been standing still. This was supposed to be research, yet her chest tightened anyway. She slowed near the edge of the courthouse lawn, and her pulse quickened with the crowd's energy. Too many people, too much noise, too much expectation pressed on her from all sides.

She drew in a slow, deep breath and held it until the dizziness eased. In. Out. She could leave. No one would stop her. But the shelter wouldn't build itself.

Come on, Deborah, you need to keep walking forward.

Forcing her feet forward toward the oak tree, she sought refuge while clutching her small notebook labeled Shelter Ideas as vendors finished setting up. The morning warmth made her cotton button-up cling to her skin. Although she should have felt thrilled by the possibilities, doubts crept in as the town hall meeting approached—practiced, well-worn doubts, as if they'd been waiting their turn. She knew whose voice they came from.

Not today. I'm not doing this today. This matters too much.

As Deborah waited for Tiffany, she scanned the blue canopies lining the courthouse square, imagining the day when jars of preserves, quilts, and soaps with The Nest Mercantile labels would be displayed among them. When she heard her name, she turned to see Tiffany approaching with a pink bag swinging from her wrist, looking so at ease in the world. Deborah felt like a stranger, even two years after leaving Chad and working for Sissy.

"Well, girl, I'm out of breath walking up here," Tiffany said, breathing heavily. She dabbed at the sweat beading on her forehead. "Oh, my, it smells like funnel cake. Wanna get some?"

"I'm good for now, but I need some coffee."

"Sounds good," she said.

As they headed toward the coffee truck, Deborah tried to catch glimpses of the vendors on each side, their tables stacked with goods. Several were carrying items such as bundles of herbs, potholders, and jars of jam. But Tiffany kept talking, circling back to the men scattered around the market, her voice chipping away at Deborah's patience. Every mention made something within her tighten. She shut her eyes for a moment and inhaled, trying to steady herself, and then she stepped up to the window.

"Caramel latte," she said.

"Deb, this is a great place to meet someone. Especially if you want to snag yourself a cowboy," Tiffany said.

Deborah curbed her annoyance. "A relationship is not something I'm looking for. I don't have time."

"Wouldn't it be great to be on a man's arm again?"

She bit her bottom lip, the metallic taste of blood filling her mouth as she fought to keep silent. Deborah had never been on Chad's arm. He would drag her to parties only to abandon her in corners, where he'd watch from across the room. If any man approached for an innocent conversation, he'd appear at her side–her body already bracing for what would follow. Memories flooded her mind–bruised wrists hidden beneath long sleeves, the suffocating grip of control wrapped around her throat. The scent of his cologne still clung to her, thick and suffocating, a reminder of accusations hissed in her ear during car rides home. She trembled at the recollection, each breath shallow as she recalled the dread that awaited her once they got home. The darkness that loomed over the familiar doorways, the weight of unspoken threats hanging in the air.

She pressed her palms against the warm cardboard of her coffee cup and focused on the heat seeping into her skin. The smell of roasted beans. The sound of chairs scraping the ground. Someone was laughing behind her. In. Out. The memories tugged her, but the present was louder.

Her next breath came easier. She pulled out a small notebook and a pen. "Okay," she said. "Let's figure out what the ladies can make in the craft barn—quilts, soaps, jams—things we can sell at the farmers' market." Tiffany nodded as she took a long draw of her coffee. "Okay, let's get to it. Did you see the booth with the quilts?"

"I was planning for it to be one of my last stops." After that, she made a note of dog treats and dog bandannas.

As they threaded through the clusters of vendors, Tiffany's chatter bounced across the stalls, noting every man that passed with breezy commentary. Sometimes, the age difference between them felt pronounced.

Oh my, she's almost the same age Shelly would be, Deborah thought, reminding herself to be patient. Maybe Tiffany lacked a mother figure in her life.

As she picked up a couple jars of jam and touched the bundles of herbs, unease settled at the base of her neck, slow and prickling. She added two bars of lavender soap to her basket, but the soothing scent did nothing to ease her anxiety. Every few steps, she glanced back, searching the edges of the bustling crowd, half-expecting Chad to materialize from between the booths. Tiffany and Deborah grabbed bottles of water and settled at a table in the shade of the big oak tree on the courthouse lawn.

"Have you seen Luke lately?" Tiffany asked.

"Not for a few days. He was working at the firehouse, and I was working on the quilts and curtains."

"Sorry, I haven't been able to help much during the weeks since school started," Tiffany said.

"I appreciate all the help you have given."

Tiffany chuckled. "It's not like I have a full social calendar."

Deborah bumped her shoulder. "Me neither."

"Why don't we go out to the Saddle Up one weekend? I'm dying to meet the redhead in there."

Deborah laughed. "His name is JW." *Finally, she's talking about guys for herself, not me.*

"Yeah, JW," she said, chewing her bottom lip. "I don't want to go in there alone."

Deborah's shoulders knotted when Tiffany suggested she go to the bar with her. It was something she had never done. Chad rarely took her anywhere, especially not to a bar. "I—I don't know if I can do that. Let me think about it," she said, glancing over her shoulder several times.

As Deborah finished her sentence, a shadow stretched over her table, long and familiar in the worst way. Her chest tightened. She was afraid to look up, afraid it was Chad. She rubbed her hand down her arm, trying to settle the tremor under her skin.

Tiffany began to speak but fell silent, her eyes narrowing as they focused on someone behind Deborah. Her posture shifted, and her voice dropped to a whisper.

"Deb...a man is walking up. Don't turn around."

Deborah froze. The oxygen in the air evaporated as she tried to breathe.

Tiffany wrapped her hand around Deborah's wrist. Not pushing or pulling, just an anchor.

"What does your ex look like?" Tiffany whispered.

Deborah swallowed and leaned in. "Tall, polo shirt, likely navy, boots polished so you could see your reflection."

"Yeah, he's here," Tiffany said, biting her bottom lip.

Deborah didn't need to turn. Chad's presence brought a recognizable unease, like a wolf among sheep. She closed her eyes and shook her head.

"Deborah, aren't you going to introduce me to your friend?" His voice sent chills through her, changing the atmosphere of the market.

Deborah's throat tightened. She reached unquestioningly for the table, digging into it with her fingers. She took shallow, uneven breaths.

Tiffany stood and stepped between Deborah and Chad. "She doesn't want to talk to you," she snapped.

Chad dismissed her with a smirk, walking past her. "This is none of your business, dear."

"I think it is," Tiffany said, loud enough that a few vendors glanced their way.

Deborah forced herself to turn. Her spine locked even though her legs were like those of a newborn foal. Chad stood in front of her like he owned the square, wearing pressed jeans, a navy polo, and sunglasses pushed up on his head. He smiled politely as he looked at her. It was a look she knew well, and it sent a sudden wave of dread through her.

"What do you want, Chad?"

"I didn't expect to see you here today." His gaze turned to Tiffany, then back to Deborah. "Or with friends."

Deborah's pulse throbbed in her ears. She took a deep cleansing breath, in through her nose, and slowly released it through her mouth. "We're just here for the market," she said, her voice even despite her inner turmoil.

"That's good," he said. His smile grew more intense. "Getting out. Hanging out with your friends. Must be nice to have all of this...free... time."

Despite the heat, Deborah had chills. He uttered the phrase "free time" with the tone of an old accusation. Her gaze swept the crowd until she found Jon, who was standing in the square. He froze when he saw Chad.

Deborah gave him a pleading look. *Help!* she screamed inside, praying he would intervene.

He approached them with long strides, his jaw clenched and his shoulders rigid. Before Chad could say anything more, Jon was at her side.

"Everything okay here, Mom?" He was calm, but the steel in his voice was unmistakable.

"I wasn't aware your mother required protection," Chad stated, his expression hardening.

Jon smiled, but it didn't reach his eyes. "She doesn't, but she's not alone."

"I see how it is." A smirk twisted his lips, and a glint of amusement flashed in his eyes. "You have Jon fight your battles. That's cute," he said, the air thick with unspoken challenge.

Deborah's hands trembled. Tiffany drew near and stood shoulder to shoulder with her, expressing her support and encouragement. Chad ignored her.

"Deborah, you look stressed," he said in a concerned voice. "I hope this project isn't becoming overwhelming. It would be awful if it fell apart."

"Deborah," a voice said from her side.

The warmth and steadiness of that voice cut through the tension.

She closed her eyes and took a deep breath. *Luke.*

With intent, Luke advanced, the gravel giving way beneath his boots, and his fire department shirt pulled taut across his large shoulders. As he approached, he placed a comforting hand on her back, his touch both soft and supportive. She gave him a pleading look, wordless but desperate. *Don't let him take control of this.*

"Is everything okay?" he asked as his eyes bore into Chad.

The smile on Chad's face vanished. In that instant, Deborah saw his mask slip. "Well, well, if it isn't the fire chief. I was unaware that my wife was among your duties. Are you all seeing each other?"

Luke's stare remained steady. "Your *ex*-wife doesn't owe you an explanation."

Chad let out a mirthless laugh. "She owes me more than you know."

Jon moved closer to Chad. "No," he said in a hushed tone. "That ended a long time ago. You will not intimidate her with your manipulative tactics."

As Chad's gaze shifted to Jon, irritation flashed in his eyes. "Careful, son. You don't know everything that's going on."

Deborah wasn't sure what he meant by *everything going on.* Something about Chad's words didn't sit right with her.

"I know enough." Jon put himself between Deborah and Chad. "I was there. I know what you did, and here's a news flash: I've grown up now. You don't get to talk to her like that anymore."

Luke positioned himself just behind and to the side of Deborah— protective, quiet, and steady.

Tiffany crossed her arms and stared at Chad. "You should go," she said. "Before someone calls the sheriff." For someone who'd been discussing cowboys all morning, her tone was surprisingly harsh.

Chad's gaze went to Tiffany. His chest expanded as he breathed in, and the muscles in his jaw jumped. He glared at Deborah, his eyes glittering with a warning she knew all too well once upon a time. "This isn't over. It's only going to get worse."

Luke stepped forward. "Chad, what you don't get is that...it *is* over."

Chad stared at Luke for a long moment. Too long. Deborah met his gaze, and a threatening message was clear in his eyes, reminiscent of a night long ago. She shivered. He turned and walked off at a controlled brisk pace.

When he disappeared into the crowd, Deborah's legs were like rubber. Jon caught her arm, and Luke steadied her on the other side.

Tiffany reached for Deborah's trembling hands, voice quivering. "Why didn't you tell me it was him you were afraid of?"

Deborah swallowed, eyes burning. "I didn't want to give him more space in my life than he had already stolen."

Luke's voice was quiet but fierce. "He's not getting another inch."

Deborah sat for a moment, taking slow, deep breaths with her eyes closed, praying her heart would stop pounding. *Luke is right; Chad isn't getting another inch.*

She opened her eyes to find Luke, Tiffany, and Jon looking at her. She took a shaky breath before speaking. "I'm okay, I came here for a reason," she said, looking at Tiffany. "Want to look at some booths with me?"

"Want me to walk with y'all?" Luke asked.

Deborah touched Luke's arm. "I appreciate you asking, but I need to do this."

He smiled and nodded. "I understand. You have my number, text if you need anything."

"I will."

"Thank you for coming to the rescue," Tiffany said and immediately bit her bottom lip. "Not that Deborah couldn't handle herself." She turned to Deborah. "I...I didn't mean it like that."

Deborah smiled. "I know. It's okay, Tiff."

"Mom, if you need us, we are just a text away," Jon said, kissing her cheek before he left. "Nice to meet you Tiffany," he called over his shoulder.

Luke gave Deborah's arm a gentle squeeze before he touched the brim of his hat and walked away.

"Come on, let's go to the quilt booth," Deborah said, looping her arm through Tiffany's, hoping that her insides would start to be as calm as her outside.

After they left the quilt booth, they continued looking at other booths, and Deborah scribbled notes on the various products and farm-fresh items at each.

One vendor, a woman in her late sixties, slipped Deborah a jar of hand lotion and whispered, "I saw what happened with that man. I've seen men like him...I was married to one. If you need anything, I'm here...every Saturday."

Deborah was speechless. She wasn't alone in her experiences. It was like a silent club of women that quietly held on, praying for someone to help them. She smiled at the woman. "Thank you...We aren't alone."

"No, honey, we aren't," she said. "I'm Loretta. Come see me anytime."

"I will."

When Deborah and Tiffany finished visiting the booths, they walked together to their cars. The click of heels on the road punctuated the silence that stretched between them. Deborah sensed that the confrontation with Chad had affected Tiffany more than she was willing to share. When she climbed into her car and shut the door, her eyes settled on the lotion and basket of soaps on her seat. Deborah gripped the steering wheel her knuckles white against the leather as thoughts of Chad's threats swirled in her mind. She knew they weren't empty; she could feel the weight of them linger, unwelcome, but familiar. The road ahead wouldn't be smooth.

A restraining order loomed in her thoughts longer than she expected, but the thought of courtrooms brought a fresh wave of dread. Eyes on her, judgments made; scrutiny that could delay permits faster than a missing signature. Chad would welcome that.

Deborah tightened her grip on the wheel, a physical anchor against the tide of uncertainty. She wasn't just fighting for herself anymore; she was fighting for the women who had suffered before her and for those still coming. With resolve, she shifted the car into gear, ready to face whatever came next.

CHAPTER 13

*L*uke could see Deborah polishing the fireplace in the living room when he knocked on the open front door. "Deb, it's Luke. Wanted to let you know I'll be in the barn."

She straightened and turned toward him, wearing Capri jeans and a tank top. Her skin was sun-kissed from yard work and gardening over the last few weeks. Luke's heart skipped a beat, like it always did when he saw her. "Oh, hey, want some coffee or donuts?" she asked, motioning toward the kitchen.

Luke hesitated, aware that saying yes would mean staying longer than he'd planned.

"Sure, do you want to go over things for the town meeting?" he asked as he entered the room. The crease between her eyebrows gave Luke his answer. "Or we could just drink coffee."

She chuckled. "I'm sorry, I'm worried. Chad has been too quiet. I'm sure he's building his army of minions. I've seen how he does business a million times. He gets quiet, then swoops in for the attack, knocking his enemy to the ground." She exhaled a long breath. "I'm his enemy. Always have been."

Luke put his hand on her arm. "You're not alone in this. So many people believe in what you are doing. Think about the day we started the renovations. How many people showed up? We have your back. Chad won't win, not on my watch." The last sentence caught in his throat.

Deborah took his hand. "Let's get some coffee." As she led him to the kitchen, she looked back and smiled. "Two sugars and a spot of plain creamer, right?"

Luke stopped, amazed she knew that. She turned to him and

stumbled into his arms. Holding her was like being wrapped in a warm blanket on a cold day—a comfort he never wanted to step out of.

"Oh, Lord, I'm so clumsy."

He smiled. "It's okay, I think you're falling for me." The words left his mouth and his gaze flickered to her face, searching.

She reached up and bopped his nose with her index finger. "Maybe."

As they drank a few cups of coffee, chatting about Cardinal Creek gossip and laughing at some of the crazy stories circulating, Luke considered how to tell her about a call he had received from the mayor. It was important for Deborah to know the truth about Chad's plans.

"I talked to the mayor yesterday. She told me that Chad has been going to various business owners trying to get the zoning for the shelter denied." Deborah's face fell, and the pain in her eyes broke his heart. Why did it hurt so badly to see her in pain? "Listen, as you said earlier, he likes to swoop in and devour his enemy, but maybe his other enemies didn't have the mayor on their side, and you do."

Deborah's eyes widened. "Wait, what? Really?"

"Yes, and you have a former council member who understands the politics of something like this," he said, covering her hand with his. Touching her settled him—a quiet, steady feeling he hadn't noticed in himself for a long time. The calm was unfamiliar, but undeniable. The warmth of her skin under his palm made the usual noise in his chest fade out, leaving him at ease.

She bit her bottom lip. "I suppose that's true. Does Jon know this?"

"I told him yesterday. He said he was going to talk to Danny and see what he could do."

Before she finished her cup of coffee, she said, "I should talk to the ladies at the quilt shop so we can be ready for the town hall meeting."

It was a sign that he should get to work. He wanted to finish painting the craft barn so they could get things set up inside. He picked up the ceramic mug he was using, rinsed it in the sink, and put it in the drainer. When he turned, she was watching him with a smile.

"What? Do I have something on my face?" he asked, wiping his face.

"No," she said. "You're amazing. Thank you for everything."

"Thank you for the kind words," he said as heat crept up his neck.

She'd completely taken him by surprise. "I really need to get to work," he mumbled while exiting through the back door.

He walked into the barn, leaned against the wall, and closed his eyes. He wasn't sure what to do with all the feelings stirring in him for Deborah. He set out to work, and over the course of the day, his mind drifted, wondering what she was doing inside. The soft rhythm of country music played in the background as he painted, forgetting to eat until his stomach grumbled. He put down his paintbrush and checked his progress before he walked to the door. The sky had shifted to a deeper blue, and a long shadow stretched across the worn red wood of the barn. Deborah's wind chimes created a melody carried by the refreshing wind. He stood with his thumbs in his pockets, gazing at the golden field and enjoying the peace the slowing pace of the evening brought.

Luke turned when he heard the squeaking of the back door. Deborah descended the stairs, and a smile spread across her face as she approached him.

"I'm the worst boss ever," she said. "I bet you're hungry."

Luke put a hand over his growling stomach. "I am."

She tilted her head to motion toward the door. "Come on, let's eat something and call it a day."

He nodded and followed her into the house. When he entered the kitchen, he was in awe at the sight. A red-and-white gingham tablecloth covered the table, and a platter of sandwiches—ham and turkey with provolone cheese—sat in the center, along with a pitcher of strawberry lemonade. Beside them sat a bowl of potato salad and a bowl of baked beans. He was amazed that she knew all his favorites; he had never told her what he liked to eat.

Deborah gestured toward the empty chair with a warm smile. "Come on, have a seat," she said, settling into her own chair at the table.

He eased into the chair next to her. "Did you know all of this stuff was my favorite, or is it a coincidence?"

A mischievous grin crossed her face. "I might have asked someone you know what you like."

He let out a long groan. "Jon."

She smiled and nodded. "I wanted to do something nice for you. I have brownies for dessert and wine if you want some."

He reached for the pitcher of lemonade. "I want some of this first. I'm dying of thirst."

Deborah laughed as she placed food on her plate.

They enjoyed their sandwiches and talked about some of their favorite places to eat and foods. As they cleared the table together, Luke touched Deborah's arm, making her jump. When she looked at him, terror filled her eyes.

"Deb, I'm sorry…I…I should have asked," he said as he retreated toward the door. "Maybe I should go."

Deborah stopped him before he could reach the door. "Luke, you did nothing wrong. Don't go. Let's have some brownies."

"Now you're talking death by chocolate."

She touched her forehead with the heel of her hand. "Exactly."

They sat at the table, and Deborah cut him a large piece of brownie along with one for herself. When he put the first bite into his mouth, the explosion of chocolate and salted caramel was the best thing he had ever tasted. He wiped his mouth with a napkin. "You made these?"

She nodded. "They're Jon's favorite."

"Now, mine too. You should sell these. I can't describe the flavor, but it's heavenly."

A blush crept onto Deborah's face. "Heavenly?"

"Yes," he said, touching her hand. "Made by an angel." *Why did I say that? It's so cliché.* He winced. "Sorry, Deb, I'm not very good with words and women."

Deborah laughed. "Luke, you are the nicest, kindest man I've ever met." She stopped and swallowed hard. "I know I jumped when you touched me, but you make me feel safe. Never doubt that."

He nodded quickly and changed the subject. "I got most of the inside of the craft area painted today. It's almost ready to put the final touches on it. Where are we with painting inside the house?"

Her eyes darted to the window, then back to him, and her lips parted slightly before she pressed them together again. The furrow in her brow deepened.

Luke reached across the table, his fingers brushing her knuckles as he took her hands in his. The touch communicated what words couldn't: he would hear whatever she needed to say without judgment.

Her gaze stayed on his hand, tracing small circles. When she finally spoke, her voice was barely above a whisper.

"Luke...do you ever stop hurting?" She blinked against tears. "Losing Shelly, it feels like the ground drops out from under me every time I think about her or what I missed."

He leaned in, drawn to her pain as his fingers continued to stroke her knuckles. "Deb..."

"I haven't been able to talk about losing my daughter. I know you were there when she died, and I know you understand what it's like to lose a child. How do you handle it? It's like a piece of my heart is missing something. I don't know how to explain it...just pain, a dull aching pain that never goes away."

A lump formed in Luke's throat. He was unsure how to respond, not knowing how to describe what had happened on the day of Shelly's accident. He'd taken Will to the hospital but had left her son to remove his sister's body. He knew that no matter what he'd said, Jon would have stayed, but if he were an effective leader, he would have taken both Jon and Will. Instead, Jon suffered because of his inability to lead effectively.

"I was at the scene of the accident, but I quickly ushered Will away while Jon stayed." He stopped and took a deep breath. "I'm sorry I couldn't get Jon to leave. I suppose...my leadership skills are lacking—"

"Luke, that's not true at all," Deborah said, cutting him off. "My son is exceptionally strong-willed. You did the right thing. My question was more parent to parent...about losing a child," she said, her eyes brimming with tears.

Luke's chest tightened whenever he talked about the loss of his son, Caleb. Losing him had shattered the foundation of his life, leaving him with grief so raw he could barely form the words to describe it. His ex-wife never missed a chance to blame him for what happened. He stared at the grain of the wooden table, tracing a finger along the dark line that split and rejoined itself.

"Caleb was his name. He was driving back from Austin." His voice came out hoarse. "February 12th. My birthday." He swallowed hard. After that, Luke hated everything about his birthday. The day felt bitter every year. "A few years after his death, nothing in my marriage was the same. It all unraveled bit by bit. Eventually, Kim packed her things. Left a teddy bear for Sammy on the kitchen counter with a note." He glanced at the calendar on Deborah's refrigerator, the kind with tear-off daily quotes. Sammy had changed after she left for college. She'd gotten close to her mom and rarely came back to Cardinal Creek to visit. "Sammy calls on Sundays now. From her mom's house."

Something about Deborah's gaze steadied him. No one had ever just sat and waited for him to find words. Not even Kim, who had screamed that he'd killed their son by expecting him to drive home for the weekend. The years after Caleb's death had hollowed Luke out, leaving him a shell that moved through life on autopilot. His marriage had crumbled, his daughter was drifting away, and he had resigned himself to permanent numbness. Then Deborah asked the one question no one had dared to ask: parent-to-parent, what it was like to lose a child.

When he looked up and met her eyes, the constant churn inside him stilled for the first time since the February night when he got that terrible call. Because he'd been broken for so long, Luke thought he might never feel anything for anyone again after his son's death and his family fell apart. But that was before Deborah. She was the only one who cared enough to ask what it felt like to lose Caleb. Even his ex-wife had never asked that question.

As Luke held Deborah's gaze, he expected her to look away or shift uncomfortably. Instead, her eyes remained steady, shining with quiet understanding. She didn't pity him, and she didn't interrupt or rush to fill the silence. She just listened as if every word mattered.

"One minute, I had a family, and just like that," he said, snapping his fingers, "it was gone..." He stopped when his voice faltered.

Deborah leaned forward slightly, then folded her hands in her lap as if she were holding herself back from reaching for him. He wanted her to touch him. He longed for her comfort—for a moment of relief from an ache in his chest that never went away. She searched his eyes as if she could read what he was feeling, then stretched her hand across the table, tentative but certain, resting it on his. A jolt ran through him at her touch—not pity, not discomfort, but strength. It radiated from her, unnerving him. He'd expected her to crumble or pull away, but instead, she seemed solid.

Luke realized Deborah might not be as fragile as she seemed, but solid—like she understood grief in her own bones. Her eyes continued to search his, communicating in a silent language that offered comfort no words could ever give.

Finally, Deborah broke the silence, and in just a few words, he learned a lot about who she really was. "Luke, thank you for sharing your pain." She squeezed his hand. "I see you. I really do."

It was then that he realized she was surviving her own battles, and that made her someone who could break through his walls if he'd let her. Luke cleared his throat. "I should head out. Do you want me to wait for you?"

"No, I'm just going to clean this up and then go home," she said, squeezing his hand. She let go, and he had to fight the urge to close his hand again, surprised by how cold everything felt without her.

"Text me when you get home."

She nodded and followed him to the door. The night greeted Luke as he stepped onto the porch—stars scattered across the dark sky like broken glass catching light. Insects pulsed a steady rhythm, matching the strange calm settling in his chest. Each step toward his truck felt heavier, weighted by something he couldn't name. Whatever had just passed between them had shifted something in him. Before climbing into the driver's seat, he turned back. Deborah stood framed in the doorway, her silhouette soft against the warm light behind her. They exchanged waves—hers lingering until she stepped inside and closed the door. In his truck, Luke stared at his hands on the wheel. The ghost of her touch still hummed across his skin. He couldn't shake the image of her steady gaze, the way she leaned forward without hesitation, or the gentle weight of her palm covering his knuckles with quiet certainty.

He muttered, "She's stronger than I thought. Stronger than I am, maybe. And that's a problem. If I let her in, I don't think I could survive losing her too." As he shifted into drive and pulled away from the farmhouse, the weight in his chest doubled. His usual hollow loneliness had sharpened into something with edges—an ache that followed him, settling between his ribs, heavy enough that he adjusted in his seat—then realized nothing eased it.

CHAPTER 14

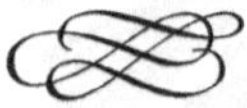

Deborah stood in the barn, paintbrush in hand, the vibrant colors of the walls reflecting her excitement. The scent of fresh paint mixed with the earthy aroma of wood shavings as she added the finishing touches to the space. Each stroke brought her closer to her dream, even as small, unwelcome tension settled beneath the excitement.

Luke entered with a playful grin, carrying a large toolbox. "Ready to work, or are you just going to paint pretty pictures?"

Deborah laughed, feeling the warmth of camaraderie. "I'm ready for whatever you throw at me."

As they worked side by side, a comfortable rhythm developed between them. Deborah glanced at the task checklist, mentally preparing for the upcoming town meeting. She knew that proving the shelter's value to the community was essential.

"Want to learn how to use a drill and saw?" Luke asked. "You might need to tackle some tasks yourself." He rolled his eyes. "I didn't mean you—"

"I know what you meant," Deborah said with a raised hand and a smile. "Yes, teach me!"

He relaxed, softening his eyes. "I need to build a few shelves, so we need to cut the wood. But first we need to measure."

Luke went to work, showing her how to measure and mark the cuts, steadily guiding her through tasks Chad had told her she'd mess up, but here she was learning. As they started building the shelf, he showed her how to use a hammer, covering her hand with his to guide it. The contact ignited something within, like a slow-burning ember. She caught the scent of cedar and clean sweat, and something warm stirred inside her that she couldn't name. Not lust. Not fear. Something gentler...and far more dangerous.

Deborah looked at him and smiled. She wasn't sure what was happening between them, but she liked the way his fingers brushed her skin, even though she knew a relationship with him was unlikely. The way he treated her and believed in her was something she never had with Chad.

While Luke cut boards for the second shelf, Deborah continued building the first one. When she finished, she stepped back, hands on her hips, pride swelling in her chest. When she looked up, her eyes met Luke's, his expression steady, unguarded, and almost reverent. The sight sent a thrill up her spine so intense that she had to catch her breath.

"That's a fine job, Deb," he said, checking her work. "Nice and sturdy."

She looked away, flustered. "It was fun. Would you want to teach some classes here for the women on using tools and things like that?"

Confidence flickered through his smile. "Sure, if you'd like to have lunch with me on the days I teach."

Deborah extended her hand, and he grasped it. "Deal," she said, smiling.

"There is something I want to teach you, and I can teach this in a class as well—fire extinguisher use," he said.

"Yes, that's important."

"I'm gonna go to the truck and get one. I'll show you now."

While he was grabbing the fire extinguisher from the truck, Deborah smoothed her hands over her jeans, trying to steady the quick, uneven beat of her heart. She wasn't prepared for the sight when Luke returned, sunlight behind him, extinguisher in hand, looking like trouble she wasn't ready to handle.

Step by step, he taught her how to use it, his voice steady and grounded. Deborah watched, noticing how good he looked in Wranglers and a cotton tee. *He certainly has muscles in all the right places. Oh, Lord, Deborah, quit staring at him.*

When he moved behind her, his breath was warm against her neck. Her pulse pounded, not out of fear but out of something she wasn't sure she'd ever felt.

"Deb, are you with me?" he asked as he handed her the fire extinguisher.

She nodded quickly.

He placed his hands over hers again, guiding her arm and showing her how to aim, squeeze, and sweep. The warmth of his body at her back felt like strength, not control, safety, not danger. She realized her shoulders were relaxed—something she'd never been able to do around a man.

"Come on, you can practice what you learned."

When they got outside, Luke stepped back so Deborah could practice what he'd shown her. When she finished, she was so excited. She'd never thought she could do the things she did today. Luke's faith in her was so foreign and scary that it made her want to flee.

They went back into the barn and spent the next couple of hours working in companionable silence. It was comforting, the kind of silence she'd dreamed of. Chad's silence had always been a warning, the calm before the storm. Luke's silence was like a shelter—a safe place.

Before they packed up for the day, they walked around, pointing out things she could do as she jotted them down in a list.

"Listen, if you need anything when you're working on this, call me. We could FaceTime, and I could walk you through it."

"I'll only do that if you aren't working."

He took off his glove and brushed his finger across her cheek. "You have a smudge right here," he said.

Her breath hitched. *He blushed...he blushed.* Somehow, it made breathing even harder.

"Thank you," she murmured as she placed her hand on his arm. "For everything. I never thought I could do any of this." She looked down and continued. "I'm very grateful for your friendship. I don't know how I could ever repay you."

He shifted closer, his voice low. "Deb, you don't owe me anything. I like being with you, and you're so easy to talk to. You're an incredibly strong and amazing woman."

Deborah's head shot up. "You really think that?" A lump formed in her throat, and tears burned her eyes. "I don't think anyone has ever said that to me before."

Luke's answer wasn't verbal. He stepped closer, slow enough that she could stop him if she wanted. Close enough that she could feel his breath. Her heart hammered in her throat. He leaned in, and she thought he was going to kiss her, but he whispered in her ear. The heat from his mouth gave her chills. "Can I hug you?"

She nodded.

When he wrapped his arms around her, she melted. She didn't mean to, but her body acted before her mind caught up. His embrace wasn't possessive or demanding.

It was calming, steady, and solid. Strong in all the right ways, gentle in the ways she hadn't realized still ached.

The hug was a lifeline. If her feelings continued to grow, Luke could be the first man she'd ever love. And that was terrifying.

Even more terrifying—she wanted to admit it.

Deborah walked into Cardinal Creek Quilting at four in the afternoon. The classroom was already buzzing with the Quiltin' Bees hard at work. Sissy greeted her with a hug, then took a step back, surveying her with narrowed eyes. "Too skinny, not enough sleep, but beautiful as ever."

Liz pulled her in for a hug. "How's my sister?"

Those words made Deborah's heart soar. She didn't know she'd ever experience the love and acceptance she had received since she walked away from Chad.

"I'm fine," she said, her voice cracking.

Liz pulled back from the hug and said, "Luke isn't giving you trouble, is he? Do I need to get after him?"

Deborah giggled, her eyes sparkling with newfound confidence. "Quite the opposite. He's great! He taught me how to build shelves today. I learned how to use power tools and even a fire extinguisher." She paused, her voice dropping slightly. "At first, I was scared to try. Chad always belittled me, telling me I couldn't do anything right. But today, I felt empowered. I asked Luke to teach classes for those who wanted to learn. I'm so excited about the possibilities!"

Tiffany walked up and gave Deborah a side hug. "Girl, that's some serious power tools energy," Tiffany joked, wiggling her eyebrows. "I'm just glad you're having fun."

Sissy cracked up, and Liz smirked at her remark. Deborah bit her bottom lip to keep from saying something back out of irritation. *I was excited. I learned how to use those tools so I can learn to do things on my own. It's not about romance. This is about me taking control of my life.*

Deborah cleared her throat. "Ladies, thank you for your help, but I need to take off soon. I have an appointment." She really just wanted to go home because no matter what she shared, someone always made it about her romance with Luke. But this was about her journey of empowerment. "We have just a few more things on the task list, and then the decorating can begin."

"How are things coming for the town hall meeting?" Sissy asked.

Deborah shuffled through the mental checklist she'd rehearsed a dozen times. "I've got the renovation numbers ready, the budget stuff, community needs assessment..." She pressed her finger against her bottom lip, eyes drifting upward. "There's one more thing. I just—I can feel it."

"We can meet up next week to go over everything if you'd like," Liz said.

"That sounds good, Liz. Thanks, y'all. See ya soon."

"Deborah," Tiffany said as she gathered her things. "I think I may be annoying with the joking about Luke," she murmured. "It's easier than talking about anything real." She shrugged. "Ignore me when I'm acting like that."

Deborah smiled and nodded.

She stepped out of the quilt shop with a chorus of goodbyes behind her. As she closed the door, irritation from Tiffany's teasing churned inside her. Deborah slid behind the wheel and shut the door, closing her eyes and taking in the quiet. The sun dipped low across Main Street, throwing shadows over the hood of her SUV as she pulled away from the quilt shop. She knew Tiffany meant nothing by it, but it still bothered her. *All the talk about romance—it's like I'm nobody without a man. My romance with Luke is our business.*

Deborah tightened her grip on the steering wheel. This chapter of her life wasn't about catching a man; it was about breathing for the first time without asking for permission. Her stomach knotted, and she needed air. When Green's Grocery came into view, she turned into the parking lot without thinking. Wandering the aisles and choosing groceries might settle her nerves. It helped a little. By the time she drove home, the sky had deepened to shades of lavender and peach, with night clinging to the horizon as she parked.

Deborah put the key in the door with one hand while balancing a grocery bag in the other. A trip to the supermarket helped Deborah clear her head. As she opened a can of soup, poured it into the pot, and absentmindedly stirred it, her thoughts went back to Luke's tender touch, and words *I believe in you. You're strong* lingered in her mind. No one had ever said that to her before–not even her parents.

But then Tiffany's words about finding romance intruded, and frustration bubbled within. The thought of needing someone else overshadowed her moment of independence. And needing someone else meant losing control.

This is about me, not Tiffany's idea of romance.

As she sat eating her soup, she eyed the shelf she had bought. She'd been waiting for Jon to hang it. After she finished her soup, she grabbed the drill from the closet and began measuring, just as Luke had taught her. She applied every skill he'd instructed her to do. His patient tone and gentle guidance echoed in her head as she hung the shelf on the brackets. When she was finished, she took a step back and admired her handiwork.

For years, Chad had held every screw, nail, and repair against her, insisting she couldn't do it. Tonight, in the quiet of her apartment, the hum of the drill in her hand felt like rebellion—like freedom. No raised voice, no criticism. Just her, the wall, and the steady thrum of her own capability.

She smiled. "I did it," she whispered. One step forward on her journey to empowerment. She grabbed her phone off the table and took a picture of the shelf. Then she sent a text to Luke.

> Deborah: This is because you taught me how to use power tools. Thank you for teaching me new skills.

After a few seconds, the three dots appeared.

> Luke: It looks great. You're an excellent student.

She sat on the couch, looking at the shelf and rereading Luke's text. Then she walked over to the shelf and set a potted plant on it, the small green sprout thriving in its new home. The shelf stood steady and strong, a reflection of the strength Deborah was learning to embrace. A sense of accomplishment washed over her, filling her with warmth and resolve.

This was her moment, the beginning of a new chapter where she refused to let Chad's voice echo in her mind. No longer would she allow anyone to make her feel less than she was. She took a deep breath, reminding herself that she had a right to stand up for herself.

With renewed determination, she headed to the bathroom for a quick shower, washing away the remnants of doubt. As she lay in bed, she envisioned herself as strong and capable, ready to face whatever challenges lay ahead. Tonight, fear wouldn't have a place in her dreams; she would build a future where she was in control. With a final sigh of contentment, she closed her eyes, embracing the possibilities that awaited her.

CHAPTER 15

Deborah's hand trembled as she applied the last swipe of coral lipstick, its bright color a stark contrast to the turmoil swirling inside her. In the bathroom mirror, the woman staring back looked put-together but nervous—eyes too wide, shoulders too stiff. She tucked a loose strand of hair behind her ear, squared her tense shoulders, grabbed her car keys, and reminded herself that today would test everything she had built. As she locked the front door, her thoughts flickered to the Quiltin' Bees waiting at the quilt shop. They were her support, her lifeline, but what if she faltered? The sky deepened from blue to honeyed amber near the horizon, clouds catching the light like slow-moving embers. She closed her eyes and inhaled, taking a moment to savor the warmth of the sun on her face, but it did little to ease the knot in her stomach.

Jon had told her he and Kati would bring Anna and Will. She needed to make this work. With the index cards peeking from her purse, she walked to her SUV, feeling the weight of expectation bearing down on her.

As she drove to the quilt shop, Deborah rehearsed what she'd say if anyone asked why the town needed a shelter for women. In her mind, Chad's face hovered just beneath the surface as her arguments tangled with memories of him, sharper than she wanted. If only she'd had somewhere to escape when Jon and Shelly were little. Maybe she could have spared them the years of fear and pain.

Scenes from those years flashed like old footage as she recalled the sound of slammed doors, the shouts that echoed down the hall, the bruises and bloody lips, and the weight of the next outburst. Even now, with no one else in her apartment, Deborah still waited for the other shoe to drop, for Chad to show up, angry and unpredictable.

She blinked hard, pulling herself back. She drew a breath and lifted her chin. "Not now," she murmured. "Today, I show up."

The quilt shop came into view, and Deborah's heart pounded in her chest. Luke stood outside the quilt shop, leaning against the wall, already looking her way. He pushed off the wall and waved when she pulled into the parking lot. She turned off the car and released a ragged breath as he approached. He opened her door, and she grabbed her purse before getting out.

"I wanted to make sure you got inside without Chad bothering you," he said, scanning the street before giving her a side hug.

Deborah smiled. "Thanks, I appreciate it. I was worried he might be lurking around here." His protection warmed her. She tensed when the thought of how his protection could later become suffocation. She'd been there before.

"I have your back. Everyone is inside waiting for you. I told Jon I would come get you," he said, placing his hand in the small of her back. A tremor ran through her at his touch. When his hand fell away, the warmth lingered like an echo, leaving her with an unexpected hollow feeling where his palm had been.

When she walked into the quilt shop, Jon greeted Deborah with a hug. "I'm proud of you, Mom," he whispered. "The place looks amazing. I drove out there today."

Kati came alongside them. "Can I break in here and give my mother-in-law a hug?"

Jon and Deborah pulled Kati into their hug. "Deborah, we saw the house. It's amazing," Kati said.

"Thanks," she said, dabbing at her eyes.

As Sissy walked up, she clapped her hands to get everyone's attention. "Okay, let's take a seat so Deborah can practice her presentation."

Tiffany raised her hand. "What about mentioning our fire chief?" she asked, nodding toward Luke with a meaningful smile. "He's well known and liked, so having his endorsement could help."

When Deborah raised an eyebrow, Tiffany added, "But only if you want to. You've done most of this."

She noticed Jon going after Tiffany. Then Kati grabbed his sleeve and whispered something in his ear. Jon nodded. Luke looked at Deborah when Tiffany yelled across the room.

She mouthed, "I'm sorry."

He just smiled and winked.

Deborah took her place at the front of the classroom and began her presentation. When she finished, the room erupted in applause. She let out a long breath, forced a smile, and prayed that her words would be enough to help the opposition understand that the shelter wouldn't pose a danger. It would provide the community with a resource unavailable to the school or hospital.

Jon drew in close, keeping his voice tight. "Is that woman the one I met at the farmers' market? I don't care who she is, but she better not say stuff like that during the meeting," he said, his words harsh and clipped.

Deborah laid her hand on his arm. "She means well," she said, with a small, weary smile. "She just has a lot of energy."

Her voice carried farther than she intended. Deborah glanced up and caught Tiffany's gaze across the room. Her face dimmed—not sharply, just enough to notice. When their eyes met, Tiffany gave a small nod, a quiet acknowledgment from someone used to being misunderstood.

"Luke is going to walk you to the town meeting, and we'll meet you there," he said.

She nodded. "I'll see ya there."

Luke stepped beside her and put out his elbow. "I shall escort you to City Hall."

Deborah clutched her notecards and intertwined her arm with his.

They walked to City Hall in silence, the light of the day fading. She glanced at his profile as they strolled. He was steady. He was always there when she needed him. Chad was never like that. He never cheered her on or touched her face with tenderness. He wasn't even there when Jon and Shelly were born. She let out a long, ragged breath, and her eyes burned with tears.

Luke stopped and turned toward her. "What's wrong?" he asked, wiping a tear that trailed down her cheek.

"Why are you so nice to me?" she wondered aloud. "Always there when I need you. I can never repay you for all you've done for me."

He placed his hand on her cheek. "You owe me nothing. Believe it or not, you've helped me too. I enjoy your company. Your friendship means a lot to me."

Before Deborah thought about it, she threw herself into his arms. He wrapped them around her and pulled her in tight. The warmth of his body against hers lit a fire inside her. His arms provided protection and a peace she hadn't ever felt. When the hug broke, Luke laced his fingers with hers as they walked the rest of the way to their destination in silence.

City Hall housed the Cardinal Creek City Council Chambers, situated off Main Street; a room built for motions, votes, and public comment rather than comfort. The odor of old paper, coffee, and furniture lingered in the air. Ceiling fans hummed overhead, and the wooden pew-style benches creaked as Deborah slid into a seat, the sound carrying farther than she liked.

Deborah's gaze drifted to the raised platform at the front of the room, where seven empty chairs awaited the council members. Gold nameplates caught the light, each positioned with a slender microphone that stood like a sentinel. The Texas flag stood in the corner, its lone star watching over the proceedings. The wall behind the chairs bore the town seal—a cardinal perched on a live oak branch, its colors faded with the years, but still keeping its dignity. Her fingers tightened around her notes as she stared at the worn wooden podium where, in minutes, she would stand to fight for everything that mattered.

As the townsfolk filtered in one by one, greetings and soft chatter filled the room before they took their spots. The room was part church, part courtroom, and part small town theater, a place where everyone knew everyone's business, and every opinion came with a story.

When the gavel struck, Deborah jumped. Luke placed his hand over hers as he leaned in and whispered, "Turn around."

She turned—and the Quiltin' Bees filled the room, joined by Jon, Kati, Will, Anna, JW, Tiffany, and Garrett—all wearing T-shirts with the words Team Deborah, in bold across their chests. Her vision blurred with tears. Then Luke stepped forward. Without a word, he unbuttoned his shirt, letting it fall open, revealing the words beneath. *Show up. Speak up.*

Deborah was overcome with gratitude. At that point, she knew she could give her presentation and win over the audience.

When they called her to the podium, Deborah's heart was beating in her ears. Sweat formed around her collar. She stood at the podium and spoke. Initially, she stumbled, but she turned to the crowd of people who believed in her and finally looked at Luke, who also smiled at her. Her knees trembled, but Luke's steady presence grounded her like his warm hand against her spine.

She closed her eyes and released a long breath. She delivered a heartfelt speech about the shelter's importance, emphasizing that it was a place for healing and rebuilding lives.

"In closing, The Nest at Cardinal Creek would be an asset to this community." When she finished, the crowd erupted in applause.

"This project is a danger to the community. It will lower property values and bring undesirable people to the area. Is that what you want?" Chad said as he headed toward the podium.

Fear crept up Deborah's spine, the old familiar kind that remembered slammed doors and whispered threats, but she wouldn't give in this time. She closed her eyes, took a deep breath, and turned around. When their gazes locked, instead of looking away like she usually did, her eyes remained on him as she squared her shoulders and stood up straight. Out of the corner of her eye, she noticed Luke standing, ready to pounce on Chad if he had to.

The townspeople in the gallery stood and applauded so loudly that the crowd couldn't hear Chad. There was a rap of the gavel, and the mayor spoke.

"Thank you, Ms. Clemmons. We will take your information into consideration."

Deborah nodded. The mayor's eyes settled on Luke, who nodded back at her. That left Deborah wondering whether there was something between them. She shook her head. That idea was absurd.

After the meeting, Deborah stood next to Luke and Jon, praying

Chad would leave the building. Tiffany stood beside her, talking a mile a minute about how much Luke was staring at her during her presentation. Deborah prayed he wouldn't hear what she was saying.

She leaned toward Tiffany. "I don't want to talk about my love life. Luke is right there, please stop," she said in a harsh tone.

Tiffany nudged her. "Hey, I know you have a lot on your mind. I'll zip it."

"Yeah, I'm sorry. I'm frazzled," she said, squeezing Tiffany's shoulder. "I'm sorry about earlier—"

Tiffany waved her hand. "Don't say it. There's no need. I know I'm a little much sometimes."

JW approached Tiffany and Deborah with a warm smile. "Deborah, that was a fantastic presentation. If you need any donations or support from the Saddle Up, just let me know." His gaze then shifted to Tiffany, a hint of curiosity in his eyes.

Deborah raised an eyebrow, then looked at Tiffany, who acted like he wasn't even there. Maybe it was because she hurt her feelings. "JW, have you met Tiffany? She's the newest Quiltin' Bee."

JW touched his fingers to his hat. "Ma'am, pleasure to meet you."

Tiffany's eyes were like saucers as she nodded. Deborah elbowed her.

"Evenin', sir. Nice to meet you."

"Ma'am, sir is my dad. Just call me JW."

She nodded but stayed silent.

Deborah was confused. Tiffany was so loud talking about men that she thought she'd be less shy around them.

Maybe Tiffany isn't as confident as she seems. Maybe all her noise is just her armor.

"Deborah, it was good to see you, and Tiffany, it was a real pleasure meeting you. Hope to see ya around," JW said before leaving.

Deborah wrapped an arm around Tiffany. "Isn't that the guy you've been looking at?"

"Yes," she whispered, "but he wouldn't like me. He was just being nice."

"I doubt it. Did you see the way he looked at you?"

"Nothing like the way Luke looks at you," Tiffany said, then she covered her mouth, her eyes wide.

"You're hopeless, Tiff," Deborah said.

They both laughed as they stepped outside to meet the others. She looked around, expecting Chad to jump out of the shadows. As she stood under a bright streetlight, she wondered if anything she did would make a difference.

~

Luke stepped out of City Hall, and the mayor's warnings about Chad echoed low in the back of his mind, like a storm brewing. He didn't want to bring it up tonight, not after what Deborah had just done. The streetlight cast a warm glow, catching the gold threads in Deborah's hair as she stood talking to Tiffany. She looked different. Steady. Stronger.

When Chad tried to speak, she met him head-on, chin lifted, and her shoulders squared. Not the woman who sat in the waiting room after Jon's injury three years ago, wringing her hands, afraid to meet his eyes.

This time, she held Chad's gaze and didn't look away.

Something steady settled in Luke's chest.

But when the crowd began to thin, Deborah's posture shifted. Her eyes moved down the street, as if she expected someone to jump out of the shadows. She twisted her fingers together, small and unconscious. Luke recognized the gesture. Strength didn't mean the fear was gone.

A sharp tug in Luke's chest urged him into action. He quickly closed the gap and took her hands in his, brushing her knuckles with his thumbs.

"I'm so proud of you," he whispered. "You stood your ground. He saw it too."

Their eyes met and held, speaking volumes without a single word. The air between them changed, carrying a possibility that made Luke's breath catch. Deborah's gaze shifted, revealing something new—like a door unlocking, opening just enough to offer a glimpse of whatever might be waiting on the other side.

Luke's heart raced, and for a fleeting moment, he wished they were alone. He thought about inviting her for coffee—either at her place or his, it didn't matter—anything to keep this moment untouched. Guilt gnawed at him. The mayor's warning pressed at the back of his mind, heavy and urgent. Chad wasn't just noise anymore. There were formal complaints. Eyes on the shelter. Real trouble brewing. Luke held it back anyway, just for now. She deserved a small victory before the next fight began.

Deborah put her hand on his arm. The fire between them was driving Luke wild. He wasn't sure what to do. He wanted to kiss her, but not in front of half the town.

"Deb, could I walk you to your car?" he asked, his heart beating like a drum.

"Sure," she said. "Hey, y'all, I'm gonna go."

Deborah slipped her arm through his, leaning on him as they walked. That single point of contact undid him. He wanted more. Much more.

When they got to Deborah's car, she leaned against the door with a small defiant tilt to her chin, an invitation that screamed uncertainty. Luke moved in close enough to hear her breath hitch. Did she want him to kiss her?

She lifted her hand and traced her fingers down his jawline. Soft and exploring.

It short-circuited any hesitation; electricity hummed between them, and for a moment, it felt as if the parking lot lights might flicker from the current.

He cupped her face, thumbs grazing her cheeks as he kissed her, soft at first, testing the boundaries she never spoke aloud. Deborah pulled him close, fists clenching his shirt, and a rush of heat surged through him, intensifying the kiss in a way he hadn't anticipated. This woman was brave, shaking, and pulling him under faster than he expected.

Then, just as suddenly as it had begun, the light went out. She stiffened beneath his touch, as if fear and hesitation were tangling between them, and she pulled back, rigid.

Fear had struck her—not of him, he knew instantly—but of what wanting could mean.

Luke pulled back immediately, shaken. He lifted his hands, careful to show her he wouldn't move forward unless she asked him to.

Movement over her shoulder made his stomach drop. He caught sight of Chad, propped against his car two spaces over, arms folded, a smirk twisting his mouth as he stared.

He was watching.

Marking his territory.

Deborah, oblivious, brushed her fingers to her lips, as if trying to cool the lingering heat. Fury simmered low in Luke's chest.

Chad smirked at him one last time before slipping into his truck and pulling away—too slowly, too deliberately.

Deborah didn't know, but the fight with Chad was only beginning.

CHAPTER 16

Deborah hovered in the doorway of the quilt shop classroom, taking one extra breath she didn't actually need. Liz looked up and smiled.

"Town hall was a win," she said. "That was a battle well fought."

"If you're standing there debating whether to come in," Tiffany said without looking up. "We voted. You're staying."

Deborah forced a smile. "I'm not sure I agreed to this quilting dictatorship."

"Oh, there was a secondary vote," Tiffany said, lifting her eyes, "about whether Luke kissed you."

Deborah stepped into the classroom in silence, the echo of Luke's kiss still humming through her. The memory flickered beneath the dull glow of the parking lot light, sending a buzz from her cheek to the tips of her fingers. No kiss had ever felt like this. She couldn't tell whether Luke had pulled back because of something he sensed in her or if she'd imagined it altogether.

On the drive over, she scolded herself, replaying moments where she wished she'd softened and stayed in the warmth of his kiss instead of jolting away in uncertainty. She longed to share more about her relationship with Chad, but shame held her back. Everything with Luke left her in a tailspin. Did love and trust mean control and abuse?

As she adjusted her bag, she felt a hand on her shoulder and flinched before she even turned.

"Oh, honey, I'm sorry," Liz said softly. "Old habits, I know."

Deborah forced a smile. "Never apologize. I just...wasn't expecting it," she said. "I didn't get a chance to talk to you last night—"

"Yeah, because *someone* disappeared with Luke," Tiffany teased with a mischievous grin. "So? Did he kiss you?"

Deborah glanced at Liz and rolled her eyes. Sleep-deprived and impatient, she snapped faster than she meant to.

"Did JW give you his phone number?" she asked sharply.

The entire table went still.

"I, uh, no," Tiffany mumbled, lowering her head as she returned to her sewing.

Deborah closed her eyes and took a deep breath. She wasn't really angry at Tiffany. She was angry at fear, at Chad, at herself. Still, the words were out, and the air was brittle. She wanted more from Luke, but it had to be on their terms, not on Tiffany's timeline. She excused herself and sought refuge in the restroom.

As Deborah came out of the bathroom, Tiffany stopped her. "Listen, Deborah, I don't mean to pry. I just...I think you might be scared to let yourself have something good. Trust me, I know, because I believe the same thing about myself." There was no teasing, only sincerity.

Deborah raised an eyebrow. "Why didn't you talk to JW? It was obvious he liked you."

Tiffany placed a hand on Deborah's shoulder. "A guy like JW would never like me," she said. "Look at you, Deb, you're beautiful."

Deborah blinked, totally taken off guard. "Beautiful doesn't keep people from hurting you," she swallowed. "Maybe we're trying to convince ourselves that we deserve better this time."

Tiffany's chin lifted. "I guess we are all a mess in our own flavors."

Deborah's phone buzzed in her pocket, interrupting their conversation.

She pulled it out. She didn't recognize the number on the screen. She pressed the button. "Hello."

"Ms. Clemmons, this is Ms. Brown at the permit office. I wanted to inform you that Chad Clemmons has filed a zoning complaint against the shelter you are trying to open."

Deborah walked into the husband's waiting room at the quilt shop and sat on the leather seat, which still carried the familiar scent of Luke's cologne. "What are my options?" "You can contest the complaint, apply for an exemption, and between you and me, have someone who knows these kinds of complaints look over it thoroughly; they may find something, but I didn't tell you that," Ms. Brown said. "I'm sorry, Ms. Clemmons."

"I appreciate your help." When Deborah ended the call, she went back to the classroom and sat alone, watching all the women as they worked on her dream that might never come true.

Deborah's dreams had faded before. In college, she wanted to become a teacher until her roommate invited her to a party. There, she met Chad, the first man to offer her alcohol. Her strict upbringing with her father, a minister, had instilled a fear of disobedience, making her hesitant, though she felt she should stay at the party. Chad had always known where to strike—not at her body, not anymore, but at her future.

When Chad approached her with a drink, she declined, feeling uncomfortable. "It's just a Coke," he insisted, and despite her reservations, she drank it.

Moments later, she felt dizzy and told him she wanted to leave, but he led her upstairs. That was the last thing she remembered when she awoke the next morning—head pounding, stripped of her clothes, and with Chad in bed beside her.

Three months later, she returned home to reveal her pregnancy. Her father's violent reaction left her battered and afraid.

"You'll marry him," he insisted, pulling her to her feet, ignoring her pleas. "You will no longer be my daughter."

Two months later, she married Chad, and the nightmare began on their wedding night. She hadn't spoken to her family since. And now here he was again—not asking for obedience, demanding her silence. Different tactics. Same man.

"Deb," Liz said as she waved a hand in front of her face, bringing her back to the present.

Deborah looked at Liz, but her chest and throat were so tight that air could barely enter or leave. "Yes," she said, unable to say any more.

"Are you okay, dear?" Liz touched her hand, bringing her back to reality.

"I'm fine. I—I don't feel well. You mind if I leave?" she asked, stumbling over her words.

"Are you okay to drive?"

"I'm fine, I just need to drink some hot tea and rest," she said, standing and slipping her bag over her shoulder. "Will you tell the others goodbye for me?"

Liz hugged her. Deborah wasn't sure how she knew that was what she needed. It was as if all the life was drained out of her as she opened the door of the quilt shop. She looked back before she walked out, trying to ground herself in the present.

When she got into her car, she pulled up Luke's number on her phone. Her finger hovered over the send button. She needed to know whether Luke would be like Chad or if he genuinely cared about her. Even as she pressed send, she still wasn't sure what she'd say if he picked up.

When he answered, she said, "Hey."

"Hey, are you okay?" His voice sounded distracted.

"Yeah, I'm on my way to City Hall to pick up the complaint Chad filed," she said, exhausted from the incessant trouble Chad caused. "Do you think you could stop by my apartment and look at it with me?"

There was a long silence before he answered.

"Yeah, sure," he said, his voice tentative.

Deborah's heart sank. "It's okay if you don't have time, I understand. I'll let you go."

She heard him let out a long breath. "Deb, wait."

Tears slid down her cheeks. She felt alone, just as she had when her father made her marry Chad. Deborah cleared her throat. "It's okay, Luke. I know I've been a bother with the shelter and all."

"No, Deb, really, I can stop by. I'm sorry, just having a day," he said.

Deborah wiped her eyes and chuckled. "I know what you mean. I can make dinner. I have wine. You can sleep on the couch if we drink it."

Luke was silent for a moment. "You know, that sounds like just what I need."

"Is six, okay?"

"Yes, sounds great."

Deborah stopped by City Hall, picked up the notice, folded it, and set it on the seat next to her. Nothing Chad did ever looked dangerous at first. The paper felt lighter, less daunting now that she knew Luke would be coming by tonight to look it over. Hope was dangerous—but she reached for it anyway. *Maybe I can still make this work.*

~

At home, while she made dinner for herself and Luke, she reflected on the day's events. Memories of Chad raised questions about the differences between him and men like Luke, who treated her with respect. Maybe a relationship didn't mean controlling someone's every move. Chad had always made her feel as if her body were his to command. Was that how all men were? If she let Luke kiss her again, would it end the way it did with Chad? No, that couldn't be Luke. He wasn't like that.

Deborah placed two bottles of wine in the refrigerator, unsure whether she should drink any. She placed two plates on the table and went back to check the oven to see if the lasagna was doing okay. It had been almost three years since she'd cooked for a man. She was nervous because with Chad, even dinner could turn into an explosion. *Stop! Luke isn't Chad.*

There was a knock at the door, and Deborah smoothed her skirt and straightened her tunic top before opening it. Luke wore Wranglers and a blue button-down shirt with pearl buttons. The scent of his spicy, woody cologne danced around her nose, taunting her. She bit her bottom lip, both hungry for him and scared at the same time. *Did I invite him here to test him? Am I testing myself too?*

He scanned her from head to toe and let out a low whistle. "You look beautiful."

"You don't look so bad yourself," she said, stepping aside to let him in. As he entered, he brushed against her arm, sending a jolt of electricity between them. "You can sit at the table. I'll put dinner out now."

She slipped on some oven mitts, pulled out the pan of lasagna and bread, then placed them on the table. "You want some wine? I know I do," she said.

"Are you sure I can sleep on your couch?"

She turned to him. "Luke, we're both adults, old enough to drink and..." She stopped, the heat creeping up her face.

Luke cleared his throat. "Yeah, sure, I know."

Deborah poured Luke a glass of Cabernet, then served him a square of lasagna, steam rising from the layers of pasta and cheese. She poured her own wine with slightly unsteady hands, the glass making a soft clink against the bottle's neck.

Luke took a bite, and a flicker of surprise crossed his face. Deborah paused with her fork halfway to her mouth, tilting her head. "Everything okay?"

He nodded, finishing his bite. "Yes, more than okay. It's amazing." He took a long drink of wine.

She smiled. "So good you had to wash it down with wine?"

"It's not that, darlin'. There are two things I'm worried about. The fact I didn't tell you that I knew about the zoning complaint—I didn't want to ruin your night. And..." He hesitated, setting his glass down. "I couldn't stop wondering if you regretted our kiss."

Deborah reached for her glass, taking a long drink. "It's not that, Luke. I liked it." Maybe a little wine would ease her fear enough to kiss him without hesitation.

"I did too," he said.

When they finished dinner, Deborah suggested they move to the living room. She hesitated before following him to the couch, wine glasses in hand, wondering if inviting him there was brave or reckless. *What exactly do I want to happen? Is that why I'm drinking wine?*

After finishing the first bottle, she retrieved the second from the refrigerator, feeling a bit disconnected from the world. She'd never drunk wine before, but with Luke there, she needed something to steady her nerves. She wanted him to kiss her, to touch her—she craved a gentle man's touch. She shivered as she poured wine into Luke's glass.

"Are you okay?" he asked.

Deborah wrapped her fingers around her wine glass and took a long sip. "I've never been with a man other than Chad. Did you know my kids weren't created out of love?" She paused, setting her wine down to pace herself. "I like you, Luke. I'm just so confused. You touch me, and my body betrays me. All I hear is, 'He's going to hurt you.'"

She returned to the couch, sitting close to him. She was scared, but her body was on fire for him, and the alcohol made her bold. She ran her hand up Luke's thigh and then lifted it to touch his face. "I want you," she slurred. "Do you want me, or am I too damaged?"

"I do, but not while you're drinking. May I kiss you?"

"I really wish you would," she replied.

When their lips met, a spark ignited, sending a low, simmering heat through them. Luke's phone buzzed incessantly, vibrating against the table, but he ignored it, deepening the kiss. A thrill ran through Deborah at his disregard for the outside world, but somewhere in the back of her mind, concern nagged at her.

Moments later, her phone chimed from inside her purse. She hesitated, torn between a flicker of worry about who might be calling and the space closing around them with the kind of closeness that made breathing feel optional. She ignored the sound and leaned into him instead, savoring the connection that made her feel alive for the first time in her life. It was intoxicating.

Suddenly, a fist hammered on the door with a determined knock that echoed through the room, shattering the moment. Deborah jerked back, breathless. They stared at each other for a moment before Luke jumped to his feet. His expression shifted from confusion to concern, the intimacy of the moment evaporating into uncertain tension.

"Come with me," he said, leading her toward the door.

Deborah's heart raced. *Who could it be at this hour?*

Luke opened the door.

Jon stood there, his face devoid of color and his chest rising and falling quickly. "Mom...Why didn't you answer your phone?" he asked as he walked past them. "It's the farmhouse."

Deborah stepped out from behind Luke. "What's wrong?"

Jon swallowed, his Adam's apple bobbing. "It's on fire."

Deborah froze. Her palms went cold, and her knees trembled as the air left her lungs.

"No," she whispered. "No, Jon...no...Jon."

She didn't realize she was falling until Luke caught her by the elbow, holding her up as her legs buckled.

He pulled her against him, and her forehead rested on his chest. "I've got you," he whispered.

Jon's voice stuttered. "Engine 7 is already on the scene, but Luke—Chief, they requested you."

When Luke shifted into command mode, it was immediate and fierce. His jaw was set, eyes burning, voice low and lethal. He was all steel.

He grabbed his radio and keys, turning to Jon. "Get her into your truck. Stay behind me."

"Roger that."

Deborah stood frozen, absently shaking her head as numbness crawled up her spine. "My plans—my everything. Luke..."

He cradled the back of her head for one raw moment, and for just a moment, he wasn't Chief Erickson but the man who kissed her like she mattered.

"It's not gone," he said passionately. "I will fight this fire with everything I have."

He pulled away and strode to his truck. Jon followed close behind him. Deborah stood frozen as Luke climbed into the cab. The engine turned over, headlights sweeping once across the lot before the rear taillights disappeared down the road.

The last thing she heard was his voice over the radio, low and steady. "He won't get away with this."

Deborah stared at Jon as tears slid down her cheeks. Her throat tightened until she could barely swallow. "You know who's responsible for this, right?" She began to pace. "He takes personal joy in ruining anything good I try to do, just to prove he has control over me. I don't know what to do from here... Let's go see how bad the damage is before I make any decisions." None of it felt real. She watched herself pace and heard her own voice, as if it belonged to someone else.

CHAPTER 17

"It's over...I can't do this," Deborah whispered, gazing at the devastation left by the fire. Hours after the flames were extinguished, the farmhouse still exhaled smoke—a mix of wet ash, melted plastic, and soaked timber that clung to her throat. In the bright morning light, the farmhouse looked battered and vulnerable, its weary frame revealed in melted siding streaked with soot and windows blown out. A sour chemical bite lingers in the air. Charred beams in the kitchen slumped inward, and the porch she once sat on, dreaming, now sagged under the weight of blackened debris. Water pooled in the yard, reflecting the idle fire truck's lights. With every step closer, her chest tightened. This wasn't destruction. It was betrayal. She couldn't prove it, but she knew this tactic. Chad. His threats. His last text. Suspicion twisted in her gut until she could barely breathe. The smell permeated her hair, clothes, and throat. The dream she imagined, full of laughter and safety, looked hollow and ruined. And worse, she couldn't stop seeing Chad's smirk in every smoldering board.

The kitchen, the mudroom, and part of the hallway bore the brunt of the damage. A small bedroom remained untouched, but she hadn't yet entered it. Above the kitchen, the roof had burned away, and Deborah stood frozen, her mind struggling to take in the damage.

Deborah trudged through dew, ash, and puddles toward the untouched craft barn, yearning to enter a space untouched by destruction. She sank into a chair and buried her face in her hands. Why does Chad keep threatening me and causing problems? He couldn't be responsible for this. Could he? Her mind raced, tangled in confusion and doubt, as if each thought slipped through her fingers like water.

There were others who opposed the shelter; were they under Chad's influence, too?

She pushed herself out of the chair and headed back outside. Deborah watched through the haze as the firefighters moved through the charred remains of the kitchen, their tools clanking. She jumped when she saw one person use a long pole to drag down pieces of the ceiling, and another wave a strange camera across the wall, which glowed with white light. She continued to watch as the firefighters checked the house for structural instability. She wrapped her arms around herself, knowing that she was on the verge of losing everything all over again.

Luke approached Deborah, looking exhausted, his soot-stained jaw tight, and he examined her as if he was trying to map the unspoken pain she was feeling. When he reached her, his face changed and softened, and her stomach twisted with both longing and dread. Three steps closer, and her body betrayed her, leaning forward before she could stop herself. His hand reached for hers, and for a heartbeat, she almost let him take it, surrendering to the comfort he offered. Instead, she jerked back, scanning the property for watching eyes while hating herself for caring. The chief's tenderness would be worse than his indifference. She couldn't bear his pity, couldn't risk the rumors, and couldn't trust the part of herself that desperately wanted to.

"How are ya holdin' up?" he asked.

"I don't know, maybe this is my sign to stop." She scanned the house again. "How did this happen?"

"Not sure. We're still investigating," he said, breaking eye contact.

Deborah narrowed her eyes, studying him. *He's hiding something. Luke doesn't avoid eye contact like that.*

"Wanna tour the outside? We can assess the damages that need to be repaired."

"Sure, but I'm not sure what I'm going to do yet," she said. "Word travels fast around here. Someone mentioned the insurance company has already been called."

He stilled. "Called by who?"

She shook her head. "That's the problem. I don't know, but I have my suspicions."

"Does Jon know?"

"No," she said. "I didn't want to bother anyone."

Luke took a step closer. "Follow me," he whispered.

Deborah walked with him toward the craft barn. Her heart was racing, and she wondered what he was going to do. When they got inside, he turned to her with his hands on his hips and his brow furrowed.

"Deb, you have to talk to someone if Chad is harassing you," he said, his voice low.

"I...I..." She stopped as tears formed, her breathing ragged, and turned away from him.

He put a hand on her shoulder and turned her to face him. The tears started to fall. "Honey, I'm not going to yell at you. I'm worried. How long has this been going on?"

"A while," she whispered.

"You don't have to tell me, but please tell Jon. Has he threatened to hurt you physically?"

She shook her head. "Mostly texts and rumors," she said, dabbing her eyes. "Nothing he could be held to."

He pulled her into his arms. This time, she didn't stiffen or pull away; she melted into the warmth of his body. The smell of soot permeated his clothing, but his arms provided a comfort she longed for. When the hug finally broke, Deborah wasn't sure how long they had stood like that. She had a hollow place inside that Luke seemed to fill when it mattered most.

"You don't have to do this alone, babe. You have so many people rooting for you." He said as he kissed the top of her head.

She sniffed and wiped her eyes again. "Let's go look at this mess," she said. "Tell me what's left, and don't sugarcoat it."

Luke guided Deborah through the farmhouse's remains, his voice steady as he pointed to the blackened beams. His voice faded in and out like a bad radio signal.

"The foundation is solid," he said, pointing to something she couldn't focus on. "We can salvage most of the—"

"I knew Chad wouldn't let me get this far." Deborah's voice was flat.

Luke's face hardened, then softened again. "He hasn't won. This is just a minor setback."

A hollow, broken laugh escaped her throat, a bitter sound. "I'm tired, Luke...so tired."

Her body swayed toward him, craving the warmth she'd felt in his arms earlier, but her feet stepped backward, creating distance she both wanted and resented. All she could think about was washing away the smell of smoke, wrapping her hands around a warm mug, and closing her eyes.

"You don't have to make any decisions right now," he murmured, respecting the space she made while his eyes searched hers for permission to cross it. "Right now, you need rest."

She nodded, staring at the blackened beams. Part of her wanted to rebuild; another part whispered it would be easier to walk away.

"Why are they measuring the porch like that?"

Luke's gaze darted away. "Um, they're checking for burn patterns."

"Does that mean something?"

"It could, but it doesn't have to."

His eyes wouldn't meet hers. The comfort she had felt in his arms moments ago soured with suspicion. Was he protecting her or hiding something?

She couldn't tell which frightened her more.

L uke swept the thermal camera across the wall studs, watching as the screen turned white where heat hid behind the plaster. "Hot spot on the left side," he muttered into the radio. As he stepped over a fallen beam, he scanned the burn patterns. The V-shaped marks went upward; a classic sign of an intentional start point. His jaw tightened. A pike pole tore open the wall where he pointed, and glowing embers rolled out of the walls. Someone started this fire on purpose. And he knew exactly who.

While he scanned the ruins with a trained eye, the acrid bite of cold smoke and wet wood filled his lungs. He wasn't looking at the destruction—he was studying the patterns: burn directions, smells that didn't belong, and points of origin. His gaze settled first on the collapsed section near the kitchen, where the charring was deepest, and the beams fanned outward in a distinct V-shaped pattern. It was another sign that echoed his suspicions of arson. *Accelerant? Intentional? Electrical?*

Glass shards cracked beneath his boots as he knelt, pressing his fingertips against the underside of a beam where heat radiated through the charred wood. Luke's gut coiled; the evidence didn't lie. It wasn't random. As his flashlight swept the room, it illuminated a quilt, its edges charred to ash. The carefully sewn seams were blackened, yet the fabric at the center remained intact. He carefully lifted it, his heart tightening as ash slid off in sheets. Someone had made this quilt to last.

As he raised it, a small, scorched recipe card slipped free and fluttered to the floor. He brushed it clean with care and let out a sharp exhale—unsure why it affected him so deeply. He draped the quilt over his arm, keeping the card secure between his gloved hands.

Behind him, another firefighter called, "Chief, you good?"

"Yeah," Luke said. He swallowed hard. "I'm good."

He wasn't good. Fury blazed in his chest. This wasn't intimidation —it was calculated destruction. Someone had targeted everything Deborah was trying to build. They wanted to reduce her dreams to ash. All the pieces added up as he looked over the scene several times. Too low, too wide, too fast for an electrical issue. Pour marks on the kitchen floor. Irregular char depth. Appliances burned from an unnatural starting point.

His jaw clenched. He couldn't tell her. Not yet. Not until the inspector confirmed it. He needed to be her anchor, not the spark that sent her spiraling.

Luke headed toward his truck, holding the quilt to his chest. Once inside, he sat behind the wheel and stared at the card. It was smoky but readable.

One side had a recipe, the other side read:

Hughes Family Peach Cobbler, "Leaving Day" Jan 1982
I think the day is tomorrow.
The house is quiet now except for the pecan tree knocking on the

window. Carl will come home late from the shop again, or at least I hope he does. I can't stand his voice.

I used Momma's cobbler recipe because she always said a woman thinks clearly with something sweet in her belly.

I hope she was right. I packed a small bag and hid it in the trunk. If he finds it, he'll drag me back inside the bedroom and do what he did last time. My arm still aches where he grabbed me. I keep touching the place where the bruise was, wondering if I imagined it.

As the cobbler sits on the stove cooling, I sit here writing on the back of this card because I don't want my fear to be the last word I leave in this house.

If this card is found, know that you are not weak for leaving. You're brave for wanting more. Take the peaches, take the sweetness, and go. A woman can start over at any age.

Leave with courage. Leave with the truth.

Signed, Etta Hughes

At the bottom of the card, there was one more sentence in smaller, shaky handwriting.

If I don't come back, I hope this house finds someone who needs a second chance as much as I did.

Luke reread the card, studying the loops of Etta's handwriting on the paper, written over forty-three years ago.

His throat burned.

He sat in his truck, fists pressed to his eyes, overwhelmed by the sudden realization that generations of hurt had a name. The weight of it crushed him. Deborah was in danger; he could sense the life she was trying to rebuild was under siege from the shadows of her past.

The tears came—quiet, angry, determined. They were for what Deborah had survived, for what women before her had endured, and for what she was trying to build, which someone was determined to destroy.

If Chad started this fire, Luke knew one thing for certain—he wasn't letting her face the aftermath alone. He started the engine, set the quilt on the passenger seat, and decided to bring her the pieces that had survived. She needed to see something that could be saved.

CHAPTER 18

$\mathscr{L}$uke's phone buzzed before he even opened his eyes. He sat up too fast and groaned as pain shot through his stiff back.

A text from Sammy.

Sammy: Not coming home again.

The words blurred as he blinked against the sting in his eyes. He found himself in the kitchen without quite remembering how he got there. The Dad mug felt heavy in his hand as the Keurig brewed a cup of coffee. When the smell of coffee filled the air, guilt weighed on his shoulders as he leaned against the counter.

He was sure he was going to lose Deborah. He didn't know if he was doing the right thing by keeping what he knew about the fire to himself. He didn't know how to tell her.

And now he was losing Sammy, too.

He hadn't seen her in weeks. She hadn't answered his texts or calls. He wasn't sure what was happening. He'd texted her again this morning before heading back to the farmhouse to investigate the scene, and now, finally, she responded. Since she'd left for college in August, Sammy had been slowly slipping away from him. She always had an excuse for not coming home. More than anything, Luke wanted to let her grow up without him hovering. But Caleb...

He lifted his coffee cup from the Keurig and stepped out onto the back porch. The door creaked behind him. Leaning against the column with his fingers wrapped around the warm mug, he looked at the horizon. The sky was a deep indigo with a light fog draping the field like a blanket.

The truth about the fire weighed heavily on his conscience. Every time he imagined telling Deborah what the investigation had uncovered, he pictured her face—the fear there, her hard-won strength dissolving. She'd fought too hard to rebuild her life for him to be the one to send her spiraling backward.

He pulled out his phone, found Sammy's number, and sent a text.

> Luke: Sammy, I miss you. I hope you can come home soon.

> Sammy: It's going to be a while. I'm really busy at school, and Mom kind of needs me.

The words landed like a punch to the gut. He sucked in a sharp breath as heat crept up his neck—anger mixed with a pain he couldn't explain. When her mother walked out and didn't call for a year, Luke was the one who did everything he could to contain the damage. Now, all of a sudden, her mother was playing games to keep Sammy away from him. He'd always known he might lose her to college or even a boy, but her mother? That cut deeper than he'd imagined.

Luke went back into the house and slammed the door so hard the windows rattled. His hand lingered on the doorknob, shame following the outburst. He stood in the shower until the hot water ran cold, his thoughts cycling between anger and regret. He dressed mechanically, grabbed his keys, set them down, then picked them up again.

A month ago, he would have driven straight to the farmhouse to help Deborah. Now he hesitated, the keys cutting into his palm. Staying away was smarter. Safer. He couldn't look her in the eye and lie. But his truck seemed to steer itself toward her property. Her SUV wasn't there when he arrived. Relief and disappointment hit him at the same time. He circled the perimeter twice, telling himself he was looking for clues, though his gaze kept drifting to the empty driveway. He walked into the wooded areas, searching for footprints, but found nothing.

When he left the farmhouse, Luke drove into town to get some lunch at the Cattle Trail Café. He dropped his head as he walked inside. The scent of country fried steak hit him first, a reminder of how hungry he was. Luke slid into a booth, trying to disappear. The smell of fried chicken and coffee clung to the air. He wanted silence. Instead, he got town gossip.

"Hey, Chief, want the usual?" the server asked.

"The country fried steak smells good, so I'll take that and sweet tea."

"Okay, I'll get this to the kitchen."

As Luke sat waiting for his food, a high-pitched laugh cut through the diner's clatter. His shoulders tensed. Without looking, he instantly recognized her—Mary Jo Rafferty, holding court three booths away. The woman had somehow transformed managing the town's library into a way to share everyone's personal affairs as her occupation.

The server barely set down his chicken-fried steak before the voices sharpened behind him.

"Anything else I can get you, Chief?" she asked.

It felt like her voice echoed throughout the restaurant—loud enough to carry straight to Mary Jo. When the server walked away, Luke dropped his head down and started eating. The whispers grew louder with every bite until he heard her mention the fire. The mashed potatoes stuck in his throat, making it hard to swallow.

Mary Jo took scandal and spread it like a fire during a drought.

"I'm telling you, Rhonda, the fire inspector said there was accelerant. You know what that means."

Luke's fork froze halfway to his mouth.

Rhonda lowered her voice to a whisper that somehow carried across the room.

"Well...bless her heart...Deborah Clemmons is new to the community since her divorce. People don't really know her. We don't know what she's capable of."

Luke's jaw clenched until it ached.

Mary Jo leaned in, her voice dropping to a theatrical whisper. "The Hughes place was practically given to her. And I heard there were irregularities with her insurance policy." She tapped her fingernail against her coffee mug. "Her agent mentioned something suspicious. What was her name again? Doesn't matter. Rick at the hardware store confirmed it all."

Luke dropped his fork. It clattered against the plate, but no one noticed.

The final blow came—Rhonda's voice, way too loud for someone whispering.

She leaned closer, her voice laced with false concern. "Oh, honey, everyone knows she's desperate. Starting that shelter? All those fights with Chad? Not to mention her troubles with City Hall." She clicked her tongue against her teeth. "When people are desperate, well...they might strike a match if you know what I mean."

They both laughed.

Her words made Luke sputter and cough as panic rose in his throat. He wiped his mouth and shot up so fast the table rattled. Heat surged through him. He slammed a handful of cash on the table and forced himself to walk out before he made a scene.

Behind him, Mary Jo's voice sliced through the café. "Insurance fraud. Shame, really. She seemed nice."

Luke's shoulders stiffened. His hand gripped the door handle so tight it hurt. After a moment's hesitation, he pulled it open and stepped outside, leaving Deborah's name undefended behind him.

His hand slapped the truck door harder than he meant. He leaned against the frame, breath shaking as rage flowed through him.

"Deborah would never," he muttered. There was no way she did it. She had been with him.

But in this small town, vicious rumors didn't need to be true to ruin a life.

And Chad knew that.

Luke cut the engine and let his hands slacken on the steering wheel. For a long moment, he didn't move. A hush seemed to seal itself around the house, so complete it seemed heavy—pinning everything down– not just the rooms and floorboards, but even the shadows pressed against the window, held captive by the weight of waiting. Luke remained motionless, as if staying still might loosen the quiet's grip. The only sound that felt alive was the cicadas carrying on their chorus. His mind circled back to Caleb and the quilt he'd found after the fire. Something about it gnawed at him. Was it a sign? Part of him wanted to dismiss the idea, but every time he looked at it, he saw Caleb's face. Nothing about grief was simple.

Inside, the air was stale, tinged with cedar polish and dust. He set his keys on the counter and grabbed a beer from the refrigerator. He twisted the cap, then stopped and slid it back inside. Drinking the night before a shift wasn't a good idea. He'd almost lost Jon because he'd gone into a fire hungover. He walked down the hall and stopped at the closet. The door creaked open, revealing the same cardboard box that had sat there for years, labeled "Caleb's things." Inside were rodeo shirts, a few rodeo ribbons, and the helmet from his junior firefighting course. He'd planned to join the department after he graduated. He died only months before graduation. Will and Jon joined the department at just befor Caleb would have. They'd all been close in age once. Same choice waiting at the edge of adulthood. Caleb had taken a different road. Maybe that was why Luke had gone easier on Will and Jon after Shelly died. She'd been Will's wife and Jon's sister. Grief like that left damage no training could fix. Luke crouched and rested a hand on the open flap. His chest tightened. He'd told himself a hundred times he'd do something with it—donate it, box it properly, anything but this slow rotting of his memory. He pulled out the rodeo ribbons and fire helmet, setting them aside. He'd keep those.

He ran his fingers over the helmet and looked back into the box. "I guess you don't need these anymore. And I can't keep staring at them," he murmured.

One by one, he folded the shirts, the fabric soft and familiar between his fingers. A blue-and-brown plaid shirt—Caleb's favorite. Another rodeo ribbon, its edges worn thin with time. Something lodged in his throat, hard and unyielding. He sealed the box with three strips of packing tape, tears blurring his eyes.

Outside, he gently placed it on the passenger seat and laid the quilt on top. The quilt would go to Deborah, and the box would be for the donation bin at the firehouse for Deborah's shelter. Someone else would button those shirts now, slip their arms through the sleeves that once held his son. Somehow, it felt right—like Caleb's warmth might still touch the world.

When he came back inside, he paused in front of the wall of family photos, brushing his fingers over the frame holding Caleb's smile—the one taken the day he'd gotten his junior helmet.

"I'm sorry, buddy," Luke whispered. "I'm sorry, Deborah. I can't do this. I can't lose anyone else."

The words hung in the air, shattering the silence like fragile glass. He slumped into his chair and cradled his head in his hands. The box and quilt waiting in the truck were physical reminders that sometimes, letting go cuts deeper than any hold.

CHAPTER 19

*D*eborah's mug clattered against the coffee table as someone pounded on the door. The tea inside had gone tepid hours ago. She ran her fingers through her hair, still damp after her second shower of the day, but the phantom smell of smoke clung to her nostrils. The insurance paperwork lay scattered across the kitchen counter where she'd abandoned it after the third phone call. She shuffled to the door, bracing for whatever came next. Instead, four familiar faces filled the doorway—relief hitting her so hard her knees nearly gave out. Liz was balancing a steaming casserole dish; Sissy clutched bolts of fabric; Peggy Sue held a notebook—what Deborah assumed were their battle plans— and Tiffany held a box of brownies.

Liz smiled. "I know you plan on arguing, but we're coming in," she said, walking past Deborah.

"You don't get to fall apart alone," Sissy said, entering behind Liz.

"We have plans we want to show you, but of course, it's your choice," Peggy Sue said as she walked in.

"Deb, we're not here to fix you, just hold the pieces together. That's what friends do," Tiffany said as she hugged Deborah.

The hug nearly broke her. Since seeing the farmhouse—once coming along just fine—she'd felt detached from everything. Now her dreams lay in ashes, and she doubted she had the strength to start over. After placing the food on the kitchen counter, they moved to the living room. Deborah took a deep breath before speaking.

"Ladies, I truly appreciate you stopping by, but I'm not sure I want to do anything right now." Her thoughts flickered to the look on Luke's face when she'd asked about the fire's cause. She sensed he was hiding something, treating her like she was fragile. She had kept the texts and threats from Chad to herself—and now look where it had brought her.

"Listen," Peggy Sue said. "We have a plan."

"Can you please listen to what we've come up with?" Liz asked.

Deborah nodded.

"I have the ladies who quilt for the church willing to help with a fundraiser to buy supplies for repairs," Sissy said.

"We can use the craft barn to get together and quilt since it wasn't damaged," Tiffany said.

When Liz opened the notebook and showed her the detailed plans, Deborah asked, "Y'all did this in two days?"

"Honey, you don't get it," Liz said as her voice cracked. "We love you."

That's what broke Deborah. The first sob didn't make a sound. It was just a sharp shake of the shoulders, her body's warning that a flood was about to come. Liz put her arm around her, and she cried until she was worn out. She rested her head on Liz's shoulder and shut her eyes, uncertain of what to say. She longed for help, but her fear overshadowed her desire for it.

"Deborah, is something more going on that you're not telling us?" Tiffany asked.

"What do you mean?"

"Is Chad threatening you?"

"No, w-why?" she stammered.

"If he is, you need to talk to someone," Liz said. "If not us, Jon."

"It's fine. Excuse me for a moment." Deborah stood, went to the restroom, and shut the door behind her, leaning against it as the panic rolled in like a tide. Her breath shortened. Her chest tensed. Sweat beaded on her forehead, while her skin was cold. Her stomach clenched. She dug her fingernails into her palms to ground herself, but the dread curled tighter until she couldn't tell if she was shaking on the outside or only on the inside. Xavier's words floated into her head. *Breathe in one, two, three. Breathe out one, two, three.* She closed her eyes and repeated it until her breathing was back to normal. She looked in the mirror. Her eyes were red and puffy. Perfect. She splashed her face with cold water and went back to the living room.

"Deb, are you hungry?" Liz asked.

"Not really."

"May I make you a plate? Please try to eat," Tiffany said with a smile.

"I'll try," she said.

"I have chocolate too," Tiffany said. "It helps everything."

"Lord, Tiffany, you aren't kidding," Sissy said.

"We should know. When Sissy got divorced, she ate Green's out of Rocky Road ice cream," Peggy Sue said.

Sissy narrowed her eyes. "And you ate them out of pecan pie and vanilla ice cream."

Deborah held her plate, amused by their banter. It always made her smile.

"Have you heard from Luke?" Tiffany asked. "I mean about the fire."

Deborah chuckled. "It's okay that you asked. I talked to him two days ago," she said. "He's been busy with the investigation."

"So, no word on what caused it?" Sissy asked.

"None," she said. She didn't want to tell them about her suspicions, but then thought that if she told them, they could help. Before she could speak, there was a knock at the door.

They all went quiet.

"Who's that?" Deborah whispered.

L uke approached the door with the half-burned quilt he had found in the fire. He needed to bring it to Deborah. It was a sign of hope, especially the card that had fallen out of it. His heart still ached from reading the card. It was like stepping inside the pain Deborah had endured at Chad's hands. Luke's hand trembled as he lifted it to knock.

When Liz opened the door, he almost dropped the quilt. Her smile widened when she saw him. "Chief Erickson," she said, raising her voice and turning her head so the ladies who were peeking around the corner could hear her. "Come in."

As he walked in, it was as if a million eyes were on him. Each of the women wore a silly grin as they watched him. When he entered the living room, Deborah was sitting on the couch with her legs tucked under her. Their eyes connected, and a fire ignited in him. He wanted to pull her into his arms and let her know everything was going to be okay. It looked like she'd been crying. He knelt beside her and opened the quilt, revealing the half-burned side.

Luke noticed her breath hitch, and he decided today wasn't the day to mention the investigation. *What if she breaks? She can't handle the word arson today.*

He carefully tucked the card into the quilt's hidden pocket, struggling to speak through the tightness in his throat. "This made it through the fire. I thought...I thought you might want it."

The women dabbed at their eyes, and Deborah whispered, "Thank you." Luke caught something in her gaze that made his chest constrict. It was hard looking at her after reading Etta's card. He had a front-row seat to her abuse, giving him a glimpse of what Deborah had suffered and was still battling with Chad. It was too much to bear.

"I should get going," he managed, walking to the door. The evening air hit his face like a slap. He leaned against the truck, clutching the door until his knuckles were white. He tightened his jaw against the rising tide of emotions—guilt, grief, and fear—hitting him like a tsunami. Leaning his head against the window, he breathed slowly before climbing into his truck.

His fingers tightened around his keys until the metal teeth dug into his palm. The fire inspector's preliminary report was folded in his jacket pocket, with the word *"accelerant"* circled in red. Every time he imagined telling her, he saw the same haunted look she'd worn three nights ago when she whispered Chad's name. Luke worked every step of the investigation alongside the fire inspector, hoping it had been an accident. The evidence told a different story—deliberate, calculated. The cigarette butt found beneath the oak tree, now in a sealed evidence bag at the lab, bore the gold band that Chad preferred.

Luke's hand trembled as he started the engine. If he told her about the arson, he'd have to watch the fear consume her again—or keep it from her and betray her trust. Either choice felt like failure. He pictured her face if she learned that he had hidden the truth...then imagined the terror if he told it.

"I can't lose her like I lost Caleb," he muttered, his voice breaking when he said his son's name. "But God help me, I don't know how to protect her without destroying what's between us."

Deborah smoothed the burned quilt, her fingers trembling. As she turned it over, she noticed a gap between the fabric layers. She reached in and pulled out the scorched index card.
"What's in there?" Tiffany said.
"I'm not sure. It looks like a recipe card," she said, staring at it.

Peach Cobbler, "Leaving Day" Jan 1982. She turned it over and read the diary entry. A woman can start over at any age. Leave with courage. Leave with the truth.

When she read it the second time, her breath hitched.

If I don't come back, I hope this house finds someone who needs a second chance as much as I did.

Deborah bit her lip and swallowed hard, running her trembling hand over the scorched card. "She was like me," she whispered, then shook her head. "I want to run. Part of me wants to disappear." She pulled the quilt close. "But if I quit, what happens to women like Etta? Like me?" She drew in a shaky breath. "I don't know if it's Chad that burned the house, but if he did...I'm terrified, but I'm not going to let him push me out."

"That's my girl," Liz said, throwing her arm around Deborah's shoulder.

Her phone vibrated on the table, breaking the silence. She reached for it, hoping it was Luke. But when she opened her phone, anxiety gripped her as a message from an unknown number flashed on the screen.

> Unknown: Deb, this can stop now, or it will keep getting worse.

Her stomach dropped, and a cold sweat broke across her brow. Deborah's fingers hovered over the delete button, hesitated on the reply, then returned to delete. Part of her wanted to hurl the phone across the room; another part wanted to call Chad and scream at him until her throat was raw. Instead, she set the phone down with deliberate care, her hands steady even as she trembled inside.

What's next? Could he really go so far as to have hurt or killed someone if he didn't get what he wanted? Deborah sat in pensive silence, the world narrowing to the glow of her phone.

CHAPTER 20

The mail hit the floor with a thud that made Deborah jump. Three weeks had passed since the fire that had destroyed part of the shelter, and the insurance company remained silent. Without that money, the rebuilding plans she'd sketched with the Quiltin' Bees were just wishful thinking on paper. Chad's text message lingered in her mind, uninvited and persistent. What would he do next? And was she wrong for keeping to herself?

Sometimes in the quiet hours, the thought slipped in—maybe surrender would be easier than this constant fight. Her shoulders tensed; her stomach tightened. Her body knew the cost of that bargain even when her mind tried to push the worst memories away. She bent to gather the scattered envelopes and froze when she spotted two official-looking ones: Cardinal Creek Zoning, and finally, the insurance company.

Deborah's hand shook as she reached for the envelope, its edge scraping her palm. She pulled out the documents. The letterhead screamed "Official Notice", and halfway down the page, her ex-husband's name leaped out at her, sharp as a slap: "Chadwick Clemmons, objector." Below it, the justification appeared in bold type: "Community Safety Concerns." The phrase glared at her, blurring as tears filled her eyes until she had to blink to focus.

She knew the script by heart. Chad always said he was "protecting" her, the kids, the town, or even himself. He never said what he really meant—that he hated losing control. Of her. Of everything. Protecting her or the kids had never been the point. It was about him. Always him.

A pulse thudded in Deborah's ears. Her throat tightened; her breath hitched and stuttered like a misfiring engine. She sank onto the couch.

Next, she opened the insurance company's letter.

Due to traces of accelerants identified during a cause analysis by a certified fire investigator, your fire loss claim has been placed in an extended review period. Claim payment has been temporarily withheld pending completion of the investigation and review of the findings.

Deborah's eyes locked on a single phrase: "Due to traces of accelerants identified." The rest of the letter blurred as Chad's last text replayed in her mind. Her stomach dropped. This wasn't a delay; it was an accusation.

"Wha-What happens next?" Deborah managed, though her voice sounded like it belonged to someone else. "Do they think I did this?"

Her hands trembled as she reread the letter. Deborah closed her eyes and drew a long, deep breath. Four seconds in, six out. It didn't help. Her chest felt crushed, as if an elephant sat on it, and the tears threatened to break loose.

She dropped the letters onto the table and whispered, "He's not done. He's coming after me."

She shook her head. "No, no, he's not going to win," she said with conviction.

As Deborah rested her head-on the couch, her mind was a clash of conflicting thoughts. One moment, she wanted to curl into the fetal position and disappear; the next, she wanted to fight back. Was asking for help a strength or a weakness? Would involving others make things worse?

She pulled out her phone with trembling fingers. The home screen glowed with a photo of her grandkids—Bobby, Caden, and Eva—grinning in their Halloween costumes, a reminder of what was at stake. She pressed the text icon and selected the shelter group, then froze. Her thumb hovered over the message field as doubt rushed in. She was always asking these women for help. Did she really need to drag them into this mess, too? But if she didn't reach out now, would there even be a shelter left to save?

She began typing before she could overthink it.

> Need Help: The zoning permit will be
> delayed due to Chad's complaint. I have ten
> days to respond. Does anyone know how to
> do this? —D

Deborah stared at the message, her thumb poised over the blue arrow. Before she could talk herself out of it, she tapped send. The message was delivered. The screen shifted to her recent contacts, Luke's name at the top—marked with a small firefighter emoji.

Two weeks had passed without a word from Luke. She told herself he was just busy—work and the farmhouse investigation—but something had shifted in him after the fire. Whenever she asked what they'd found, his gaze drifted away, finding interest on the ground, the ceiling, anywhere but her face. That wasn't like him.

For a moment, she watched the screen, waiting for someone, anyone, to answer. The response was almost instant.

> Sissy: We're on it, honey. Meet at the Cattle
> Trail at noon tomorrow.

> Peggy Sue: Sending prayers. And pie always
> helps.

> Jon: Garrett, JW, and I will be there
> tomorrow.

Tiffany's response was a string of expletives, followed by a row of exclamation marks.

Deborah let out a long, ragged breath. She wiped her eyes and picked up her phone to call Luke. He'd served on the city council and knew how these things worked. Maybe he'd have some information about the investigation. *Anything.*

She pulled up Luke's number and stared at it until the light from the phone blurred. *No, I'm not calling. I'm not going to be a burden to anyone.*

The unspoken question haunted her. If Chad would go this far, then every step forward mattered. And stopping now would only teach them one thing—that fear still worked.

❧

By noon the next day, Deborah pulled into the Cattle Trail Café parking lot, her palms damp against the steering wheel. The café sat on Main Street in a low brick building with a large picture window, its hand-painted letters touched up over the years. The lot was already full of the lunch crowd, with pickups, SUVs, and sedans parked nose to tail.

Deborah lingered in her car, watching people bustle along Main Street to the boutique and bakery across the way.

When she stepped inside, the room was thick with coffee and fried potatoes, and the steady hum of conversation filled the room. It was more crowded than she expected for a Wednesday. As she scanned the room for Luke, she spotted a flash of red hair belonging to JW Walker, who leaned against the counter, talking to Garrett. Luke hadn't replied to her text, but she hoped he'd show up. He could really help her.

A cluster of voices floated from the back. The Quiltin' Bees—Sissy, Liz, Peggy Sue, and Tiffany—occupied a line of tables pushed together, their arms waving over carafes of sweet tea. Jon and Kati sat beside them. Garret had squeezed in too, his posture military straight.

Sissy leaped to her feet, arms wide. "There she is. Deborah, how are you?" She drew her into a cinnamon-and-laundry-scented hug, patting Deborah's shoulder until she managed a weak smile.

"You look like you could use some sweet tea, a piece of apple pie with ice cream, and a seat," Liz said, shoving a glass of sweet tea—garnished with a lemon wedge—across the table before sinking back into her chair.

"We are all furious about this," Peggy Sue whispered. "I heard Chad has a few of the Main Street shop owners rallying behind him. Rumor is it's a couple of the newer stores. Sissy and I don't know the owners."

Deborah tried to catch Jon's eye, but he was busy feeding Bobby, who wore more food on his face and bib than in his mouth. Kati reached over and squeezed her hand.

"We're not going to let Chad win," Sissy said, shaking her head. "No one messes with one of ours."

JW cleared his throat. "Deb, there are rumors flying about the fire."

Deborah's stomach clenched. She'd seen the insurance letter. She knew who had started those rumors.

Garrett leaned forward, arms braced on the table. "Have you heard anything official about the investigation? The guys downtown are saying it was flagged by the insurance company."

Deborah managed to nod. "I got the letter yesterday—along with the zoning notice."

A hush fell over the table.

Liz tapped her mug. "Whoever's stirring this up is doing it on purpose—and the insurance red flag and zoning notice weren't coincidences." Her voice dropped to a whisper. "Danny and I did a little online digging. Turns out Chad's in the middle of a permit battle in San Antonio." She glanced at Deborah. "If Chad is fighting permits there, it wouldn't be hard to see a pattern."

Despite everything happening, Deborah smiled. "You're spending time with Danny?"

"Stay on task," Liz said as blush rose to her cheeks. "The documents, Deb."

"Yes, ma'am."

Peggy Sue slid a notepad toward Deborah. "We already have a list of ideas for the appeal." She lowered her voice. "And Danny said he'd help talk to the mayor if it comes to that."

Deborah was amazed. The practical way they approached the problem should have reassured her. Instead, it made the situation more real. Her plans were on hold, and there was nothing she could do about it yet. "Thank you," she said, her voice distant.

Peggy Sue cleared her throat to get everyone's attention. "Now that we're all on the same page, how about making it official?" She pulled a sheet from the notebook in front of her. A hand-drawn logo in bold marker read "Team Deborah," surrounded by purple hearts and a needle and thread.

"I redesigned the logo for the T-shirts we can wear to the appeal,"

Peggy Sue said, grinning. "We need something to let Chad know that you don't mess with one of the Bees."

"You mean hens," Jon said.

"Jonathan, don't make me smack you," Liz warned.

Sissy elbowed Liz. "You know he likes it when we pinch his cheeks."

Jon shook his head. "Ladies, how many times do I have to tell you I'm a married man and a father?"

"Pinch away, ladies," Kati said, pulling Bobby onto her lap. "Have at it, Peggy Sue and Sissy." Everyone laughed.

"Traitor," Jon muttered, leaning in to kiss Kati.

Deborah leaned back in her chair, the warmth of laughter and banter soaking into her bones. For a moment, she wanted to believe she could win, that all this fighting might amount to something. She scanned the table, noting fierce loyalty in Sissy and the watchful support of Jon.

A familiar ache lingered in her chest—the fear that at any moment it could all fall apart. But beneath it, a quiet persistence stirred in her ribcage. Was it hope? Or stubbornness?

After the laughter faded and they went their separate ways, Deborah took the long way out of town. She rolled down her windows and let the breeze flow through her hair; the rush of tires over asphalt filled the quiet. The late September sky glowed gold, fading into lavender that poured over fields and caught on fence posts. She could smell rain in the air.

The farmhouse looked different in the light—wounded but still stubbornly standing. Charred beams along the left side of the porch caught the last streaks of sun, turning blackened wood ember orange. Someone had swept away most of the debris, propped a few boards, and hammered new treads onto the steps. It wasn't enough to hide the fire, but it showed someone cared.

Deborah parked beside the old garden fence, its weathered pickets untouched by the fire, and walked up the repaired steps. She sat on the top one, slipped off her sandals, and curled her toes over the edge. Her arms rested on her knees as she gazed at the horizon. The sunbathed the hills in fiery orange. She had always liked this time of day—a pause to see what the day had become before nightfall, a breath between what had burned down and what could still be rebuilt. Tonight, it felt different. This wasn't just a project anymore. It was a question: Was she brave enough to fight for it again?

Jon's truck idled up the driveway. When he appeared, he stood at the base of the steps, hands in his pockets, chin tilted toward the sky. Without a word, he climbed up and settled beside her, close enough that their shoulders touched. For a long time, they didn't speak. The crickets started up, tentative at first, then bold and insistent as dusk thickened. Deborah watched the grass wave in the wind as the monarch butterflies danced through it, bound for Mexico for the winter. She looked at her hands and realized they weren't shaking anymore.

"Mom, I know you're worried," Jon said, breaking the silence. His voice carried a rasp since the fire three years ago—the one that almost killed him but saved her life and brought him back into hers. "I talked to a lawyer on the union board. He's going to help us pro bono." He met her eyes. "You don't have to do this by yourself."

Deborah nodded, watching the sun slip behind the trees.

"You know this isn't just about the shelter," she said. "It's Chad— he haunts my dreams, and now he's back in my life because I'm trying to do something good. I keep thinking, what if I lose no matter what we do?" Her voice dropped, raw and thin. "What if this is it for me...being alone?"

Jon didn't speak at first. The porch seemed to hold its breath with them. He finally shifted, brushing his thumb across the worn seam of his jeans.

"First of all, you're not going to lose," Jon said. He held her gaze. "But when you say you're alone—are you talking about the fight, or about your life? Tell me what's really bothering you."

Jon shifted beside her, but Deborah kept her gaze fixed on the horizon. The words crowded her tongue, begging to be spoken—the messages, the warnings, the quiet manipulations that had started long before the fire. She opened her mouth.

It wasn't one thing—it was all of it. The rumors. The call to the insurance company. The nonstop messages. The way he'd pulled Jon into it. Chad was everywhere now, and she was unable to see an end in sight.

She took a shaky breath, her throat tight as she forced down the rising tide of emotion. Old habits of protecting her children from Chad kept resurfacing, relentless and familiar. She wanted to tell Jon the truth, to let him in on what was really happening, but she carried the weight of it all on her shoulders. Yet she knew it was time to confront certain aspects of this battle of her own, but for now she chose silence, clinging to the hope she could handle it without involving him.

"I—no. Not right now," she whispered. "It's just...everything feels like too much."

Jon stayed quiet, waiting. She didn't speak. Her silence should've been enough. Finally, Deborah wiped her cheeks, embarrassed by how quickly the tears had come.

"I haven't seen or heard from Luke in a couple of weeks," she confessed. "He was the one helping me with repairs and the fire investigation, and then he just...disappeared. He didn't even come to the café today." The night he dropped the quilt off replayed in her mind. He gave it to her and mumbled an apology, then left. "I must've said something wrong or scared him off. Is it so hard for someone to love me? Or am I just someone he wanted to fix and then leave?"

Jon inhaled slowly, deeply. "Mom...there's something you need to know about Luke. He's not like Dad. He's not even like me." He leaned back, eyes narrowing at the fading streaks of orange in the sky. "Luke's son, Caleb, died just before he was supposed to start the fire academy. When he died, Luke froze. Kim left him with Sammy, and he had to keep going as if nothing had collapsed. He hasn't let anyone in for a long time."

Deborah understood freezing and retreating. She'd done both. Still, a gnawing feeling told her Luke was hiding something from her. She didn't know what. Then it hit her—after everything with the fire, it was too much for him.

"Maybe I'm too much for him," she whispered.

"Maybe he's afraid of losing someone else," Jon countered softly. "Or maybe you're the first person in years to make him want to try." He nudged her gently. "Guys like him don't talk about pain. They fix stuff. And when they can't fix what hurts, they run."

Deborah let out a shaky laugh.

"Sounds like you've been to therapy."

"You were my partner a few times," Jon said with a smirk. "We're healing together."

Before she could respond, he hopped up and headed over to his truck, saying he'd be right back. He returned with two heavy boxes. The cardboard thudded against the wood when he set it on the porch.

"These are donations we're collecting at the firehouse for the shelter. Clothes, bedding. Look at the one marked Caleb." His voice dipped. "You'll understand when you see what's inside."

A lump rose in her throat. She touched the nearest box, her fingers trailing over her name, handwritten in bold black marker. Luke must have written it himself.

"Thank you," she whispered.

Jon stood, dusting his jeans. "Kati made dinner. You want to stay with us tonight?"

Deborah shook her head. "I need to do this alone. Just for tonight."

"Okay." He hugged her, strong and deliberate. "Call me if you need anything. Anything."

"Jon..." Her voice cracked. "The investigation..." She swallowed hard. "Have you heard anything? What was found?"

Jon hesitated long enough for her stomach to drop.

"They're still looking into it."

Deborah stood, dread crawling up the back of her neck. "Do they think I did it? Not the rumors, the investigators."

His eyes flickered with restrained emotion—anger, pity, and something else she couldn't make out.

"No," he said. "I don't. And Luke—" He stopped, bracing himself. "He doesn't think that either, but..."

Her breath caught, the ache in her ribs pulsing sharper. "But what?"

Jon didn't answer, but he didn't have to. The silence pressed in, heavy and deliberate. She recognized that kind of quiet. It was the kind that meant something wasn't being said.

CHAPTER 21

Deborah curled her hands around her coffee cup, letting the warmth steady her. A stack of mail slumped on the couch, half-opened envelopes sliding against one another. She wasn't ready for bad news. Even junk mail was safer than the truth. It had been two weeks since she'd filed her response to Chad's complaint, and she hadn't heard a word from zoning, the insurance company...Luke.

Silence from the others, she expected.

Luke's silence lingered.

She replayed the night he dropped off the quilt a hundred times, the careful way he held it, the quiet in his eyes, and the abrupt departure. Since then, nothing. No visits. No texts. No calls. It was impossible to believe he knew anything about the fire and hadn't told her. Her eyes roamed over the stack of mail, and she saw it: an official envelope from Cardinal Creek Planning and Zoning.

Her stomach dropped.

She lifted the envelope; the paper stuck to her damp palm. The longer she waited, the longer she could pretend her dream was still possible.

She tore open the envelope. Inside lay a single sheet of paper. She pulled it out and unfolded it.

"Application Denied. The proposed project does not comply with zoning ordinances."

Deborah's vision blurred. The letter crinkled in her trembling hands before she hurled it across the room.

"I built my hope on something the town doesn't want," she whispered, retrieving the letter from the floor. "It's over."

As her tears slid onto the page, the ink bled as if the words were trying to escape.

Her eyes darted around the room. She needed air. Noise. Relief from everything.

Before Deborah knew it, her keys were in her hand, and she was out the door. She drove on instinct, straight to Cattle Trail Café—the place everyone went to talk, whisper, and judge.

She pushed through the door with her chin up, daring anyone to meet her eyes. *Let them whisper. Let them stare.* Standing up to Chad wasn't a sin—it was the first right thing she'd done in years.

The café fell silent for a moment as she entered. Then the whispers began. Mary Jo Rafferty—the town librarian, who trafficked in rumors more than she shelved books—leaned across the table, her voice carrying in the hush. Deborah caught her name in the stream of words, saw the glances darting her way, and felt judgment press tight against her throat.

Then she saw him.

Chad sat alone in a booth, owning the space as if every inch of the place belonged to him. Their eyes locked. His lips curled into that familiar victory smirk, his gaze tracking her like wounded prey. He stood, straightened his shirt, and crossed the room with a slow, controlled stride.

He leaned in close, his breath brushing her ear. "Deborah," he whispered. "We need to talk."

She didn't want to. Every instinct screamed for her to run.

But people were watching.

Mary Jo's whispers stopped. All eyes were on her. That old, ingrained obedience coiled around her like a snake.

Her body moved on autopilot, sliding into the booth opposite him. The corner of his mouth twitched upward as he watched her comply.

Chad draped an arm across the back of the booth. "Zoning board giving you trouble?" he asked, his voice velvet smooth.

Deborah's lips pressed into a thin line.

"It's a real shame about the fire." He lowered his voice to a concerned murmur, but nothing reached his eyes. "The rumor is you started it yourself. Desperate times, desperate measures?"

The accusation hung between them. Her stomach knotted as she realized what he was doing.

His hands shot across the table, capturing hers before she could retreat. The familiar weight of his fingers—the same ones that had shattered her favorite mug against the wall—tightened around her wrists.

Deborah yanked her hands free and tucked them under the table, her skin still burning from his touch.

Chad casually slid into the booth beside her, trapping her. His thigh pressed against hers. His hand dropped onto her leg, heavy and possessive. When his palm slid upward, nausea rolled through her.

Nowhere to run.

She froze. Her body remembered how it was to be powerless.

His breath brushed her ear. "You'd better come home, sweetheart," he whispered. "Or you're going to lose everything."

His grip tightened so hard it made her wince.

"I'm in control of this," he murmured. "Stop fighting me, or everything you're clinging to goes up in flames...maybe the Chief too."

Flames.

The air rushed from her lungs.

Flames!

Her blood went cold. Deborah glanced around for an escape and pulled back, trembling.

He leaned closer, and something in his smile—something in the certainty of his threat—clicked into place. *Chad started the fire.*

He burned the farmhouse.

He tried to destroy her dream, her reputation.

And now he sat here, touching her as if he owned her; like he'd done her a favor.

Deborah swallowed the bile rising in her throat. Fear and fury and something sharper burned inside her.

This time, she stood. Not quickly, but with a strength she'd never felt before.

"I'm not yours," she whispered. "Never was."

Chad's smile didn't falter—the practiced one that hid the monster within.

"Oh, sweetheart," he murmured, sliding his hand down her thigh. "We'll see about that."

She remained standing and inched into his space, forcing him to slide out of the booth. "Someday you'll choke on that arrogance," she said, her voice steady as she shouldered past him and walked out the door. The hushed whispers of the café trailed behind her like ghosts.

And for the first time since the fire, she knew.

Chad was the real enemy.

When Deborah slid into her SUV, she slammed the door so hard the interior rattled. The first sob tore from her throat, raw, guttural, uncontrolled. She gripped the steering wheel until her knuckles whitened, her breath hitching in jagged bursts. Her trembling finger found the start button.

She drove on autopilot, hardly aware of the road. Her thoughts looped between Luke's silence and abandonment, City Hall's rejection, and Chad's laughter.

Now, the whispers followed her everywhere. She was an arsonist. The shelter she'd poured her soul into lay in ashes, and they believed she did it.

Between shuddering sobs, she choked out, "Why did I ever think anything could change?"

Twice, she missed her turn. The street signs blurred through tears that dripped onto her tunic, darkening the soft pink fabric. Every blink brought Chad's face into sharp focus—his breath against her ear, his fingers digging into her thigh with possessive force.

And now the gossip. People actually thought she'd set the fire. Some claimed she did it for insurance money.

The money she might never see. There'd been no word since the letter, and silence was never a good sign.

"Stupid," she croaked, smacking her palm against the wheel. "Stupid."

By the time she reached her apartment complex, exhaustion had settled deep in her bones. The walk to the stairs was like wading through mud.

The key jammed, scraped, then slid home on the second try. Inside, she paused in the entryway, staring at the small, quiet apartment that had once felt like freedom—and now felt like failure.

Part of her wanted to march straight to Luke's, shove the zoning letter into his hands, and demand the truth about the fire. The other part already knew the answer: he believed the rumors. Or at least, he didn't trust her enough to say otherwise.

Her purse slipped from her shoulder onto the couch, spilling the city's letter onto the carpet—the word *denied* taunting her. She snatched it and started toward the trash, then turned and shoved it into a drawer instead, slamming it so hard the silverware rattled.

"Maybe I should call the permit office," she said.

She paced.

"No," she said, shaking her head. "They're probably already laughing at me."

She sank onto the couch. Her mind ricocheted between fight and collapse until nausea crept up her throat. Her gaze snagged on a water stain in the ceiling, slowly spreading—like her hope thinning under pressure.

Her phone vibrated.

Then again.

Then again.

Jon. Liz. Tiffany.

And the fourth—

> Unknown Number: I know where you live. If I want in, I'll get in.

Her stomach churned.

She flipped the phone facedown, but the vibration kept coming, worming through the silence, needling her resolve. She grabbed it again—

> Unknown Number: I told you before. This isn't over. I can get in whenever I want. You know what happens then.

With shaking hands, she pressed the power button and held it down until the screen went black.

Silence.

Heavy.

Absolute.

The refrigerator hummed. The clock ticked. Those were the only signs the world existed at all.

Deborah curled onto her side on the couch, pulling her knees up. Tears soaked the pillow under her cheek. Every breath felt razor-thin. It was all too much to handle: the rumors, the accusations, Luke's disappearance, and Chad tightening the leash, inch by inch. Everything she built—the shelter, her safety—was gone. Suddenly, she felt small and fragile in Chad's shadow.

She reached for her phone, then yanked her hand back. No. Yes. She needed to call someone—or did she want to be alone? She needed to scream. She wanted to disappear.

"I should fight," she whispered. Then she shook her head. "I can't. I —" Her fingers curled into fists, then loosened. "But if I don't..."

The next breath cracked in her chest.

"I can't fight," she said softly. "Not anymore."

Tonight, she shut everyone out.

Tonight, she folded in on herself.

Tonight, the world slipped away.

CHAPTER 22

*D*eborah blinked awake on the couch, mascara crusted at the corners of her eyes, jeans digging into her hip bones. A thin blade of sunlight cut through the blinds and across the coffee table, dust motes dancing as she stared at the blank television screen. She picked up her phone, turned it on, then set it back down. Moments later, it buzzed with notifications.

There was a voicemail: "Ms. Clemmons, this is the fire investigator. During the investigation, Captain Luke Erikson assisted with the scene assessment, and we identified possible traces of an accelerant. The samples have been sent to the lab. We'll contact you when the results come in."

Deborah froze. Luke knew and didn't tell her. Why hadn't he told her everything? Did he think she was too fragile to handle the truth? She had a right to know.

She scrolled through her contacts, her finger hovering over his name before she typed out an angry message. She deleted it. Then she typed again.

> Deborah: You had NO right keeping things from me!

Three dots appeared.

Deborah dropped her phone onto the couch. She didn't want to hear what he had to say.

Yet when it vibrated, she snatched it up.

> Luke: I'm sorry. I didn't know how to tell you.

Deborah: I trusted you. This is something
Chad would do. I'm not fragile, Luke!

Luke: Can I call you?

Her jaw locked, teeth grinding until pain shot through her temple. Her fingers clenched the phone, its edge biting into her palm, as something volcanic and unfamiliar erupted within, scorching every rational thought.

Deborah: Now you want to talk. Wow. No, I
don't want to talk to you right now. Maybe
never.

She glanced at her notifications—two from Liz, one from Tiffany, one from Peggy Sue, and five from Jon.

Her thumb hovered for a moment, then she deleted them all.

"Even Luke doesn't believe in me," she whispered to the empty room. She pressed the power button until the screen went black, then tossed her phone onto the coffee table. It skidded across the surface and came to a stop, resting against her notebook labeled "The Nest at Cardinal Creek," the name she'd chosen for the shelter.

Outside, traffic rumbled toward jobs and futures while hers remained frozen. Her fingers twitched toward her phone again. The refrigerator kicked on with a shudder, rattling the empty apartment. Yesterday's coffee mug sat abandoned on the side table, its contents cold and forgotten.

Deborah retreated into the shadows of her small apartment, heavy curtains drawn tight to seal out any hint of sunlight. Hours bled together as she sank deeper into the darkness of her failures. She slouched into the couch, wishing she could disappear into its cushions, pressing the television remote without really watching anything. Her thoughts drifted to Luke—to the farmhouse, preparations for the town hall meeting, and that kiss—the first time she'd felt safe in a man's arms. Then he'd abandoned her, vanishing without a word. Chad's voice surfaced, cruel and familiar: *No one will ever want you.*

When Deborah left Chad, she'd been a scared, timid woman who jumped at the sound of anyone's voice. She stayed with Liz on Will and Anna's ranch after Jon got hurt. Tragic as his injury was, it became a blessing in disguise. It allowed her to spend time with him and begin healing the years of pain they had both endured. She attended therapy, joined a domestic violence survivors group, and found love and understanding among those who shared her struggles. That was what she wanted to provide for other women.

With therapy and the support of friends, she rebuilt her life on her own terms, vowing to never let anyone make her feel small again. Yet somehow, she had let it happen—by Chad, by the town, and, in her mind, by Luke too.

Deborah pressed the remote so hard her nail bent. *Click.* A soap opera filled the screen. The images blurred with the words burned into her mind: "Application Denied." Two simple words had crushed the only dream that felt like hers alone—one that mattered not just to her, but to the women it would support.

Three soft knocks echoed through the silent apartment. Deborah tensed, her breath catching as the sound fractured her isolation. She went still, hoping whoever stood on the other side would drift away. Pulling her feet up onto the couch, she tucked them beneath her, trying to make herself smaller.

A gentle voice filtered through the door. "I just wanted to check on you. I left something at the door, okay? Please call someone to let them know you're alright."

When the footsteps faded, Deborah cracked the door open and froze. A box sat on her welcome mat, the scent of banana bread wafting up. Her stomach growled despite herself. Inside were a foil-wrapped loaf and a thermos of coffee, still warm to the touch. She grabbed the box and brought it inside. A folded note lay on top in Tiffany's loopy handwriting:

I'm here if you need me. —Tiff.

Deborah's eyes stung. She almost tossed the note into the trash but set it on the counter instead. She stuck it to the refrigerator with a magnet, took it down, tucked it into the drawer with the denial letter, then moved it back to the counter when she couldn't stop seeing it. It was the kindness she craved and resented at the same time, like a woman dying of thirst who feared drowning. She rested a hand on the still warm bread but didn't eat it. She hadn't eaten since breakfast yesterday, yet her appetite was nonexistent. *People can't abandon you if you push them away first.*

Deborah returned to her spot on the couch, sinking into the cushions. Hours later, she cranked the shower knob all the way to the red line and stepped under the spray, wincing as the scalding water stung her skin. Steam billowed around her, thick and suffocating. Her shoulders slumped as water streamed down her face, mingling with tears she hadn't realized were falling. As the heat reddened her skin, she closed her eyes. *What if every man she lets close ends up being like Chad?*

Her fingers curled against the shower wall, steadying herself. *No one stays. Not really.* Her lips moved as she silently argued with herself in the steam. She twisted the faucet with a squeak, making it hotter. The burn felt right, grounding. She reached for the soap, then let her hand fall. *I can't keep hiding like this. I did that through years of abuse with Chad—trying to disappear, to survive.*

When the water finally stopped, the sudden silence echoed in her ears. She grabbed the towel from the hook and wrapped it around herself, shivering.

"You're doing it again, Deb," she whispered, shaking her head. "No more. I'm not going to push away people who love me."

She stepped out of the shower, finished drying, and pulled on a pink robe. The soft fabric whispered against her skin, a fragile barrier between heartache and whatever healing might come next. For a moment, it gave her a quiet space between sadness and hope. She wiped a clear path through the fogged mirror. Red-rimmed eyes stared back from beneath dripping strands of hair that framed her determined jaw. Deborah held her gaze, refusing to look away this time. "You've survived worse," she said, steady now. The words anchored her, cutting through the panic.

Determination flared—a stubborn beacon against the darkness. The weight of past battles pressed in, but her voice rose to meet it.

"Show up. Speak up."

There was no hesitation–no flinch. Just the command to keep moving forward, even with the ghosts at her back.

As Deborah stepped out of the bathroom, a soft knock stopped her cold. She hoped whoever was there would go away. Another three quiet knocks followed.

"Mom? Please open the door. I need to know you're okay." Jon's voice filtered through, gentle but insistent.

Deborah opened the door, her robe cinched tight, damp hair clinging to her cheeks, her eyes still red-rimmed.

Jon stood on the welcome mat, silent and unmoving. He simply held out a brown bag. The scent of fries and burgers filled the entryway. Deborah's stomach gurgled, loud enough that she pressed a hand to her robe. Her mind might have forgotten hunger, but her body hadn't.

"Figured you might not have eaten," Jon said.

She took the bag. "You figured right. Tiffany dropped off some banana bread and coffee. It's on the counter if you want some." She turned toward the living room.

When she glanced back, he was still by the door, watching her with the same pity he'd worn as a boy, hiding in the closet to protect his sister. "Are you coming?"

He followed her inside. "We're all worried about you. Why do you have your phone off?"

"I didn't want to talk to anyone after what your dad did at the café," she said, sinking into the couch.

"Mom, it's been over a week. Do you want to talk about it?"

She rolled her eyes, pulling a burger and fries from the bag. "It doesn't matter. Chad always wins." Bitterness edged her voice. "I'm going to sell it," she said.

"Listen," Jon said. "Mom, remember how I spoke to an attorney who represents firefighters? He knows about and specializes in this sort of thing and offered to represent you pro bono. He wants to meet with you. The Quiltin' Bees are planning things, but Mom, you have to decide to put yourself out there. All the help in the world won't work unless you stand up and fight."

Deborah knew he was right. She needed to fight. But right now, she was just too tired to fight with Chad, the town...or Luke.

"There are more people on your side than you realize," Jon said, sitting beside her and leaning close. "Even Luke."

She snorted. "Yeah, right. He's been ignoring me. Didn't even care enough to text me back. Then, to top it off, he didn't tell me he knew about the arson." The words tasted bitter.

"He cares more than you think." Jon pushed himself off the couch and left the room.

Deborah heard movement near the door. Then he returned from the kitchen with the box he'd brought her at the farmhouse and set it on the table.

"Please look in the box. The shirts inside belonged to Luke's son, Caleb. When I brought them to you, I thought you might find a use for 'em."

Deborah froze mid-bite and looked at him.

"Caleb's?"

Jon nodded. "Don't tell Luke I told you. He's been...off." He turned to leave, then stopped. "I thought maybe some of the guys from the firehouse were doing repairs, but it's been Luke all along."

Before leaving, he kissed the top of her head. "I love you, Mom."

"I love you too, Jon."

When the door closed, she was left with just her thoughts.

Deborah set her food aside and opened the box. She pulled out a faded plaid shirt with rodeo patches, faintly scented with Tide and cedar—the familiar scent of Luke. Beneath it lay a blue-and-white plaid shirt with pearlized buttons at the cuffs. As she unfolded it, she found a note tucked into the pocket.

Hey Dad,

I know I don't say it enough, but I'm proud to be your son. You always show up for everyone, no matter what, and that's something special. I can't wait to put on the uniform and work alongside you at the station. I hope I can be half the man you are. See ya soon. Love you.

Caleb

Tears slid down Deborah's cheeks as she read. Had Luke known this was hidden there? The weight he carried after Caleb died—the way his wife had left him alone with Sammy with no communication—it all pressed heavier now that Sammy was off at college. The house must have felt massive without her. It made sense that grief would echo louder in all those empty rooms.

Deborah's gaze drifted toward the doorway, where her sewing machine waited, its familiar silhouette promising purpose, healing. "I know what to do with these," she said, lifting the box and carrying it to her sewing room.

She unpacked the shirts one by one, laying them across the table until they formed a patchwork of memories in navy blue, crimson red, soft gray, and cream. The colors glowed softly under the work light. She moved them around, separating the shades and arranging them from dark to light. Then she turned to her fabric stash and drew out pieces that coordinated with the shirts. The rotary cutter whispered through cloth, her hands sure and steady as she imagined the blocks taking shape, fitting together just right.

When she finished the first block—Caleb's flannel pieced beside one of her own fabric scraps, two lives woven together—night had fallen. Deborah kept working, the hum of the sewing machine the only sound in the house, a steady pulse, mending more than fabric, something within her that had been torn for far too long.

CHAPTER 23

*L*uke slammed his office door so hard the glass rattled. Deborah's last text still burned on his screen:

Deborah: Now you want to talk. Wow. No, I
don't want to talk to you right now. Maybe
never.

He collapsed into his chair, elbows braced on his knees, breath quickening. A stack of shift reports slipped from the desk and scattered across the floor, but he didn't move to pick them up. He couldn't. His hands shook. He'd faced fires that moved faster than a rattlesnake coiled to strike, but nothing hit him like the look he imagined on Deborah's face as she typed it.

He was losing her.

First Caleb...then Sammy started slipping away...and now Deborah felt out of reach.

His phone buzzed. He didn't want to look. He turned away.

It buzzed again. He picked it up. Sammy's picture filled the screen.

"Hey, darlin', are you leavin' yet?"

Sammy let out a long sigh. "Mom told me that if I come home this weekend, you won't have time for me. She said you never had time for us after Caleb died."

Luke was speechless. He stared at the ceiling, fighting the urge to hurl the phone across the room. He and Sammy had always had a good relationship. But her visits had grown rare, the calls and texts coming only when he initiated them. He'd told himself it was college, that she was adjusting. Now he knew better. His ex-wife had poisoned her against him because she blamed Luke for Caleb's death.

"What's going on?" he asked, trying to hide his irritation. "I don't understand where this is coming from." He wanted to fist his hands in his hair and scream words he couldn't take back.

Sammy sniffed. "Mom said you wouldn't let me see her. Why would you do that?" Her voice cracked.

His mind spun. What was his ex-wife doing? Why now? She'd walked out years ago, leaving Sammy behind without so much as a phone call. He'd received the divorce papers and nothing else—no communication—until Sammy left for college. Luke had survived by locking his grief down with the discipline of a firefighter: routine, order, purpose.

"Sammy, you know that isn't true. Is that why you haven't been coming home?" A knot formed in his stomach.

"Listen, Dad. I need some space. I'll come home when I sort through things."

Luke's chest tightened. It seemed like everything was slipping away, leaving him alone. He bit his lip to keep his temper in check and the hurt from spilling out.

"I can take time off and come to Austin."

"No, I don't want to see you right now," she said, hiccupping through sobs.

His throat tightened. His stomach twisted, like he'd taken a punch.

"I gotta go."

"Love you, Sammy."

"Goodbye, Dad."

The phone went dead. Luke stared at it, the realization settling in that she'd hung up as if it were the last time they would ever speak. *She didn't say I love you. She always says I love you to me. Have I lost my daughter, too?*

He grabbed his bag, climbed into his truck, and sat with his hands wrapped around the steering wheel until his knuckles turned white. Everything was slipping away. Caleb was gone. His wife had left. Now, Sammy was pulling away too.

On the drive home, he thought about the things he could get done at the farmhouse, but he really just wanted to go home. Being at the farmhouse only made him think of Deborah. He longed to see her, to be with her, but that was a risk he wasn't willing to take, not just for himself, but for her. She didn't need the weight he'd been carrying since Caleb died.

Before getting out of his truck, he sent a quick text to try to explain.

Luke: I'm sorry. I didn't know how to tell you.

Deborah: Simple. Just say it and trust I'm strong enough to handle it. The whole town is talking about me. Did you even defend me? No excuses.

Luke: Deb, please…

Silence. He waited for fifteen minutes. When he tried to call, it went straight to voicemail.

He wasn't just losing Deborah–he was losing Sammy, too. He'd already buried Caleb. Now the rest of his world was slipping through his fingers.

Everything he loved—everything he tried to love and protect—slipped through his fingers, lost forever.

When Luke stepped out of his truck and crossed the yard toward the barn. As he pulled the door open, the familiar scent of hay enveloped him. He mucked the stalls, the rhythmic shoveling of manure a distraction from his racing thoughts. After feeding the horses, he saddled one and went for a ride to clear his head. As the hours passed, he followed the fence line, checking for places where his cattle or horses might escape. He replayed his conversation with Sammy. How could she believe he'd keep her from her mother? She was old enough to remember the day her mom left. Why trust the woman who deserted them when they needed each other most? Doubt crept in, sharp and relentless. Maybe he had never known how to hold a family together. It had been a downward spiral since the day they left the hospital after Caleb died. Now Sammy was gone too.

As Luke rode back to the house, twilight settled over the pasture. He climbed off his horse, Peanut. Sammy had named him. Peanut was a muscular chestnut horse with a deep chest, sloped shoulders, and strong hindquarters. His gait was smooth, his head nodding in an easy rhythm with every stride. Every time Luke rode him, the same memory surfaced.

He and Sammy are hauling a travel trailer to Black, Missouri. A week-long camping adventure that smelled like rain and damp earth. Spring-fed creeks winding through the Ozarks. Old barns and forgotten structures tucked into the woods. They'd hiked until their legs ached, laughing as the rain poured, then watched the sun break through the clouds, creating rainbows. It had been beautiful.

He finished brushing down Peanut and patted his neck before giving him some feed. When Luke exited the stall, his legs ached on the walk back to the house. Riding for hours hurt more than it did when he was younger, but he still loved it. It helped him clear his head. He sat on the porch as the sun slid across the rolling limestone hills, turning everything gold and amber. As the crickets hummed and a coyote howled in the distance, Luke found comfort in the noise outside.

Inside was different.

Silent. Lonely. Just him and the walls.

When the sun finally dipped behind the hills, he pushed himself up off the chair and walked to his truck for his workbag. He slipped the key into the lock and turned it, then paused, his hand resting on the handle. He wasn't sure he wanted to step back into that quiet. He opened the door and was greeted by the familiar scent of cedar from his cologne, which lingered throughout the house.

He dropped his bag at the door and muttered, "It's just me and these walls again."

His boots echoed through the house as he crossed the floor. The closet door stood open, and a bare patch marked the space where Caleb's box of shirts had sat before he'd taken them to the firehouse for Deborah's shelter. He approached the closet and knelt in the empty space, his fingers tracing the outline of dust. Panic overtook him. Had he really given away the physical reminders of his son? His throat closed, and his hands shook as he traced the space. Dust coated his fingers.

"Caleb," he whispered, the name barely making it past his lips as his shoulders curled forward and his chest hollowed. He closed his eyes, remembering the faded plaid, the worn cuffs, the way Caleb used to roll his sleeves before chores.

It wasn't just about the shirts. It was everything he'd tried to box up and give away because keeping it hurt too much. He grabbed a forgotten shirt, still hanging in the closet, and crushed it in his fist.

"I gave away the last pieces of him," he said, his voice cracking for the first time in years.

He shuffled to the worn leather recliner in the living room, Caleb's shirt pressed to his face. The chair creaked as he collapsed into it, shoulders shaking. He buried his nose in the fabric and breathed in—cedar, Tide, and that hint of teenage sweat. His fingers traced the frayed collar, worn thin from too many washes. After all these years, Caleb's scent still clung to the fabric. He thought of the Christmas receipt in his wallet—$42.99 for the same bottle he'd caught Caleb sneaking from his bathroom drawer three Sundays in a row.

Luke sank lower into the chair, clutching the shirt. His eyes drifted to the mantle lined with pictures of Sammy and Caleb as babies, then as older children, the years passing too fast. The last photos of Caleb sat frozen in time: high school graduation, Junior Fire Academy. He picked it up, his thumb tracing Caleb's smile.

He whispered, "You would've told me not to let go so easily, wouldn't you?"

When he finally moved, the floor groaned beneath his weight—not loud, but just enough to make it feel like the house itself carried his son's memory in its bones.

Luke's phone buzzed, pulling his attention back to the table next to his chair. He picked it up. It was a message from Sammy.

> Sammy: Mom has been telling me so much stuff. Why would you keep me from her? I know I asked on the phone, but I'm just so angry that you would do that.

Luke slammed his phone down, unsure how to respond. What was his ex-wife doing? And how could he answer without sounding defensive or worse, like he was demonizing her mother? He picked his phone up again.

Luke: Sammy, if you want to talk about this, we need to do it in person. Either I come to Austin, or you come home. But I'll tell you this. I loved your mother even after she left. Why would I keep you from her? It took me a long time to stop loving her. Am I married again? She is. Have you seen me dating? She moved on.

His finger hovered over the button before he pressed send. He wasn't going to be painted as the villain.

Sammy: Whatever, Dad. Jealous much.

Luke rolled his eyes. For a moment, he wondered if he was arguing with his ex-wife instead of his daughter.

Luke: You know what happened between your mother and me is our business. But I did everything I could to be a good father. I'm not perfect, but I did my best.

Luke's anger simmered as he waited.

Sammy: Pack up my room and send my stuff to Mom's house. I'm moving in with her.

Luke read the message again. And again. His thumb hovered over the keyboard, then fell away. Part of him wanted to drive to Austin tonight, force her to understand. Another part wanted to text back that she was acting just like her mother. Instead, he set the phone face down on the table.

"If she wants her stuff..." he muttered, then stopped himself. No. He should pack it carefully. Show her he cared. But wouldn't that prove she could walk all over him? His jaw clenched as he stared at the silent phone, torn between rage and desperate fear that this might be permanent.

His little girl was slipping through his fingers like his ex-wife, and now Deborah. These thoughts were on repeat, circling through his mind.

He picked up the remote control and turned on the television. The silence was deafening. A Western hummed in the background, but he didn't watch it. His gaze stayed fixed on the closet where Caleb's shirts were once stored. The empty space where the box sat felt like a void in his heart, as if Caleb had slipped away like Sammy and Deborah. Each absence weighed heavily on him, a stark reminder of the connections he feared were fading.

His mind shifted to Deborah. First, he hadn't been able to stay away, and when she finally trusted him, he'd withheld the truth about the fire.

"Deb, you deserve better than me," he whispered. "I'm sorry."

Luke checked his watch. It was after midnight. He pushed himself out of his chair, turned off the television, and headed to his bedroom. As he passed Caleb's room, he stopped. After a moment, he turned the knob and pushed the door open. It was a time capsule. The bed was neatly made, his guitar untouched, the air heavy with dust and old wood. He sat on the edge of the bed, elbows on his knees, exhaustion settling deep into his bones.

"I'm sorry, Caleb. I'm sorry, Deborah, I can't lose anyone else."

Tears trailed down his face as his fingers clutched the frayed edge of the quilt, his ex-wife's handiwork from happier days. Moonlight spilled through the blinds, casting silver bars across the floor. His gaze settled on Caleb's prom picture, his carefree smile frozen in a world that had moved on without him. Luke twisted his hands together until his knuckles whitened, the emptiness of the house echoing with all the conversations they would never have.

CHAPTER 24

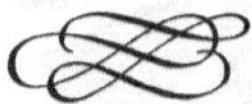

Luke's thumb hovered over the screen, scrolling between Sammy's and Deborah's texts, the light harsh in the darkened room. His eyes burned from a night spent staring at the ceiling, then the phone, then the ceiling again. Maybe he should call Sammy...no, that would make it worse. Or would it? She might listen if he caught her at the right time. But Deborah...he could still fix things without a conversation, couldn't he? Or would that be another mistake? His stomach knotted as he set the phone on his nightstand, then stopped, his hand lingering there, knowing that not choosing was still a choice.

He got out of bed and went to the kitchen. Caleb's chair caught his eye on his way to the coffeepot, a familiar ache tightening his chest. When the coffee finished brewing, he leaned against the counter, drinking it as he stared at Caleb's and Sammy's empty chairs. The silence, the empty chairs, and his now-empty coffee cup reminded him of everything he'd lost. He turned toward the window. *I can't save Caleb. I don't know how to save Sammy. But I can save the house for Deborah.*

He dialed Jon's number.

"Hey, Chief. What's up?" Jon queried when he answered.

"Can you meet me at the fire station?" Luke asked. "Bring Will, JW, and Garrett if you can. I need help fixing the farmhouse."

Jon hesitated. "Even if she doesn't want your help?"

"She'll never need to know it's me."

"The insurance money hasn't come through," Jon said. "But I can put some in. Maybe JW and Garrett, too."

"I have some savings I'll put in too," Luke said. "Meet me in a couple of hours?"

"Yep, see ya then."

Luke left without eating breakfast; his stomach was too knotted to hold food. Was this the right thing to do? The guys at the firehouse would help, but should they? They'd pool their money for repairs as the investigation dragged on, but what if Deborah found out? She'd hate him for interfering. No, she'd hate him for lying again. He should have told her everything from the start, instead of deciding which truths she could handle. That was what Chad had done—manipulated her with selective information. Wasn't Luke doing the same thing now? He tightened his grip on the steering wheel. No, this was different. This was protection, not control. Wasn't it? He loved her. God help him, he loved her even though he'd sworn he'd never love anyone again.

The station kitchen hit Luke with a wall of noise when he walked in —laughter, raised voices, and the clatter of dishes. Sounds that usually faded into the background scraped against his raw nerves. The smell of coffee permeated the air—familiar, automatic, and suddenly unbearable. He shrugged off his jacket, wincing at the stiffness in his shoulders, and went for the coffeepot without meeting anyone's eyes. Without turning, he sensed Jon and Will sharing one of their wordless glances—the kind men gave each other when they recognized a storm brewing.

Jon slid into the chair across from him. "You look like you fought a mountain lion and lost."

Luke stared into his mug, the dark liquid reflecting nothing back. His battles weren't against anything with claws—just memories of the son he'd lost, the daughter pushing him away, and Deborah, angry with him for good reason. His jaw tightened, a sharp retort forming, but he swallowed it down with a bitter sip of coffee.

Jon lowered his voice. "Look, Chief. I'll support you on this. We all will."

Luke looked up. "Fellas, I need your help fixing Deborah's farmhouse." Then, quieter, as he met Jon's eyes, he added, "I'm just not sure if I should be doing this."

They exchanged glances. JW placed a check on the table, then Garrett and Jon did the same. "This should cover supplies," JW said.

A voice called out from the back of the room. "Count us in, Chief." Luke turned to find three rookies standing shoulder to shoulder, their faces earnest beneath their department-issued haircuts. The one in the middle—Ramirez, if Luke remembered correctly—stepped forward. "Whatever you need, sir."

A smile tugged at Luke's mouth. This was just the thing he needed to climb out of the darkness that had been settling inside him.

He stood and faced the group. "We'll start tomorrow," he said, pushing down the voice warning that she'd hate him for this. "Jon, can you head out to the farmhouse with me and help figure out what supplies we'll need?"

"Let's do it," Jon said. "I'll tell Momma D we'll need food from the Hens."

Will and Garrett chuckled.

Luke shook his head, grateful for the moment of lightness. "We're doing this for Deborah," he said, then hesitated. "Even if she'd rather do it on her own."

"Yes, Chief."

A glimmer of hope settled within as Luke left the firehouse, determined to get this project to a better place than it had been before the fire.

~

By noon the next day, a cloud of dust rose over the gravel drive like a storm warning. One by one, pickup trucks rumbled in. Doors slammed, and boots hit the ground. Jon's F-150 sagged under the mountain of lumber strapped down. JW's truck carried boxes of nails, tools, and ladders. Garrett's hauled enough power tools to rebuild half of Cardinal Creek. The Quiltin' Bees' minivans arrived last, packed with folding tables that wobbled as they were set up, followed by casseroles wrapped in foil, jugs of sweet tea, and cleaning supplies.

After a few hours of restless sleep, Luke finally felt steady enough to act. This— building something, fixing something—he could do. It was the only thing that made sense.

They started with the porch supports, the ones that had taken the worst of the fire. Luke ran his fingers along the charred beams, flakes of carbon breaking loose and clinging to his skin like ash tattoos. When they removed the supports, the wood groaned, cracking open to reveal the deep, brittle black that meant the fire had gotten hotter than it should have.

Garrett and JW handled the joists; their T-shirts darkened with sweat despite the autumn chill. Will's shovel scraped against the metal wheelbarrow as he mixed concrete.

Luke's boots left a zigzag trail across the yard as he moved between tasks. He crouched over a section of subflooring, running his thumb across a burn pattern, the result of a fire that burned too hot, too fast, and too clean. The kind of burn no faulty wiring could pull off.

He snapped two photos with his phone, then slipped it back into his pocket without comment. The pattern matched what he'd seen before —too clean, too deliberate. Something to keep to himself for now, another piece of the puzzle he wasn't ready to complete.

He kept glancing at the tree line, half-expecting Deborah to appear with her hands on her hips, angry, accusing him of meddling. He wished she would. Anything would be better than the silence.

By evening, the farmhouse had gradually transformed under their hands, its silhouette straightening against the darkening sky. It was still wounded but no longer broken.

As Luke stood there, taking in the progress they'd made, Jon came up beside him and placed a hand on his shoulder. "You're doing this for her?"

Luke's brow furrowed. "Of course. But I'm also doing it because someone should've helped her a long time ago."

Jon let out a low breath. "You won't get any argument from me." He clapped Luke on his back and headed toward his truck.

Luke watched the last pickup pull away, trailing dust clouds that caught the evening light. He ran his calloused palm along a fresh porch post, feeling the grain beneath his fingers. The rebuilt steps, the new beams, the replaced boards—each one said what he couldn't.

The farmhouse stood straighter against the darkening sky, still damaged, still healing, but no longer broken. Luke stared at the structure in front of him. Something inside him shifted, a misaligned piece setting into place. Whether that meant he was no longer broken, he didn't know.

∼

After a week of work, Luke's hands were blistered and raw, but the porch stood rebuilt with new posts and fresh paint, just as it had been before the fire. Inside, the kitchen was beginning to take shape, though the cabinet he hung made him wonder if Deborah would tear it all down when she discovered his involvement.

He'd tracked down an electrician he'd worked with as a rookie to do the wiring at no charge as long as they supplied the material. Luke took a week's vacation, working from sunrise until his vision blurred, collapsing into his truck each night to drive home for a shower and a few hours of sleep before returning at dawn.

On Saturday, three trucks rumbled up the driveway, kicking up dust that glittered in the morning light. JW's old rodeo buddies—men with sun-leathered skin and hands shaped by honest work—climbed out with tool belts over their shoulders.

"We'll have this roof done by sundown," the tallest one promised as they went to work.

As Luke watched them work, something unfamiliar bloomed in his chest—a fragile hope that maybe, some broken things could be made whole again.

True to their word, the men packed up their tools as dusk arrived. Luke stood back, watching the last rays of sunset catch on the new metal roof, turning the farmhouse proud and defiant against the darkening sky. Two weeks of sweat and sacrifice had erased most of the fire's damage: new glass gleaming in the windows, kitchen cabinets hanging square, and the floor replaced with clean, solid planks. He pictured Deborah walking through the front door, imagined her face softening with surprise, then hardening again when she realized who was behind it.

He sank onto the porch steps, watching fireflies rise from the tall grass like embers floating upward. Part of him wanted to be here to explain himself, but the coward in him wanted to vanish before she found out. The rebuilt porch, the new roof, the repaired kitchen—they were the only language he had for the words stuck in his throat. Maybe someday those words would come. For now, this house stood as his confession, his penance.

"Damn it, Deb," he whispered into the empty yard. "Please let me in."

His phone buzzed. Morales.

"Hey, what's up?"

"Lab results confirmed accelerant," Morales said. "It wasn't an accident, Luke." His voice was tight. "It matches the pattern from another case filed six months ago. A house fire outside Cardinal Creek. Judge's residence. It's the same accelerant signature as the Holcomb case."

Luke blinked hard, his pulse spiking. *The judge...Holcomb. Was that the judge who finalized Deborah's divorce?*

"And Chief," Morales added, lowering his voice, "we're treating the fires as related. Not accidental. The cigarette is part of the evidence we are waiting for."

Luke's grip tightened until his knuckles hurt. His pulse hammered in his throat as two terrible truths collided: someone had deliberately targeted Deborah, and the connection was something he couldn't tell her.

"Does Deborah know?" His voice sounded strange, distant.

"She will when the letter goes out. Her name is on the property. She may be questioned," Morales said.

"Is she a suspect?"

"Not at this time. But there's interest..." Morales paused. "Be careful who you tell. We'll be in touch." The line went dead.

Luke lowered his phone, his hand shaking. Behind him stood the farmhouse, its new beams and unfinished spaces like a wound hastily closed before the bleeding had stopped.

His stomach churned. He'd rebuilt her house while hiding the truth that it had been arson.

His heart hammered in his chest.

Someone with ties to both Judge Holcomb and Deborah had set the fire. Someone seeking revenge.

Luke swallowed hard as he scanned the property, no longer looking for Deborah as he had all week, but for threats, for footprints, shadows, anything that didn't belong.

Chad.

The fireflies continued their silent dance, indifferent to the weight crushing Luke's chest.

"I should have told you from the start, Deb," he whispered. "Now I can't."

He couldn't give her the truth, but he'd stand between Deborah and Chad, no matter the cost.

CHAPTER 25

Deborah's eyelids fluttered open, her cheek creased from the edge of the sewing table. Dawn painted her sewing room in honeyed gold, catching on the first quilt block she finished—a heart, pieced from Caleb's shirt. Her eyes burned, her body ached, but as she ran her fingers over the fabric, something inside her felt lighter. The heart she'd sewn felt warm beneath her hand. She whispered his name, hoping he could hear. She carefully laid the quilt block on the bed next to the others waiting to be sewn. Her finger traced the pocket that had held the letter that never reached Luke. The next block she'd make would incorporate the pocket so that she could place the letter inside for Luke.

Deborah made her way to the kitchen to make some coffee. She hadn't bothered making any in days. She placed her favorite French vanilla pod into her Keurig and grabbed the creamer from the refrigerator as it brewed. The scent filled the kitchen, the familiar ritual warming the space more than she expected. She cut a slice of banana bread and fished the denial letter from the drawer. The paper crinkled in her grip. Sitting at the table, she set her coffee aside, and set the letter squarely in front of her, daring herself to read every word and let the bad news soak in. The banana bread tasted bland and heavy. She took a sip of coffee, bracing herself. Exhaustion had consumed her, but she wasn't done yet. In thick black marker, she wrote: "We Fight. Stand up. Speak up."

She flipped her planner open and started a new page. She numbered her ideas, all clear and practical: a fundraiser featuring a quilt auction, a petition with a goal of at least five hundred signatures challenging the zoning board's decision, and possible partnerships with the school and firehouse. Call Fire Chief Erikson. A fundraiser would open the shelter's doors to the community, letting them see its purpose firsthand. People rarely fear what stands in plain sight.

Deborah picked up her phone and powered it on. It was time to face the world again. There were several missed texts and calls. She opened her messages and started a group text with Liz, Tiffany, Sissy, and Peggy Sue.

> Deborah: I'm sorry for being MIA. Are you busy today? Bring your sass and caffeine. We fight!

> Liz: On my way. Better be dressed and determined.

> Deborah: Will be dressed and ready to fight.

> Tiffany: On my way too.

> Sissy: Me too.

> Peggy Sue: Me too.

Deborah slipped into a pair of jeans and her favorite blue sweater with the tiny pearl buttons. In the kitchen, her hands trembled as she washed the dishes, rehearsing what she'd say. She scrubbed the coffee rings from the table and set out mugs. The knock came at 10:17. Her stomach knotted—part dread, part a desperate longing for connection. Deborah's breath caught as she opened the door. She stood frozen as four pairs of arms engulfed her at once, the scent of Peggy Sue's lavender perfume mingling with the warm scent of cinnamon rolls Tiffany clutched to her chest. Her quiet sobs dampened Deborah's neck.

"Seven voicemails," Liz whispered, holding Deborah's shoulders firmly. "Seven."

Their embraces both comforted and overwhelmed her, their tears mirroring the ones she'd shed in the dark. She hugged them back, fighting the urge to retreat into solitude.

Sissy gave her a playful slap on the arm. "Honey, you scared me. When I couldn't get a hold of you, I thought Chad snatched you up."

"He didn't hurt you?" Peggy Sue asked.

"I'm sorry I worried y'all. He didn't hurt me physically," Deborah said.

Tiffany pulled her into a side hug. "I'm just glad you are okay." She held up a pan. "I made cinnamon rolls."

"Jon told us he talked to you," Sissy said. "Otherwise, one of us might have broken down your door."

Deborah chuckled.

They chatted as they made coffee and cut the pan of cinnamon rolls. When they finally sat, the mood shifted—this was business. Deborah presented her idea for a fundraiser, *The Nest Revival: Quilts for Courage.*

Tiffany clapped her hands. "I love it. I can talk to the school and see how we can get involved."

As they continued to plan, Deborah's voice grew steadier and more confident with each detail. The women divided the tasks. Liz and Sissy would handle the quilt auction. Peggy Sue and Sissy would use their chamber connections to secure signatures for the petition. Tiffany handled the coordination with the school district.

"Liz," Deborah said, "do you think Kati would talk to the hospital?"

"I'll ask her later tonight," Liz said.

"I know she's busy with Bobby, so let her know she can call me whenever."

When they had each completed their tasks, they gathered their things and pulled Deborah into a hug filled with love and hope. She stood in the doorway and watched them go, her shoulders straighter than they'd been in days.

Alone again, Deborah's fingers trembled as she threaded the needle. The fabric squares cut from Caleb's shirts lay before her like an unfinished confession. She pressed her palm against the pieced pocket that would hold Caleb's letter, her pulse quickening. Reba McEntire's "Is There Life Out There" played from her "'80s Ladies" playlist, and Deborah found herself humming along, her foot tapping the sewing machine pedal in rhythm. With each stitch, the needle pierced her hesitation. She'd spent over thirty years retreating from what scared her. Not this time.

Deborah worked methodically, arranging and rearranging the blocks until the pattern felt right. As darkness crept through the blinds, she switched on a small LED lamp, illuminating her work. The sewing machine purred beneath her hands, keeping time with Reba's voice. Her foot eased onto the pedal as she guided the fabric through, her fingers tireless. Memories of Luke surfaced—his laugh, his quiet strength—and suddenly she was back at the farmhouse, feeling the warmth of his hands covering hers. His voice, tender and reassuring, danced in her ear as he patiently taught her how to use the fire extinguisher. At that moment, a sense of comfort washed over her, a contrast to the chaos around her.

Then there was Luke's grief. The grief that made him hide things from her. She poured herself into the quilt, into creating something that might offer him comfort when he wrapped himself in pieces of Caleb. When the quilt top was finished, she held it up and examined her work with a critical eye. There was one more thing to do. She prepared the quilt to finish it herself. Sissy had taught her free-motion quilting a while ago, and she'd practiced on a few smaller projects. Now it was time to make this quilt special for Luke. Deborah worked until early morning. When she was done, she laid the quilt across the bed and admired the work. Then she turned it over. A quilt tag sewn on the back read, "For Luke. For Caleb. For starting over."

She folded the quilt, slipped it into a bag, and set it by the door before going to bed.

As she folded fabric and placed it in a bag, she knocked the Hughes cookbook onto the floor. She picked it up and sat on the bed, the weight of it settling in her lap. Opening it, she flipped through the recipes until she reached Etta's first entry.

June 3, 1945
Married today. Momma cried. Daddy told me I made my bed, and now I must lie in it. I hope he's wrong.

Deborah turned the page, her mind drifting back to her own wedding day. Her daddy had said the same thing.

December 19, 1946
I burned supper again. He threw the plate at me. I picked glass from my hair. It cut my cheek. Our nearest neighbor is two miles away. No one can hear my cries.

Deborah skipped a few entries. It was like someone had witnessed what she went through with Chad.

December 11, 1952
In the summer heat, the bruise showed up faster than I expected. Harder to hide. My momma gave me a recipe, and on the back, it read, "A man who raises his voice will one day raise his hand." There was no greater truth than what she wrote. Daddy hit her. Now Henry hits me.

Deborah bit her bottom lip as she continued reading. She squeezed her eyes shut, memories flooding back—her daddy striking her momma if supper was late or his shirt wasn't pressed just right. She had sworn she'd never get married. Her ticket out was college but look how that turned out.

March 4, 1958
Baked peach cobbler to keep the peace. Sugar and silence are my survival.

June 22, 1961
Peach cobbler for Leaving Day. I have a bag packed under the bed. I need to get Ruth out of here. This is no way for a child to grow up. I wonder if she's as terrified as I am.

April 5, 1967
Ruth asked why Daddy yells so much. I didn't have an answer. I just whispered, "You deserve better than this." She's only seven.

January 14, 1974

He broke a chair last night when he found my suitcase. Ruth stayed in her room pretending not to hear her daddy drag me up the stairs...and what happened next. This morning, I wore sunglasses. We pretended nothing happened while I cooked breakfast and the Carpenters played on the radio.

August 30, 1980

I started writing recipes again. I'm learning who I used to be or who I want to be. Is it time to start over?

January 9, 1982

Last entry. Tomorrow, I leave. Peach cobbler is cooling on the counter. My final offering. Ruth has grown now. I hope she finds true love. I don't want her to repeat my mistakes. I'm 57 and hope it's not too late to start over, but it's what I'm gonna do.

Deborah closed the book, tears streaming down her face. Etta's words had reached across time to touch her heart. The parallels were uncanny—both women taking decades to find the courage to leave abusive husbands, both watching their children grow up in the shadow of fear. For years, Deborah had carried her pain like a secret shame, but here was proof she wasn't alone. She wiped her eyes with the back of her hand and took a deep breath. For the first time in a long time, her hands were still. She straightened and looked forward, not questioning it. Chad might have stolen years from her life, but he wouldn't take one more day of her future.

～

The next morning, Deborah loaded her SUV with purpose: first, the quilt, carefully folded; then her planner, an overnight bag, and finally a travel mug of steaming coffee. Gravel popped beneath her tires as she navigated the winding dirt road toward the farmhouse she hadn't visited in weeks. This journey was different. She was driving toward something rather than away from it.

The Nest Revival. When the farmhouse came into view around the final bend, Deborah eased off the gas. Her breath caught. The fire-gutted house she remembered had been transformed. The house that once smelled of smoke and rot now had fresh paint covering the burn marks. The wild grass had been tamed, and rocking chairs stood in formation along the porch, anchored by a swing that hung beside the picture window. As she drew closer, she noticed the roof had been mended too.

"Luke," she whispered.

The sky bloomed with lavender as Deborah pulled to a stop. Her fingers lingered on the quilt beside her, drawing resolve from each carefully sewn stitch. She stroked it and whispered, "You'll have your home too."

As she climbed the porch steps, her spine straightened on its own. She was no longer a woman running from her past, but one returning to fight for the new life she was building—not only for herself, but for women who needed refuge. The sight of the restored farmhouse blurred through sudden tears. Luke had thought of everything, down to the smallest detail. Something unfamiliar unfurled in her chest, warm and certain. No one had ever created something this beautiful just for her.

Inside, Deborah busied herself setting up for her presentation. She unfolded the display board and smoothed the edges, then picked up a marker and carefully wrote *The Nest Revival* across the top. Each letter landed with deliberate care, the words standing proud and clear for everyone to see. Her hands trembled slightly as she rehearsed what she wanted to say.

The hinges creaked as the door swung open, and Liz balanced a peach cobbler still steaming in its dish. Behind her, Sissy and Peggy Sue filed in, while Tiffany slipped by quietly and set down a tray of brownies cut into perfect squares. Anna and Kati followed, struggling with a cooler and a bag of ice between them. More women came in after. Faces Deborah didn't recognize scanned the room with purpose before introducing themselves as supporters. Deborah stood, stunned. No one had ever shown her this kind of attention before.

Deborah folded Liz into a hug. "I suppose you know about all of this," she said, gesturing at the transformed space around them.

"Guilty as charged," Sissy called over her shoulder as she set down the spaghetti.

"But who paid for it?" Deborah asked.

Peggy Sue joined them. "Jon, JW, Garrett, and Luke all chipped in for materials."

"The labor was all done by volunteers," Liz added.

Deborah's chest tightened with something between gratitude and disbelief. "Jon put this together?" she asked, her voice unsteady.

Liz touched her shoulder. "Honey, Luke organized it. He worked day and night to get it done."

Understanding settled over Deborah. Only Luke would have poured such attention into every detail, from the rocking chairs to the porch swing positioned exactly where she'd mentioned wanting one. The words caught in Deborah's throat as silence fell over the room. A woman she'd never met before reached out, her fingers warm against Deborah's wrist.

"When my sister had nowhere to turn," she said softly, "there was no place like this. That's why I'm here today."

The ladies settled into their seats, giving Deborah their full attention. She stood beside her presentation board and began to outline her vision for the fundraiser and auction.

"The fundraiser and auction will be a catalyst to raise awareness," Deborah said. "I'm hoping it rallies city support to overturn or amend the zoning restrictions." She took a deep breath and continued. "The event will center on the shelter's mission: Empowering Women to Rebuild."

She opened the quilt she'd made for Luke and set it on the table. "Each quilt tells a story." She said, her voice firm now as she gestured to the quilt. "When people bid on these at the auction, they're not just buying fabric—they're helping us fight those zoning laws."

The room erupted in applause, hands coming together in a thunderstorm of support.

When Deborah finished, each woman volunteered for a task, voices overlapping with ideas and offers of help. After the presentation, Jon and Will arrived. Jon greeted Deborah with a hug. "You know you've got the support of the fire department, right?"

Deborah thought about all the work Luke had done while she was away and nodded. "Thanks," she said, hugging him tight. "Thank you for working with Luke to fix the house."

"Mom, you know he loves you, right?" Jon said.

She hugged him tighter and whispered, "I love him too."

"He's not Dad."

Deborah nodded. "I'm sorry you spent your childhood afraid."

He eased back, offering a small smile. "We covered that in therapy."

She smiled. "We did." Etta's entries about Ruth had made her want to apologize again.

After the meeting, the craft barn buzzed with women's voices and busy hands, breathing life back into the shelter Deborah had almost given up on.

As twilight settled over the farmhouse, the group dispersed, leaving Deborah alone on the porch. She sank into one of the rocking chairs, savoring the solitude. The gentle creak of wood beneath her weight matched the rhythm of her breathing. After moving in with Liz, she'd discovered a peaceful sanctuary, but only recently had she learned to embrace these quiet moments on her own. Luke's quilt rested on her lap, each seam a silent promise. Her fingertips traced the patterns she'd sewn with care, hoping the thread might somehow mend the broken pieces of his heart.

A warm breeze stirred the wind chimes. Thunder murmured across the darkening sky, and Deborah watched the approaching clouds without tensing her shoulders. The Nest still had a future, and so did she.

CHAPTER 26

*D*eborah woke just before dawn, renewed purpose stirring within her. In the dim kitchen, she worked the cinnamon roll dough with steady, practiced hands, mapping out her day as the soft mound rose beneath a checkered cloth. When it doubled, she rolled it out and brushed melted butter across the surface, letting it pool in warm, golden streaks. Cinnamon and sugar filled the air, wrapping the room in a comfort she hadn't realized she needed.

Her gaze drifted to the quilt she'd made for Luke. She brushed her fingers across the quilting lines, each one carrying a piece of her heart. Beyond it, the message board Luke had replaced after the fire still stood —cluttered with sticky notes for the Nest, yellow squares blooming around the one labeled "Luke."

There were still things to do before she could deliver the quilt. She wanted it waiting when he woke—private, quiet, meaningful. Maybe it would matter more that way. Or maybe—her stomach tightened—she wasn't ready to face him, not with her heart this exposed, not with his grief still raw, and the memory of him pulling back, leaving her cautious. A sliver of fear whispered, *What if he's angry?* She pushed the thought aside, but it clung and refused to let go.

Her fingers trembled as she wrapped the quilt in brown craft paper, smoothing the edges and creasing the corners with her thumbnail. The twine bit gently into her palm as she looped it twice and cinched the knot tight. She paused with the pen over the small quilt block card, then wrote.

It's not about mending what is broken. It's about honoring what survived. —Deb.

Her handwriting looked small and unsure, but she tucked the card into an envelope, punched a hole near the corner, and threaded the twine through it. She felt like she was tying a piece of herself to the package.

She plated a warm cinnamon roll on a navy paper plate, covered it with foil, and added a Post-it:

Enjoy. —Deb.

With everything tucked under her arm, she reached for her keys on their familiar hook. But as the latch clicked behind her, a sudden thought rooted her in place.

Luke might answer the door.

She froze at the top step, keys dangling from her fingers. The cool morning air scraped her throat, and her pulse quickened.

For three long seconds, she considered retreating inside.

Then she whispered, "Sometimes you do things even when afraid," and walked toward her SUV, shoulders squared, choosing to move forward anyway.

She set the plate and quilt on the passenger seat before pulling out onto the quiet road. Dawn unfurled across the sky—lavender melting into rose, then into the fiery edge of the rising sun. Country music hummed in the background as she gripped the wheel tighter. Her nerves buzzed, imagining Luke opening the door in his grief, in his silence, in that way he had of pulling inward when the world hurt too much.

But she knew one thing for certain: Luke wasn't Chad. He wouldn't lash out or twist her intentions. He wouldn't hurt her for caring. She finally understood why he'd stepped back—pain like his cut deep and didn't heal well. She knew that kind of wound. She carried her own: Shelly's wedding, the funeral Chad had forbidden her to attend, years she could never reclaim.

Her breath trembled as she whispered, "Maybe this will help him."

Fog clung to the pastures lining the road to Luke's ranch, soft and silver as the world shifted from night to morning. Birds began their chorus, their music lifting as Deborah's heart hammered faster.

His house appeared simple and rustic, with a full porch wrapping around it and a swing beneath the picture window, much like the farmhouse she'd fought to save.

She parked and stepped out, drawing a deep, steadying breath.

"Thank you for the repairs," she murmured as she walked toward the house. "And for believing in me when I couldn't."

Her pulse raced as she climbed the porch steps. She set the quilt carefully on a chair, placed the foil-covered plate beside it, then turned away without daring another glance. She hurried back to her SUV, walking fast, breath trapped in her chest—praying he wouldn't see her, and praying just as hard that he would.

~

Luke opened the front door into the crisp, clean air, which woke him fully. It smelled of grass and woodsmoke, the season unmistakable. Mist hovered over the pasture while dawn spilled honey-colored light across the hills. A distant rooster crowed, nudging the world awake.

He stepped onto the porch in jeans and an old Levi's jacket, and steam rose from the coffee, warming his hands against the brisk morning. Inside, the silence had been too loud.

He froze mid-step. A package sat on the porch chair, tied with simple twine and labeled with an envelope—his name written in Deborah's gentle, looping script. Beside it, waited a foil-wrapped plate with a yellow note:

Enjoy.

His heart lurched.

His fingers trembled as he untied the twine and peeled back the brown craft paper. A sharp gasp tore from him. Caleb's shirts—flannel, denim, and the faded cotton rescued from the wreck—had been pieced into a quilt, each square a memory he thought he'd lost.

A small Post-it peeked from a stitched pocket: "Open me."

He pulled out the folded note. Caleb's handwriting punched the breath from his lungs. When he could breathe again, he slipped the paper back into the pocket with reverence, letting the words settle like a new weight against an old wound.

He traced a square of faded red plaid, soft as breath, each thread humming with memory. His mind drifted to their last autumn trail ride

—Caleb leaning into the saddle, eyes bright, wind tugging at that same flannel. "Just like you, Dad," he'd said.

Emotion broke over him. He sagged into the chair, the quilt settling around him with the warmth of a long-missing embrace. Tears carved silent paths down his face. The faint scent of cedar rose from the stitches, wrapping around him like the ghost of his son's arms.

And for the first time since the funeral, the pressure in his chest eased; it was still there, just quieter.

A cardinal perched on the feeder, tilting its head. Luke's breath caught, and for a moment, he wasn't alone.

This quilt wasn't just what remained of Caleb. It was a bridge between what he'd lost and whatever might still be ahead.

He clutched the quilt tighter.

"Thank you, Deborah," he whispered into the morning air.

⁓

The automatic doors of Green's supermarket parted before Deborah, releasing an air-conditioned blast of chilled air that carried the weight of small town scrutiny. Near the bakery counter, two women exchanged knowing looks over a fundraiser flyer.

"Deborah," one of them said, leaning in. "You know folks are talking, right? Chad's been spreading rumors."

Deborah tightened her grip on the cart. "What kind of rumors?"

"That the shelter will bring undesirable people to town. Some think you're doing this to spite him," Mrs. Steele said, her voice low.

The words stung, but Deborah blinked and swallowed hard. No. She wouldn't let Chad's voice control her anymore. She gathered her bags and stepped out into the sunlight

That afternoon, as Deborah drove home, sunlight poured across the farmland, illuminating the farmhouse as it came into view. The once-weathered structure stood resilient. Beyond it, the craft barn buzzed with activity as preparations for the fundraiser unfolded.

By the time she grabbed her notebook and stepped inside, the space hummed with purpose.

Liz rushed in with an armful of business cards scrawled with donation promises from Cowgirl Sweets and Treats, Saddle Up Bar and Grill, and half a dozen other Main Street shops. For the past two weekends, the craft barn's windows had glowed until midnight with silhouettes of the Quiltin' Bees bent over fabric in warm yellow light.

In the corner, Tiffany hunched over a table piled with paperwork, phone pressed to her ear as she tried convincing yet another school board member of the shelter's importance. When she hung up, she showed Deborah a string of photos: —flyers taped to bulletin boards, storefronts, and gas stations from one end of the county to the other.

"I've called almost everyone on the school board," Tiffany said. "If they don't understand the importance of the shelter, I'm appealing to their desire for reelection."

Deborah slipped an arm around her shoulders. "I can't thank you enough for everything you're doing."

Across the barn, Liz, Sissy, and Peggy Sue gathered around the long wooden tables, fingers steady as they guided fabric through humming sewing machines. Blocks of intertwined hearts, log cabins stitched with heart centers, friendship stars, and bear paws emerged beneath their needles—symbols of love offered freely, a home reborn with purpose, a community linked together, and courage softened by compassion.

The once-abandoned farm now pulsed with life—steam rising from coffee mugs with half-eaten cinnamon rolls beside them, rotary cutters sliding cleanly through bright fabric, and laughter echoing through rooms that had forgotten the sound of joy.

As Deborah worked with each woman, the plan came together piece by piece. The community that once doubted her was beginning to see the shelter's importance. But the fight wasn't over—not by a long shot.

~

As the fundraiser drew near, everything began to fall into place like puzzle pieces. One morning after his shift, Jon arrived with items from the hardware store, including a flat of seedlings and gardening tools from Mrs. Schneider.

Deborah covered her mouth in surprise. "She was completely

against the shelter! And I'm pretty sure her husband was standing with Chad at the café."

"I don't think Dad told them the whole story," Jon said. "Most of the firehouse—everyone not on shift—will be here to cook for the fundraiser. JW donated a huge amount of meat, and Mr. Alvarez from Green's is giving you all the fresh produce you need."

She smiled. "Really? He was right behind your dad that day."

Jon snorted. "After Uncle Danny and the attorney finish with him, Dad will be lucky to find someone willing to share a pew with him on Sunday." His tone softened. "Kati talked to the hospital administration. She gave them statistics on women who come into the ER with nowhere safe to go back to. It opened some eyes."

Deborah exhaled, her breath shaky. The thought of another confrontation with Chad sent her pulse racing. "He's never going to leave me alone," she whispered. "He never loved me. He despised me. Why won't he just let me go?"

Jon gently lifted her chin until she met his eyes. "Control. Remember what Xavier told you?"

She nodded, swallowing hard.

He kissed her forehead. "I'm proud of you, Mom. I love you."

Deborah pulled him into a tight hug. "I love you more."

She watched him drive away, then turned to speak with the reporter about her vision for women rebuilding their lives. The Nest was no longer just a dream. —Cardinal Creek was bringing it to life.

After talking with the reporter, Deborah sank onto the porch steps, her journal open across her knees, and she wrote with a steady hand.

Fear kept me small. Faith stitched me back together.

The words rang true, sending a quiet warmth through her.

Fireflies blinked across the pasture as twilight thickened, their tiny lanterns glowing. The farmhouse windows shone, casting golden light on a display of quilts stirring in the breeze. Crickets filled the quiet with their steady song.

Deborah looked toward the hills. In the distance, a house light glowed—soft, steady, like a star sewn into the quilt of the sky.

She traced her written words with her fingertips, feeling the rough grain of the paper. She thought of the woman she used to be—the one who froze at the sound of Chad's voice, who apologized for taking up space, who mistook obedience for peace.

The work of rebuilding the farmhouse had done more than create a shelter. It rebuilt Deborah.

She stood a little taller.

And when doubt whispered, she didn't listen.

CHAPTER 27

Deborah knelt on the freshly painted boards of her front porch, knees dusted with damp earth, as the morning sun rose. The air was thick with the scent of moist soil and the promise of a new day. She coaxed basil seedlings into a row of terra-cotta pots, the leaves brushing against mint shoots. Each inhale was a thread of calm, but the tranquility was short-lived.

A low rumble shattered the quiet, sending a jolt of tension through her. Deborah stiffened, dirt clinging to her palms as she wiped them on her spattered jeans. "Luke," she whispered, heart racing. Leaning against the sun warmed white railing, she braced herself for what was coming.

He slid out of his red pickup, moving slowly and stiffly as if trying not to draw attention, the quilt balanced in the crook of his arm. Amber light caught in his hair, but his face remained still—an unreadable mask—as their eyes met across the gravel drive. Silence stretched between them, wide and uncertain, holding everything they couldn't say. This wasn't the face of a fire chief, just a father in pain.

Luke cleared his throat. "You didn't have to do this." His voice trembled.

Deborah stepped closer, her boot heel tapping against the wooden porch. "I did."

He draped the quilt over the railing and leaned in, fingertips tracing the stitches. "You even included his letter. The one in the pocket you sewed into the quilt." He pressed a hand to his chest. "Where did you find it?"

She ran her fingers over the pocket. "It was still in the shirt."

Luke swallowed. "You have no idea what you did for me."

Deborah ran a thumb along the stitches. "I thought it was beautiful."

"He must have written it the day he was killed. That shirt was in his bag." He swallowed hard. "It was like he knew I'd need it right now. And I did."

Deborah stepped closer and touched his arm. "I'm sorry, Luke."

He lifted a hand to her face, his touch gentle. "After everything you've been through with the shelter and Chad, you still took the time to make this for me after I lied to you about the investigation and disappeared."

Deborah smiled and took his hand. "No, you didn't disappear." She gestured toward the porch. "Look around. This was all you." She pointed out the repairs and the fresh paint. "You've been with me all along, just not physically." She placed her hand over his heart. "I was right here."

For the first time since he arrived, his body relaxed, as though a heavy burden had finally lifted. "Would you mind if I hugged you?"

Her smile deepened. "I'd love that."

Luke pulled her into his arms and held on tight. The familiar scent of cedar was like home for Deborah. His breath hitched against her hair, the first crack as the grief he'd been holding together finally broke.

When they pulled apart, Luke cupped her cheek. "You've got this, Deborah."

"I hope you can come to the fundraiser. I could use the fire chief's support," she said with a wink. "We're meeting at the Cattle Trail Café later if you want to join us for the last big meeting."

Luke looked down, scuffing his boots against the porch boards. "I'll try. Either way, Deb, you're going to win."

"Not alone this time," she said, smiling.

He hugged her again and whispered, "Thank you."

As he stepped away, something fragile flickered in his eyes—hope, struggling to break free beneath the weight of grief. He clutched the quilt to his chest, knuckles whitening, as if letting go might make everything vanish. It was a lifeline, a gift Deborah was grateful she'd been able to give him. She placed a hand over her heart as she watched him drive away. It was hard to know what Luke was thinking, but she'd leave the door open for him while he grieved his son. Quilts were meant to provide warmth and comfort. This one mended something back together for both of them.

~

As Deborah stepped into the Cattle Trail Café, the buzz of the dinner crowd surrounded her: dishes clanking, laughter swelling, the smell of coffee and fried pies in the air. The last time she'd been here, Chad had humiliated her. Today, she was here to finalize plans for the fundraiser and auction.

In the corner booth, a flash of familiar navy caught her eye. She let out a long sigh as his gaze landed on her—sharp and assessing—before he turned back to his phone. She forced herself to look away and kept walking. He wasn't going to ruin tonight, not this time.

Liz waved her over to their usual booth, but today it held more than just the Quiltin' Bees. Community members were there alongside Jon and Kati. Deborah took a deep breath, opened her notebook, and pulled out a stack of notecards, ready to dive into the meeting.

"Did y'all see Chad in the corner?" she asked.

"Yep," Liz said. "But in all my years of teaching, I learned that if you ignore a child's bad behavior, they eventually stop." She glanced pointedly in his direction. "In his case, I'm hoping he leaves."

"Yes," Sissy said. "Leave."

"Okay, ladies, let's not start a brawl as you did in our senior year," Peggy Sue said.

Deborah giggled, easing the tension.

She slid cards across the worn tabletop, her fingers lingering on each one.

"Liz, the silent auction needs your eagle eye. Last one we did, you got Mrs. Henderson to bid on her own pie plate three times."

Liz's laugh lines deepened as she tucked the card into her purse.

"Sissy, no one knows quilts like you do." Sissy nodded, already sketching the display layouts on a napkin.

"And Peggy Sue," Deborah said, "those raffle tickets won't sell themselves." Peggy Sue winked, her fork poised over flaky crust as steam curled from their coffee cups.

Across the table, Jon's thumb traced the list of firefighter names on his clipboard. His eyes flicked up once—not at the paper, but toward the far corner booth. Chad sat there nursing a cup of coffee, pretending not to watch her.

Jon didn't say a word. He didn't need to. His jaw tightened—a small, unspoken promise—before he looked back down at his list, as if Chad were nothing more than a smudge on the wall.

Beside him, Kati's phone lit up with texts. "Another nurse is donating snickerdoodles," she whispered, eyes bright, either unaware of —or choosing to ignore—the tension humming at the table.

As they sat planning, the mayor approached the table and took a seat. "Deborah, I wanted to introduce myself. I'm Olivia Sanders. We saw each other from afar at the town hall meeting." She smiled apologetically. "I'm sorry about the zoning issues, but I assure you I'm working behind the scenes to get them resolved."

"It's a pleasure to meet you, Ms. Sanders," Deborah said.

The mayor took an envelope from her purse and handed it to Deborah. "This is a donation—so you know I truly support you. The few naysayers from the city council are beginning to turn. Don't lose faith. I believe in this project. Luke has told me so much about it."

A lump rose in Deborah's throat. Luke had gone to the mayor on her behalf. He never ceased to amaze her. She took the envelope and managed, "Thank you so much, ma'am."

"Call me Olivia." She squeezed Deborah's shoulder as she stood. "I'll see you at the fundraiser."

"Thank you again, Olivia."

After the mayor left, the café door jingled, and a man in dusty Wranglers and a sweat-stained Stetson approached their table. His Adam's apple bobbed as he cleared his throat, knuckles white around a stack of green vouchers from Hank's Feed & Supply.

"These are good for chicken feed," he mumbled, eyes fixed somewhere past Deborah's shoulder. "Or horse feed, if that's what they bring with 'em." He set the vouchers on the table with calloused fingers.

"Never thought I'd say this, but Luke made some sense at the Elks Lodge last week."

"Thank you, Mr. Hank," Deborah said softly. *Luke again.*

As he shuffled away, a woman with silver-rimmed glasses perched on her nose slid into his place, clutching a choir hymnal to her cardigan. "First Methodist is with you," she whispered, her perfume carrying hints of talcum powder and peppermint. "Twenty voices strong for your fundraiser. My sister needed a place like yours back in '86."

Deborah was overwhelmed by the community's outpouring of support. She looked up to find Jon watching her, his expression transformed. The boyish pity was gone; in its place was the steady gaze of a man who regarded her with unmistakable admiration. Her throat tightened. He smiled, winked, and shaped his fingers into a heart. She returned the gesture.

The bell over the diner door jingled, and Deborah turned to see Luke walk in, hat in hand. He didn't come to the table, choosing a stool at the counter where he could still see her.

Luke's gaze flickered toward the corner booth, where Chad sat, his attention fixed elsewhere. Not once did Chad didn't look over; he didn't need to. The tension hung in the air, thick and undeniable.

When Deborah didn't flinch or follow Chad's movements with her eyes, the silence deepened. Finally, Chad pushed back his chair and slipped out of the café without a sound, leaving no trace of his presence, as if he'd never been there at all.

Luke smiled and nodded at Deborah, who returned the gesture, but thoughts still remained on Chad. The message was clear: Chad was watching, lurking in the shadows even when he wasn't physically present.

Liz leaned close and whispered, "Well, look who emerged from the smoke."

Deborah's pulse quickened as she pretended Luke wasn't there, though his eyes never left her as they continued to work on things for the fundraiser.

"Does anyone know who could be in charge of the cook-off?" Deborah asked the group.

"I think JW said he could do it," Jon said.

"Could you text him and ask?"

Jon nodded, pulling out his phone to send a text.

She was just about to ask if anyone had seen Tiffany when the bell over the door jingled again, and Tiffany burst in like a tornado.

"Oh my gosh! I'm so sorry I'm late," she said, breathless. "I was putting up the rest of the flyers and organizing the volunteers." She rummaged through her bag and pulled out a paper. "Here's the list."

When she finished, she collapsed into the chair next to Deborah. "I know I'm too much, Deb. I'm sorry."

Deborah slipped an arm around her shoulders. "You're fine just the way you are. Thanks for all you have been doing."

"Girl, you are like the sister I always wanted."

Tears stung Deborah's eyes. "Thanks, Tiff."

Tiffany bumped her arm. "Not trying to stir the pot or anything, but did you see Luke over at the counter? Because either I'm losing my mind, or he's been staring at you."

Deborah smiled, amused. "I think he has been."

Tiffany laughed. "You do whatever you want, honey. Who am I to fix your love life? Mine is in shambles."

Deborah squeezed her hand, then glanced at her watch. "Okay, y'all, I think I've taken up enough of your time. Does anyone have any questions? Everyone clear on their assignments?"

The group nodded. In just days, it would all be real, and the prospect both scared and thrilled her.

"I can't thank you enough for all your help and support," Deborah said. "I love each and every one of you."

As everyone cleared out, Deborah sat alone at the table, her fingernail tracing slow circles on her coffee cup that had gone cold. Her phone buzzed on the table.

She picked it up and sighed, rolling her eyes. "Why don't I block his number?" she mumbled, knowing he'd find another way.

Chad: Nice little group you've formed. Looks like you've even got your baby boy involved. It would be a shame if the fundraiser didn't go well.

Her stomach dropped. Just enough venom to curdle her confidence. She locked her phone and placed it face down on the table. She wasn't going to give him the satisfaction.

The dinner rush had faded, leaving just the hum of the cooler and the soft squeak of the waitress's rag against Formica. Her chest tightened as she thought of Olivia's envelope, Hank's feed vouchers, the choir director's perfume. The same people who'd once whispered behind her back that the shelter would bring trouble were standing beside her now. Then there was Luke, working behind the scenes the entire time. He hadn't abandoned her after all. Her feelings for him have grown, but she wasn't sure if he was ready for her. Her stomach fluttered. Ridiculous at her age. A throat cleared nearby, and she looked up to find Luke watching her, his eyes warm as embers.

"Bad news?"

"Nothing that matters." she lied.

His jaw flexed slightly, but he didn't press. She'd always appreciated that about him. He knew when to step back and let her process things.

"May I?"

Deborah nodded.

She watched him settle into the chair beside her, unable to look away as he turned his hat over and over in his hands. The silence between them was comfortable yet charged. Finally, he reached across the table and gave her hand a steady squeeze.

"Do you still need the fire chief's support?"

Her throat tightened, but she managed a small, wobbly smile. "Only if he's willing to take orders."

He chuckled, eyes glistening. "Guess I could handle that."

Through the café window, amber light from the streetlamp caught the fine lines around Luke's eyes. His thumb traced slow, hesitant circles against her palm as the neon sign flickered, briefly casting a rose-colored glow across their intertwined fingers resting on the worn Formica.

CHAPTER 28

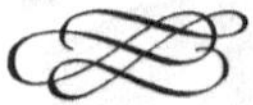

$\mathcal{D}$eborah's hand trembled as she poured coffee, spilling a few drops onto the counter. Outside, the Hill Country glowed warm and calm, as if the last week hadn't happened. The upcoming town council discussion weighed on Deborah's mind. They needed a loophole. Danny and the attorney had been digging, but what if there wasn't one?

Deep down, she knew she had more supporters than enemies, but Chad's name flashed in her mind like a warning siren. He had half the town's influential men wrapped around his finger—the ones who drank expensive scotch with him every Thursday at the country club. That kind of power didn't disappear.

Deborah drained her coffee cup and arranged the color-coded folders on the table in the formal dining room, her neat handwriting visible on each label. Until a final denial was issued, they had to keep planning the grand opening. An engine approached, low and steady, and she froze. She prayed it wasn't Chad coming up the driveway to make good on his threats. When Luke's pickup came into view, she sighed with relief. A smile tugged at her lips as she watched him park, her fingers gripping the edge of the table, afraid he might turn around and drive away.

She stepped outside and crossed the drive toward Luke's truck. Luke climbed out, adjusting his department cap and giving her a smile she felt more than saw. "Figured the fire chief might have something useful to contribute this morning," he said

"I could use all the help I can get."

"The mayor called," he said, lowering his voice. "There might be a way to reclassify the shelter. Before you panic, it's a good thing."

She blinked. "Reclassify how?"

"I'm not sure yet. That's what I wanted to go through with you." He scratched his jaw. "I thought maybe we could look over the deed together."

When he said "together," her heart skipped.

"Thank you, Luke," she said softly, touching his arm.

They worked side by side in silence, the comfort of it as unsettling as it was welcome. Deborah found herself watching his steady hands as he sorted papers, so different from Chad's sharp, impatient movements. Her stomach knotted. Despite their time together, a nagging doubt lingered. Was Luke's calm just another mask waiting to slip?

Luke inhaled twice, as if about to speak, then closed his mouth and returned to the papers. Deborah shifted her chair an inch away without meaning to, a reflex leftover from life with Chad. She regretted it instantly.

Luke noticed. His jaw flexed.

After five strained minutes, he slid the deed toward her.

"Look, Deb!" he said, leaning closer. "This clause might let you operate without a variance."

"Do you think it's a mistake?"

"Or something zoning overlooked." He tapped the line. "Agricultural with auxiliary purpose. It's rare."

Deborah's eyes widened.

"Auxiliary purpose includes housing for seasonal work and community-related residence."

"Luke, that means—"

"You're exempt from zoning review."

"We did it."

"You did it," he said quietly. "I just read the fine print."

Silence settled between them, warm and charged.

"I never meant to lie to you. I just—"

Deborah leaned in and pressed her fingers to his lips.

"Luke," she whispered.

His gaze traveled from her mouth to her eyes, slow, deliberate.

"Deborah," he murmured, closing the distance.

Time slowed as the space between them disappeared.

A car door slammed outside. Heavy footsteps crossed the porch, and the front door flew open, shattering the moment.

Tiffany burst in first, breathless, hair wild, stumbling forward with knuckles white around her purse strap as if she'd sprinted all the way from town. She froze, eyes darting to Luke and Deborah, inches apart. Luke's low laugh mingled with Deborah's nervous one, their gazes locked, and she found herself hoping the moment wouldn't end.

"Hey... were you two doing zoning research?" Tiffany asked, air-quoting the word "research."

Jon came in behind her, with Liz, Sissy, Peggy Sue, JW, Will, and Garrett close on his heels. They froze when they took in the scene.

Deborah jumped back, and Luke cleared his throat. Her cheeks burned as she stared down at the deed without seeing a word.

"Anyway, y'all, I have news!" Tiffany said, breaking the tension when she noticed everyone staring.

Luke raised his hand. "We found something too." He turned to Deborah. "Tell them."

Deborah swallowed. "The deed has a clause! The land was originally classified as agricultural with auxiliary residential use. Meaning the shelter may fall under permitted use without a zoning variance."

Tiffany blinked and grinned. "That's the same clause I found at the courthouse this morning. Deborah, this is happening. Your dream is real!"

"The denial letter is invalid," Luke said. "I'm calling the mayor."

When he returned, he slipped an arm around Deborah's shoulders. "I left a voicemail with the details," he said, checking his watch. "If she doesn't call back within the hour, I'll try again."

Deborah bit her bottom lip. "Do you think there's gonna be a problem?" *It can't be this easy.*

"I hope not, darlin'," he said, taking her hand.

Jon stepped closer. "What's going on?"

"Luke called the mayor, but he got her voicemail," Deborah said, wringing her hands.

Luke covered them with his own, giving a gentle squeeze.

His phone buzzed in his pocket. He answered and put it on speaker. "Hey, what's the word?"

"I've never seen anything like this clause," the mayor said. "Deborah, your shelter was meant to exist. You don't just have legal standing; you have history on your side."

The room erupted as voices overlapped, hugs were exchanged, and cheers filled the air. Everyone celebrated except Luke, who watched Deborah with a quiet, admiring smile while she pretended not to notice.

"Well, this calls for a celebration," Liz said, clapping, "and planning the grand opening."

"Looks like you finally caught a break," Luke said.

"We," she corrected, "we caught a break. You showed up, Luke. You've been showing up."

Luke didn't respond. The others pretended not to watch, though Deborah sensed none of them missed the moment.

For the rest of the afternoon, they huddled around Deborah's dining table with calendars and notepads, mapping out every detail of the fundraiser set for Friday and the shelter's grand opening just fourteen days later. Deborah drifted through it all in a daze as teams were formed and task lists were assigned. She and Luke collaborated on the tour schedule, a quiet momentum building as the plans came together.

As they prepared for the celebration, Deborah looked at each person there who'd been such a large part of her journey. They'd believed when she'd been afraid to, which brought her right to this moment. She held her head high, knowing that it could lead others without fear.

By evening, the farmhouse transformed under strings of lanterns hanging from the porch eaves, glowing against the clearing evening sky. Music drifted from portable speakers while the scent of barbecue filled the air. Firefighters took control of the grill, Quiltin' Bees arranged food on tables covered with checkered cloths, and townspeople milled about with plates and drinks.

Tiffany was wearing a sundress instead of her usual teacher clothes, flirting confidently with JW near the refreshment table.

"For a city girl, you've got sass," JW teased, his red hair catching the lantern light.

"And for a small town bartender, you've got charm," she said, laughing as she touched his arm.

Deborah watched from the porch steps, a plate balanced on her knees, taking in the scene with quiet joy. Her gaze swept across the property—the renovated farmhouse, the barn with its new roof, the cleared garden space—all evidence of how far they'd come.

The celebration dwindled as guests drifted into the night, leaving Deborah to find Luke alone on the porch. His silhouette was outlined against the darkening sky as he rocked gently in one of the wooden chairs, the boards squeaking under his weight. She handed him a mug of coffee and sat in the rocker next to him. The moon shone bright, and the stars looked like diamonds. They sat in silence, listening to the cicadas.

Luke finally spoke. "So, what happens now?"

"With?" Deborah asked, unsure where he was headed with this conversation.

"Everything," he whispered.

"You know what's happening with the shelter. Do you mean something else?"

He took a long drink of coffee and stared straight ahead. After a moment, he said, "Us?"

Her brow furrowed. "Do you know what you want, Luke?" His hesitation only deepened her own confusion.

The rocking chair stilled as he set his mug down.

Is he going to get up and leave? Deborah stood and stepped in front of him.

Luke rose to his feet. "The problem isn't not knowing what I want," he said, his gaze drifting from her eyes to her lips, as he'd done earlier when they almost kissed. "I know exactly what I want."

Deborah's heart fluttered as she stepped closer. "Luke, I have feelings for you."

The air between them crackled. "If I start kissing you, I might not be able to stop," he admitted, his voice barely above a whisper. "I want whatever we do to be special. You deserve that." He placed his hand on her cheek, and she leaned into his touch, wishing for a deeper connection. She knew he was fighting something; she didn't know what.

"I'm your friend first, Luke. I'm here if you need to talk," she said, caressing his face and silently hoping he'd kiss her. Instead, he exhaled and stepped back.

"I'm sorry, but I need to slow this down. I don't want to complicate things—or hurt you."

Her chest ached, but she nodded. "I'm here for you," she said, hoping to encourage him without revealing her own vulnerability. "I'll see you at the fundraiser?" She managed a smile, though her heart sank at the thought of another missed opportunity.

Luke brushed his thumb across her cheek, his eyes filled with warmth. "You have a strength that I envy."

"You do too," she said, "but fear is driving you away. I won't give up on you."

He kissed her forehead and held her gaze for a moment longer. "I'll see you at the fundraiser. I'm proud of you."

"Night, Luke."

"Night."

Deborah watched him walk across the gravel, questions churning. *Is it fear of losing me...or fear of losing someone again?* She knew her own fear lingered too—of his kindness being a mask. But Chad had never pretended to be patient or gentle. And Luke was.

As he drove away, she realized fear was holding them both hostage. She'd let Luke process things until the fundraiser.

Deborah's phone buzzed—unknown number.

A chill ran down her spine.

> Unknown Number: Have you had enough?
> Nothing is going to stop me, not even a
> loophole. Not even your boyfriend can
> protect you from me.

Chad.

The text sent a jolt of anger through her, igniting a fire she'd long kept smothered. He had no clue that his actions, words, and texts had only fueled her determination. With each breath, the weight of his threats lifted, replaced by the strength she was beginning to embrace. A newfound confidence swept through her, strengthened by the support of her newfound friends. She straightened her shoulders, a tight smile forming on her lips. This time she was ready. She wasn't backing down.

CHAPTER 29

*L*uke sat in the rocking chair, listening to its familiar creak in the quiet morning. The Hill Country glowed with orange and pink, but the knot in his stomach stayed tight. He hadn't felt right since the night he walked away from Deborah, even though all he wanted was to kiss her.

Mockingbirds and cardinals called to one another, their songs drifting on the breeze, yet his mind lingered on the café—on Deborah standing tall, her voice steady as she directed volunteers. He admired the way she had transformed, exuding a confidence he'd never seen before.

But beneath that strength lay a fragility he couldn't ignore. He glanced at his forgotten coffee, a thin skin forming on its surface, and at the memorial quilt beside it—patches from Caleb's faded Levi's, his little league jersey, and the flannel he wore while horseback riding.

Luke's fingers brushed against the hidden pocket with the letter inside. He unfolded it for the tenth time, his son's handwriting blurring as tears threatened. Pressing the letter to his chest, he felt his heart pound against his ribs. He had to make this right—not just for Caleb, but for Deborah too. She was counting on him. He couldn't let her down.

The memory of pain in Sammy's voice during their last conversation twisted in his gut. Her harsh words stung. He smoothed the quilt across his lap, thumb tracing a crooked seam where Caleb's rodeo patch had been sewn. The fabric warmed under his touch, almost alive, while the grief he buried stayed heavy in his heart. He pictured Deborah's eyes searching his face for answers he didn't possess, comfort he couldn't summon, reassurances trapped behind the wall of his grief.

How was he going to repair his relationship with his daughter? That was the real question. Deborah had transformed his mourning into something living by stitching together Caleb's shirts, patches, jeans, and including his letter. She'd made grief tangible, something that could be held and felt. Luke buried his sorrow deep within, locking away every trace. He had been physically present for Sammy but emotionally distant–a ghost haunting the room. Was his ex-wife fully present for Sammy? Perhaps she wasn't asking too much; she wanted something he didn't know how to give–not for her, and not for Deborah.

Luke closed his eyes and lay his head back on the rocker, contemplating whether he should go to the fundraiser today. Deborah had said she wanted him there, but after he'd left, the doubt had crept back in. The guilt from walking away had been eating him up. He wanted to spend time with her; he loved her company. But how could he risk hurting her when he was so emotionally unavailable, even to his daughter? How could he have a relationship? He'd watched his marriage crumble when he'd shut down after Caleb's death.

Do you need a fire chief? His words at the diner lingered in his thoughts. They'd sounded braver than he felt. She'd searched his eyes for an answer he still didn't have. One thing he knew for sure, Deborah was stronger than he was. Maybe the question had given her something to hang onto. He'd always tried to support her from a distance, staying in his lane as fire chief. But what would it say if he skipped the fundraiser? Would Chad be there? He pressed his lips together, uneasy. The old rocker creaked faster as his foot tapped an anxious rhythm, his thoughts spinning with every back-and-forth.

Luke's phone buzzed. Sammy's picture lit the screen, and he closed his eyes, taking a deep breath. His finger hovered over the answer button before he pressed it.

"Hey, darlin'. How are you?"

"Hi, Dad. I was thinking of coming in a couple weeks to get my stuff," she said. Her voice cracked.

"Are you going to stay the weekend?"

"I was thinking I might. Are you free?"

"I'll be free." Luke paused, trying to swallow the lump in his throat. "Sammy?"

"Yeah, Dad."

"I'm sorry. There's no handbook for surviving your life when one of your children dies. I messed up after your mom left, and I can't say I'm sorry enough. It won't happen anymore."

"I love you, Dad. We'll talk when I get home."

She had said "home." Tears rolled down his cheeks. He cleared his throat. "We will. I love you, and I'm so proud of you."

"See you in a couple weeks, Daddy."

Daddy. She hadn't called him that in years. Was it a sign she was understanding? Could they work things out? The phone call gave Luke hope, and he needed it more than anything. The walls he'd built cost him his wife. He'd let grief rule him long enough to nearly lose his daughter and Deborah. The memorial quilt was a reminder that Deborah had forgiven his failings. Sammy's call and wanting to come home were proof that they were working toward forgiveness.

Luke folded the quilt with careful hands and tucked it under his arm, leaving the cold coffee forgotten on the porch. Inside, he stood before the hallway mirror, straightening his collar, rehearsing words that wouldn't come. His reflection stared back, eyes clearer than they'd been in months. He grabbed his jacket from the hook, fingers lingered on the worn denim before slipping it on.

As he reached for his keys, the quilt on his recliner caught his eye. "If I'm going to show up for anyone," he said to the empty house, "I have to start now." The keys jingled as he locked the door behind him.

His boots hit the gravel driveway when a flash of red caught his eye —a cardinal darting across his path to perch in the oak in his front yard. Its bright presence was like a torch against the pale blue sky.

Deborah's fingers trembled against the porch railing as she watched Sissy direct volunteers toward the parking area, Liz's clipboard catching sunlight as she checked off names.

Around her, the farmhouse buzzed with movement. Peggy Sue balanced on a stepladder, her silver bracelets jingling as she strung lights through the porch rails while Tiffany held the cord below. Anna arranged blueberry muffins into spirals on a red-checked tablecloth as

Kati adjusted the hand-lettered price signs. Smoke curled from the barbecue pit where Jon flipped burgers and Will directed firefighters in their *Cardinal Creek Heroes* t-shirts.

Dawn broke over the farmhouse, illuminating dew-kissed grass and carrying the scents of coffee and fresh-baked goods through the air. Deborah's heart fluttered, quick and steady.

Beyond them stood the craft barn with its fresh red paint, empty quilting frames waiting by the windows. In the garden plot, soil stretched in neat rows. The chicken coop's new wire gleamed. Deborah's throat tightened. She inhaled slowly, counting to five, one of the tools she'd learned in therapy. It was all here, ready to help women get back on their feet and learn to survive without needing someone to do it for them.

She took a steady breath, nervous about having people come to the Nest, but opening the doors to the community was necessary so they could see the value of what she was doing. Months of planning, rehabbing, painting, and cleaning had transformed this place into her dream. Now the farmhouse pulsed with color and movement. It had come to life.

Deborah's heart swelled when she spotted the quilts hanging across a clothesline like they were being aired out. A hand on her shoulder startled her. She turned to find Liz holding out a shirt.

"This is for you," Liz said.

Deborah held it up. The front displayed a log cabin quilt block with the words "Cardinal Creek Stands." Together. Her eyes filled with tears.

"I don't know how to thank you for everything you've done."

"Just keep getting stronger," Liz said, pulling her into a hug. "I'm proud of you."

Deborah slipped the shirt over her head and checked her watch. *What if no one comes? No—stop.* She forced the thought out of her mind as the first trucks began pulling into the parking lot Jon had set up. Garrett and JW headed toward the barbecue pit. Deborah noticed JW scanning the crowd, searching for someone. She smiled to herself, wondering if he was looking for Tiffany.

As more people arrived, her nerves calmed, especially when she saw the kids having a good time playing games, and people dancing to music. A crowd gathered around the silent auction table, bidding on the quilts. While Deborah worked the baked goods table, the superintendent approached with a letter of support.

"Ms. Clemmons," he said. "Tiffany has told us about your vision. This shelter is a much-needed service to the community. The district is committed to helping in any way we can. Several teachers have already volunteered to tutor students." He handed Deborah the letter.

Her hands trembled as she received it. "Thank you, sir," she said, sounding more confident than she felt.

"You have the full support of the PTA as well. We should meet soon to discuss plans."

"I'll call next week to set something up."

"Perfect. It was nice meeting you." He shook her hand and excused himself.

Deborah looked around until she spotted Tiffany in the craft barn working with the kids to make picture frames. She smiled, knowing she'd misjudged her and needed to thank her for all her hard work and support.

The fundraiser was in full swing, and there were people everywhere. The community had shown up in full force. Several attendees wore the "Cardinal Creek Stands Together" T-shirt, showing solidarity. As the morning wore on, Deborah looked around to see if Luke had arrived. It had been two days since she'd seen him. She hoped he would show up, but if he didn't, she'd stand on her own two feet with the group that had supported her through it all.

As she walked around shaking hands and greeting families, she noticed Luke's truck pull into the driveway. Her heart began to beat faster. A smile spread across her face as he climbed out of his truck, solid and familiar in a way that made her breath catch. He looked good. One kiss, and everything it promised had branded itself into her memory, heating her like July in Texas. Their eyes met as he approached, and her heart skipped a beat.

"Hey," he said.

"Luke," she whispered.

"This looks fantastic. You did it."

"I hear you've been talking to people too."

He shrugged, flashing a crooked grin. "Maybe."

Deborah laid her hand on his arm, resisting the pull to step closer. "Luke, we need to stop dancing around this."

He nodded. "Walk with me a sec?" he asked.

She nodded, her pulse quickening.

He led her to the oak tree across from the farmhouse, where the noise faded and the shade wrapped around them. He shoved his hands into his jeans' pockets, his jaw tense.

"You look like you're holdin' your breath," Deborah said softly.

He chuckled. "Maybe."

A breeze lifted a stray hair from her cheek. Luke reached for it, then stopped himself, his hand hovering before dropping back to his side.

"I need to ask you something before the day gets crazy." His voice was low and gruff. "Do you trust me?"

Her breath hitched. "I want to."

"But you don't."

She didn't answer, and the silence built a wall between them.

Luke glanced toward the farmhouse, then back at her. "I know you've heard rumors about the investigation. I know you're scared, and you deserve answers. I just can't give you everything yet." His Adam's apple bobbed as he swallowed. "Not because I don't want to. I can't."

Deborah folded her arms across her chest. "You kept things from me before. You lied. An omission is still a lie. You didn't tell me that someone may have done this on purpose."

He recoiled at her words, as if they were physical blows. "I thought I was shielding you from more pain," he said, voice catching. "I convinced myself that was protection."

She narrowed her eyes. "Yeah, that's what Chad would say."

Luke kicked the ground with his boot. "That's not fair, Deb."

"I know," she said. "But when you shut me out...it felt the same."

He stepped so close she could smell his soap. "I'm not him. I would never be him. And I swear on all that I love...I'm not going to abandon or hurt you."

"How can I trust that this ends well?"

"It will," he said with conviction that warmed her heart. "And when this is over, I'll tell you everything. I promise."

Their eyes locked, the pull between them undeniable. This time, Luke brushed her cheek. Her breath caught as he leaned in—

"Deborah! The reporter from San Antonio is here."

They both exhaled in frustration as the spell shattered.

"We'll finish this later," Luke said.

"When?" she whispered.

"Tonight," he said, then paused. "If you want to."

Before she could answer, Sissy was already steering the reporter toward her.

Luke squeezed her arm before heading toward the barbecue pit where he stayed, though his eyes followed her. Deborah needed to trust that he'd tell her everything. Maybe there was more happening than she understood.

Her pulse roared as the reporter strode toward her—not from interview jitters, but from the echo of almost a kiss still warming her skin. She squared her shoulders, pasted on a smile, and moved to meet him.

She walked with the reporter from San Antonio toward the newly built porch, her voice steady despite her heart pounding. The reporter nodded and scribbled with genuine interest, a small mercy that soothed Deborah's nerves.

As the breeze shifted, she caught a familiar scent of musk.

She held her breath. It was Chad. His cologne was forever imprinted in her mind. Her spine stiffened.

Boots scraped the gravel. The low laughter of men followed.

The reporter's brows drew together. "Is that...?"

Deborah closed her eyes. She didn't need to look. Her body already knew who it was.

Chad strode up the drive, two of his cronies flanking him in their pearl-buttoned shirts and black Stetsons. Chad's lips curled into a smirk that didn't reach his eyes beneath the brim of his hat.

"Well, bless your little heart," he drawled. "Showin' off the place for the news? You've always been dramatic."

Deborah's breath caught. She prayed he wouldn't make a scene. Her eyes darted toward Jon, JW, Garrett, and Luke, who were closing in from different angles, positioning themselves between her and trouble.

The Quiltin' Bees moved in from the opposite side. Liz and Sissy lifted their chins, ready for a challenge. The wall of support behind her gave Deborah the strength to stand tall. On the outside, she looked confident and unafraid. Inside, she trembled, reduced to the timid woman she'd been with him.

The reporter whispered, "Is this your ex-husband?"

Deborah swallowed. "Yes."

Chad's long stride stopped just short of Deborah, but behind her were all her supporters. Jon placed his hand on her shoulder, and she patted it.

"Do you think a bake sale and some quilts will erase the law?" Chad sneered. "Are you gonna cry pretty to bend the zoning? It won't work."

The reporter stepped back.

Jon stepped forward.

Luke edged closer, jaw clenched, his eyes locked on Chad.

Deborah lifted her chin, hands trembling firmly behind her back. "Chad, you need to leave. You're not welcome here."

He smirked, leaning closer until she could smell his cologne, which she used to scrub from his clothes.

"You've always needed a man to fix things, starting with your daddy. What are you going to do when this place burns again, let your boyfriend fix it?"

Silence fell so complete that she could hear an acorn fall from the oak tree.

Luke and Jon surged forward, the kind of movement that made a man rethink his life choices. But they never reached Chad.

Flashing lights tore up the drive, leaving a cloud of dust behind them.

Deputy Wilson's cruiser slid to a stop, and two uniformed deputies stepped out, hands resting on their revolvers.

"Chad Clemmons?" Deputy Wilson called.

Chad turned, irritation sharpening his voice. "What now? —"

"You're under arrest for arson," Wilson said, his voice carrying across the fundraiser. "You willfully and intentionally set fires resulting in property damage."

"Fires?" Chad scoffed.

Gasps rippled through the crowd.

Deborah's stomach churned.

The deputies moved in, grabbing Chad's wrists. He jerked in protest. "Do you know who I am? This is crazy. She set the fire. I told y'all she—"

"Save it," Wilson snapped as he patted Chad down, removing cigarettes from his pocket. "Next time, don't leave a cigarette at each of the scenes. DNA's a hell of a thing."

The world seemed to hold its breath, the silence so complete it pressed against Deborah's eardrums.

Scenes? What do they mean?

It was as if all the air had been squeezed from her lungs. She swayed, and Luke was at her side, steadying her without touching her.

"This isn't the end, Deb. You'll see," Chad yelled as they shoved him into the back of the cruiser, door slamming while he yelled something she couldn't hear.

There was a hush over the crowd. Slowly, the clapping began. First, one person. Then the whole fundraiser roared in applause.

Deborah blinked as her knees nearly buckled from the weight of months of terror lifted from her shoulders. Her breath hitched as relief washed through her.

She turned to see Luke smiling. "Deb, I'm so proud of you. That was amazing."

"I'm pretty sure throwing up right now would ruin the moment," she whispered.

They laughed.

As the sun started setting, the farmhouse glowed with string lights, and the air smelled of barbecue and cedar. Deborah wiped down tables while Luke coiled the last of the extension cords. Jon and the firefighters worked to clean up their area. As they worked side by side, Deborah thought about all the times people had mentioned Luke talking up the shelter. He needed to know that she knew that he hadn't deserted her.

"Thank you for your help with the shelter. You know, talking to people in town," she said.

He shrugged. "You would have found a way. You're much stronger than you think. Stronger than me, but I'm working on that."

She touched his arm. "I can see that."

"We'll talk," he said as he started to leave.

"I'd love that."

His smile was small, but sure. "Good night, Deb." He leaned in and kissed her cheek.

A gesture so small ignited a fire inside her. Deborah knew that her feelings for Luke had grown into more than she'd ever expected.

CHAPTER 30

*L*uke's phone buzzed against the arm of the rocker, jolting him awake. Sammy's name lit up the screen as morning light crept over the porch, brushing over his unshaven jaw as he blinked awake. He must have drifted off sometime after midnight, still wrapped in Caleb's quilt like armor against everything that hit him at the fundraiser. He still hadn't talked to her since the fundraiser, and the silence was much heavier than he wanted to admit.

"Hey, pumpkin. How are you?"

"I saw the news feature about the shelter. I'd love to meet Deborah. I'm doing a project for school, and I'd like to interview her for my project."

Luke's heart soared. *Even if she just wants to come home to meet Deborah, it's a start for us.* "Of course. The grand opening is this afternoon. You can come to that."

"Are you sure you have time?"

"I'll always make time for you. You're the most important person in my life," Luke said, the words catching in his throat.

"I know you and Deborah went out to eat before I left for college. Do you like her?"

Luke swallowed hard. *Do I like her? I more than like her.*

"Dad?"

"I do, Sammy. More than I even realized."

"Did you push her away, too?"

"Too?" Luke was shocked at what she was saying.

"Yeah, too. You pushed everyone away after Caleb died."

Anger flared, then faded as Luke took a deep breath. *Listen to her. She lost her brother, then her mom, and in a way, her dad, too.*

"I didn't mean to, I swear," he said, his voice cracking.

"I need you, Dad," Sammy said. Her voice broke, and sobs followed.

"God, Sammy, I'm so sorry. I didn't..." Tears rolled down his cheeks as his words failed him. He leaned back against the chair and closed his eyes. "Can you forgive me?"

"Of course," she said, hiccupping. "I love you, Dad. I know you tried to hold it together, especially after Mom left. It was hard for you, but I never wanted for anything."

There was a moment of silence, then Sammy cleared her throat. "I'll see you at the shelter this afternoon." Her voice softened. "And Dad? Someone who builds a place like that for others—someone who understands broken pieces—might be exactly what you need right now."

"I do," Luke said, trying to compose himself.

"I may have been young, but if I learned anything after Caleb died," she continued, "it's that life is unpredictable. We don't know when the people we love will leave us, so we can't run from them."

"But what if I lose her?" Luke asked, the words tumbling out before he could stop them.

Her voice softened. "Dad, I'd rather have those years with Caleb than none at all. Remember how you used to play 'The Dance' when Mom was gone? That song got me through the worst nights. Even with all this pain, I wouldn't trade a single memory of him."

Luke pressed his lips together. "How did you get so smart?"

"Genetics," she said, laughing.

"God knew what he was doing when he blessed me with you," he said as tears flowed down his cheeks.

"I'm glad we talked."

"Me too. See you at the grand opening."

When Luke pressed the end button, he placed his palm against his chest and took a deep breath, filling his lungs for the first time in months. Sammy was coming home. He opened the photos on his phone, landing on one of Deborah at the fundraiser—her smile cautious but genuine. He ran his thumb across the screen, reminded of her willingness to give him a chance after years of abuse from Chad. She was ready to open her heart. He was the one who remained closed off.

The events of the fundraiser weighed on him. Pride swelled at how Deborah stood up to Chad, but it tangled with the memory of her searching the crowd for him.

His back ached from sleeping upright. The fire investigation weighed on his mind, the constant reminder of the guilt he carried for keeping the truth from her. He replayed the fundraiser again and again, still unable to name what kept him away.

He smoothed his palm over the quilt, tracing the stitches of Caleb's rodeo patch. The contrast of rough denim and soft flannel made his throat tighten. This wasn't just a quilt; it was a part of Caleb he'd locked away. And, for the same reason, it was every part of Sammy he'd almost lost. When Deborah made the quilt, she'd handed him a piece of himself. Now he had to find the courage to give her something in return —the truth: about the fire, about Caleb, about Sammy, and the reason he ran.

Luke pushed himself out of the chair and went inside. In the kitchen, he rummaged through the cabinets.

"It's here somewhere," he murmured. He found it tucked in the back—an old Stanley thermos with firefighter and rodeo stickers peeling at the edges. "It's time to stop running."

He set a pot of coffee brewing, then showered. When he returned to the kitchen, he filled the thermos, the rich scent flooding the room. Memories followed: camping with Caleb, long horseback rides, traveling to rodeos in other towns. He'd only had twenty-two short years with his son, but they were great ones.

He grabbed the thermos and his truck keys and headed out the door. As he drove up to the shelter, it buzzed with activity. Jon and Will hung lights while the Quiltin' Bees set up. tables. Anna and Kati chased their babies in the yard. Inside, volunteers hung pictures and curtains in the living and dining areas. Luke paused in the entryway. The peeling wallpaper had been replaced with fresh paint. The once-rotted floorboards now lay sanded smooth beneath his boots. Sunlight streamed through windows that, just months earlier, had been so caked with grime that light could barely pass through. Like this old farmhouse finding new purpose, Luke was being rebuilt from the inside out, too.

Jon walked through the door and clapped Luke on the back. "Hey, Chief. Mom's upstairs. Go on up."

"Thanks," he said, gripping the thermos as his heart hammered in his ears.

As Luke climbed the stairs, soft humming drifted down to meet him, growing louder with each step. He paused in the doorway of the Hope room, gripping the thermos tighter. Deborah stood with her back to him, smoothing her palm over a quilt scattered with wildflowers in buttercream and robin's-egg blue. Her shoulders rose and fell as she tucked corners, her humming steady and unbroken. Sunlight from the window caught in her hair, turning the edges golden. A wooden sign hung above the freshly made bed: "New mornings, gentle starts." Luke's throat tightened. He shifted his weight, and the floorboard beneath his boot groaned. Deborah's humming stopped mid-note. She turned, fingers still clutching the quilt, eyes widening when they met his.

Luke held out the old Stanley thermos, hoping she'd take it. His fingers trembled against the worn metal. "I stopped using this after Caleb died," he said, forcing the words past the tightness in his throat. "But today, it felt right again. The quilt brought back the best parts of him. The things grief stole from me included Sammy. He cleared his throat. "And you."

Deborah's lips parted, but she didn't speak. Her glistening eyes held his gaze, urging him forward. He took a step closer, then another step. There was barely space between them now, the scent of vanilla and cinnamon wrapping around him. He tucked a loose strand behind her ear, his heart pounding.

"There's so much I need to tell you. Mostly, I need to say I'm sorry. No excuses for my behavior, but can I explain?"

She nodded

"When I found the quilt at the fire, something in me unraveled. It wasn't until I stood in Caleb's room and saw the quilt my ex made for him as a baby that it hit me." He swallowed hard, fighting the tears. "The grief came like a freight train. Then the evidence from the fire, my fear of you getting hurt, and Sammy pulling away—it was too much."

Deborah took his hands and held them, grounding him.

"When you found out, and I thought I lost you, all I could do was fix the house for you to show you I was sorry."

"I so love the work you did," she said, touching his face. "And how you did it."

His cheek melted into her palm, the warmth of her skin breaking through months of loneliness. "I pushed you away because I was more afraid of losing you than of losing myself."

Deborah's fingertips traced a path down his forearm, leaving sparks in their wake. "Then don't lose me," she whispered.

Luke moved closer, his thumb brushing the corner of her mouth, pausing for just a heartbeat before he leaned in. Their lips met—gentle at first, then deeper, weighted with all those empty mornings behind them. She tasted like coffee and cinnamon. For a moment, hope slipped past his guard. When she sighed against him, her warm breath brushing his skin, whatever had been holding him back finally loosened its grip.

CHAPTER 31

 *D*eborah stood on the farmhouse porch, taking in the freshly painted sign for The Nest at Cardinal Creek sign, the colorful quilts draped over the railings, and the volunteers arranging flowers and baked goods. At the same time, people chatted and laughter rang out behind her. A banner reading *Healing Starts Here* fluttered in the breeze. Things had really come together, slowly and stubbornly, the way real healing did. Her stomach flipped as she remembered the kiss she and Luke had shared earlier.

She traced her fingers along the porch railing he'd repaired months ago, remembering how uncertain she'd been back then. It amazed her that they'd both run in opposite directions, trying to outrun pain, only to be wounded by loneliness instead. Now Luke was here by her side, steady and present, and her dream was solid beneath her feet. Her life had changed drastically since the night, she'd left Chad and gone to Liz's house, shaking, alone, with nothing but her purse and borrowed courage. Friends, love, and a lot of therapy carried her through. Because of that, she wanted to build something to help other women the way she'd been helped. She thought the best repayment would be to pay it forward.

Luke came up behind her and wrapped his arms around her. "You did this," he whispered, his warm breath brushing her ear. "I'm so proud of you."

She rested her head-on his chest. "We did this. You were with me every step of the way."

"I have something to tell you," Luke said.

Deborah stiffened, closing her eyes before turning to face him. "What?" Her voice came out breathless.

"I love you, Deborah." He kissed her then—warm, tender, and full of a passion that left no room for doubt.

When the kiss ended, Deborah struggled to catch her breath. "Oh goodness," she said, swallowing. "At sixty, this is a day of firsts."

Luke's lips twitched into a grin. "Good ones or bad ones?"

"Good. Very good." Her voice trembled. "I've never felt anything like that. It started in my head and ended with fireworks in my toes." Tears welled in her eyes. "No man has ever told me they loved me and meant it." She brushed away a tear. "I love you too, Luke Erikson."

He pulled her into his arms, and his familiar scent wrapped her in a comfort she hadn't known was possible.

Deborah rose onto her toes and whispered in his ear, "You can kiss me like that anytime you want."

Luke laughed. "That won't be a problem."

They walked hand in hand as the crowd gathered for the ribbon-cutting ceremony. The mayor shook Deborah's hand, then stepped up to the microphone.

"Today, we open this shelter, which will offer hope to women who believe hope no longer exists. Thanks to Deborah Clemmons, there is hope." She gestured toward the building. "While these women are here, they'll learn how to survive by learning skills or reclaiming ones they haven't used in years. Deborah has thought of what an abused woman truly needs." She turned to Deborah. "Thank you for having the courage to stand up."

The crowd erupted into applause, and Deborah was overcome with emotion. Luke squeezed her hand. "You got this."

As Deborah approached the podium, she shook the mayor's hand and took a steadying breath. "Over thirty years ago, I was a young, naive college freshman who went to a party. I was drugged. I was assaulted. And when I became pregnant, my very strict father forced me to marry the man who hurt me." Her voice wavered, but she pressed on. "That was when my nightmare began."

She glanced toward Jon, who nodded encouragement. "My children were victims too, hiding in a closet, seeing things no child should ever see. We suffered. And we had nowhere to go. Even after my children escaped after graduating from high school and leaving home, I stayed."

She drew a ragged breath. "I stayed because I didn't know there was another option. I even missed my daughter's funeral because he wouldn't let me go."

The crowd was silent.

"Hope didn't exist for me until my son's best friend and the fire chief rescued me. From that moment on, I began to heal. My mission is simple: no woman should suffer that long. To every woman who thinks they can't start over, our door is open to you. Hope and healing are what the Nest is about. Thank you for the support. And to Team Deborah, I love you all."

Applause thundered through the crowd. Jon rushed the stage and pulled Deborah into a fierce hug, squeezing so tight she could barely breathe.

"Jon, what's wrong?"

"I love you," he said, his tears warm against her neck.

"I love you more than you know."

"I know, Mom. You had choices when you got pregnant with me," he said, pulling back to look at her.

She smiled and wiped the tears from his cheek. "No," she said gently. "Either way, I wanted you and Shelly."

Kati stepped forward and hugged her. "You did great."

Deborah noticed Luke standing off to the side. When their eyes met, she tilted her head and motioned him over. When he joined them, she slipped her hand into his. "I have something to tell you both," she said, smiling. "Luke and I are in love. So, you'll be seeing us kissing because he's really good at it."

Jon's face twisted in horror. "Mother. Absolutely not."

Luke and Deborah laughed. "Yes. Absolutely."

"Not the loving each other part," Jon said. "I just don't need visuals. Or details. Gross." He shook his head as he walked off. "The chief kissing someone, okay, fine. The chief kissing my mom? Hard pass."

Deborah, Luke, and Kati burst into laughter. It felt wonderful.

"Deb, you made Jon speechless," Luke said.

"Yeah, that's rare," Kati added, laughing as she walked away. "Don't get into trouble, you two."

Luke wrapped an arm around Deborah and pulled her close. "You're a little frisky, aren't you?"

She laughed. "Another first. I have a lot of firsts to catch up on."

"Like what?"

She leaned in and whispered, "Making love."

Luke flushed, and Deborah's stomach tightened. *Did I say something wrong?* She searched his face.

"I assure you, when that happens, it will be special for both of us," Luke said, hugging her.

"We should probably go mingle." Deborah winked at him as they headed toward the craft barn, where Liz was giving a large crowd a tour of the areas where goods would be made for the Nest Mercantile and the farmers' market. Liz nodded at Deborah, who smiled back at her before heading inside the farmhouse to begin her own tour. The house smelled of fresh-baked goods that Tiffany had been working on all day. In the kitchen, Tiffany and JW were baking together. She stirred the dough while directing him on how to put the chocolate chip cookies on the baking sheets. Deborah stood in the doorway, smiling as she watched JW, an apron tied around his waist, scoop dough onto the pan. As Tiffany mixed the next batch of cookies, JW stole a glance at her, smiled, and said, "Like this?"

She set the bowl down, checked the tray, and nodded. "You're doing great for a guy who doesn't bake."

Luke stepped up behind Deborah and whispered, "They're waiting. Something's definitely blooming there."

Deborah nodded and backed away from the doorway. She met her tour group in the living room and proudly showed off the bedrooms, each adorned with handcrafted quilts in colors meant to offer comfort, hope, and renewal. They moved onto the porch, lined with rocking chairs and boxes of herbs for cooking healthy meals, meant to turn dinnertime into fellowship instead of fear. At the craft barn, sunlight poured over the quilting area, where machines waited for women to learn not just the art of quilting, but also the connection and friendship that came from working alongside a group of women like the ones Deborah had when she needed them most.

Throughout the tour, she noticed Luke standing in the back of the group, watching her with pride. When their eyes met, sparks flared. He winked and smiled. She winked back.

The fear and tension that once lived between them was gone. Their journey together and apart had been rough, but it proved their love could stand the test of time. His steady presence grounded her, offering a warmth and security she'd come to love.

When the tour ended, Luke joined her, beaming. "Wow. Seeing it all on a tour is amazing. You did it."

Deborah shook her head as she reached for his hand. "No, we did it."

A fter many tours and conversations that left their throats dry, Luke took respite from the celebration on the porch with Deborah. His heart swelled as he watched her dream come true when he spotted a familiar figure approaching. It was Sammy. His heart raced as he stood and went to the railing, not believing she was really walking toward them. He hurried down the steps, anxious to hug his daughter, and Sammy picked up her pace to meet him.

When they met, Luke pulled her into a tight hug. Tears streamed down his cheeks. "I'm sorry I hurt you."

"Dad, it's okay. Let's start over."

They clung to each other, neither willing to let go.

After a moment, Sammy leaned back and smiled. "Want to introduce me to Deborah?"

Luke chuckled. "I do," he said as he draped his arm around Sammy.

As they walked toward the porch, Deborah sat, smiling. Her eyes were red from tears. She stood as they ascended the stairs. "You must be Sammy," she said, extending her hand.

Sammy stepped forward and shook it. "Yes, that's me. Dad's told me so much about you." Her gaze swept across the grounds of the shelter, eyes widening with genuine admiration. "What you've built here—it's incredible."

"Well, your dad helped a lot."

Sammy ran her fingers along the smooth porch railing. "He always did have a way with wood. I bet his fingerprints are all over this place."

Deborah gestured toward the door. "Come on. Let me give you a tour."

She took Sammy's hand and led her inside, Sammy's steps light, almost eager. Luke followed close behind, smiling. He hadn't seen his daughter this animated in ages. It was as if the shelter hadn't just brought Deborah to life, but breathed energy into Luke and Sammy too.

Inside, Sammy and Deborah stopped in front of a framed piece on the wall. When Luke joined them, all the air left his lungs. It was a quilt, thoughtfully pieced and familiar. It resembled Caleb's quilt but carried new elements woven in—a family tree, its branches marked with names: Luke, Sammy, Jon, Kati, and Deborah. Luke's eyes filled with tears; the words couldn't get past the lump in his throat.

Sammy turned to him. "Dad, this is the kind of woman who stays, not just when things are good, but when they get hard. She brings torn things back together and makes them stronger. She doesn't walk away." She let out a long, ragged breath. "Like Mom did."

She wrapped her arms around Deborah. "No matter what, you're family to me. Thanks for helping my dad."

Deborah hugged her, then looked up at Luke. "I love Luke. And if he wants me, I'm not going anywhere, for better or worse."

Luke wrapped his arms around Deborah and Sammy. "I love you too, Deb," he said, kissing her forehead. "My kid is super smart."

"She is," Deborah said. She brushed her cheek with the back of her hand. "There's something I want to show you."

Sammy and Luke followed her into the bright farmhouse kitchen. Sunlight pooled across the butcher-block counters and the glass-front cabinets that Luke had helped install. In the corner where a breadbox once stood was a small display, featuring a framed photograph of three generations of Hughes women, a stack of recipe cards, and a small black notebook with masking tape on the spine.

"I found this when I first came to the farmhouse," Deborah explained, running her fingers down the spine. Three generations of

Hughes women kept recipes and diary entries of the abuse they had endured."

"This goes with the burned quilt I found after the fire," Luke said.

Deborah nodded.

Sammy leaned against her. "It's like the house knew."

"Even after the fire, the house stood tall," Deborah said. "I wanted you both to know this house exists for broken people to find their footing again. You belong in its story just as much as I do."

Luke ran his fingers across the cookbook, then studied the ladies in the photo as if he could absorb their history through his fingertips. "Thank you for showing us this. And thank you for including us."

They moved back to the entryway and stood before the quilt once more—a testament to what had been lost and lovingly mended, its blocks symbolizing friendship, courage, and home. Life could break, but with love and family, it could be mended and begin again.

EPILOGUE

*F*ive Months Later

Luke's hands were sweating as he prepared the porch for Deborah's proposal. The Quiltin' Bees, Jon, Kati, and Sammy, had worked like crazy to get everything ready, while Liz took Deborah on a much-needed spa day Luke had arranged.

Kati set a mason jar of wildflowers on the table beside two glasses and a bottle of Moscato. Beyond the house, bluebonnets spread across the field in full bloom. The steady cluck of chickens near the craft barn provided comfort to Luke's frayed nerves. What if it was too soon? They'd been together for five months and had learned the give-and-take of a relationship. There was nothing he wanted more than to wake up beside Deborah every morning and have her be the last thing he saw every night before he drifted off to sleep. He patted his pocket, checking for the ring. His hands trembled when he looked down at them.

"Caleb, you'd be proud of me. I'm doing this right," he whispered. He never imagined he'd be asking someone to marry him at sixty. He'd been fine with living the rest of his life alone until he saw the quilt in the shelter's entryway. In that moment, he knew he wanted to be with the woman who'd included him in her family tree without being married. She'd chosen him long before this day.

Jon stepped onto the porch. "Chief, I think everything is in place."

Luke turned to him. "Jon, I've told you a thousand times to call me Luke."

He clapped him on the back. "Maybe we could chat sometime about me calling you *Dad*."

Luke swallowed hard. "You're kidding, right?"

Jon shook his head. "Actually, I'm not. You and Robert Deluca have been more of a father to me than Chad ever was."

Luke put a hand on his shoulder. "It would be an honor. Besides, we already got through the teenage years."

Jon chuckled. "The drinking and not listening on the job."

"That's in the past," Luke said. "It's behind you. Even then, you were saving lives."

Jon smiled. "Look at us now. I know you'll love my mom, so this makes me happy." As he walked away, he glanced back. "Oh, don't forget you're a grandpa too. And another one's on the way."

"Wait—what?" Luke said.

"Kati's pregnant," Jon said, stepping off the porch. "But that's for later. I think I hear Momma D's car."

Luke turned as Liz's car came up the driveway. His heart pounded and sweat dripped beneath his pressed white shirt. He wiped his hands on his Wranglers and swallowed hard. Deborah stepped out of the car and smiled as she took in the lights strung across the porch. She narrowed her eyes when they landed on Luke.

"Luke Erikson, are you up to something?" she asked, smiling.

"Maybe," he said, walking to the steps and offering his hand. "Come sit with me." He led her to the spot where he'd repaired the railing months ago. Draped over it was Caleb's quilt, something Luke kept close for those hard days, a reminder that Caleb was never far and that Deborah loved him. She took a seat, her eyes scanning the glowing lights, the fading afternoon sun, and the bluebonnets, which he knew were her favorite. Luke dropped to one knee and took her hand. Deborah gasped, covering her mouth. Behind them, muffled laughter and excited whispers carried from their giddy, not-so-hidden audience, who were supposed to be making themselves scarce.

Luke drew a deep breath. "Deborah, our journey really began that night at the hospital. I was really into you even then. We've both suffered the loss of a child and a spouse, and we survived. We learned the importance of family, community, and forgiveness. I knew I loved you when, despite your own pain, you brought my son back to life with a quilt. When you made a second quilt and hung it in the shelter—when you included Sammy and me in your family tree—I knew I wanted to marry you." He reached into his pocket and pulled out the ring. "Would you make me the happiest man on Earth by becoming my wife? I want to spend the rest of my days with you."

Tears streamed down Deborah's face. "Yes...a million times, yes."

Luke wrapped her in his arms and gave her a passionate kiss, the kind that curled toes and left them breathless.

When they finally broke apart, Deborah wiped the tears from her eyes. "That's another first for me," she said, running a finger down his face. "Someone asking me to marry him because he loves me."

"And I do, Deborah. I love you."

"I love you too."

Deborah's eyes were still damp with tears when she turned to her quiet onlookers—who were anything but quiet—wiping their eyes and cheering for her. This porch had once been a broken place. Now it was a place where her life could begin again.

"Oh, there's a couple more things," Luke said, looking at Jon, who nodded. "It seems our son Jon is going to make us grandparents again."

Deborah's eyes widened. "Our son? Kati's having a baby?"

Jon stepped forward. "I asked Luke if I could call him dad. And you are going to be a grandma again."

Deborah's heart soared. Her son finally had a good man in his life—someone steady, someone he could lean on, even now, as a grown man. She turned to Luke. "I'm gonna be a grandma again."

Jon said, "And our new kid doesn't need an aunt or uncle the same age." His face twisted. "Oh God, why did I say that?"

The group burst into laughter.

Luke squeezed Deborah's hand. "Grab a jacket and lock up. I have another surprise."

She went inside, intrigued by what he had planned. She slipped on a jacket and turned on the porch light. *Some lights never go out...They find new homes to shine from.*

As she started out the door, Luke handed her Caleb's quilt. She ran her hands over the quilt's surface. Their journey had been long and painful, but today they have love, family, and a community that believed in them. She carefully laid the quilt on the bench beneath the hanging quilt in the entryway. She looked up and smiled. Life could bring pain, but through love, it could be pieced back together into something even more beautiful.

When Deborah stepped back onto the porch, she stopped short. Waiting in the driveway was a party bus with the words "She Said Yes" painted on the windows. Everyone piled onto the bus. Deborah looked around at all the people who meant the world to her, who stood behind her, providing light and love, when life was at its darkest. She looked at her son, whom she once believed hated her, but it turned out he loved her so deeply that it hurt to watch her suffer. Today, she welcomed Luke into his life with the highest honor of all: Dad.

When they arrived in town, they entered Saddle Up Bar and Grill. There was a banner stretched across the room that read "*Congratulations, Deborah and Luke.*" Deborah pressed a hand to her chest, overwhelmed in the best way by the kindness and love, all woven together into one beautiful quilt.

Luke leaned in and whispered, "For the rest of your life, you don't walk into anything alone."

~

As the celebration for Luke and Deborah's engagement moved into full swing, Tiffany drifted between tables, offering her congratulations with a smile she'd perfected years ago. It was the same smile she'd learned to plaster on her face when she was married to her high school sweetheart—a man who abused her for much of their marriage. His cruelty worsened when she gained weight and couldn't give him a child. She wrapped her cardigan around herself. Rooms filled with women like Kati—skinny, beautiful, effortless—made her want to crawl out of her own skin. She'd once been the cheerleader with the perfect body. Then a health issue stole that from her, replacing it with weight she couldn't lose. Tiffany edged toward a corner table where she could disappear. Head down, she set her drink on the table and tugged her cardigan closed as she sat down.

Across the room, Deborah and Luke slow danced, his lips brushing her temple. The sight twisted something deep inside Tiffany. She remembered her husband sneering, saying that no one would ever want someone so big. Who would want to take someone to bed who disgusted them when they were wearing clothes? During the last four years of their marriage, he openly cheated on her in their home. Tiffany turned a blind eye until the girl became pregnant. She twisted her empty ring finger, avoiding her reflection in the mirrored wall behind the bar across from where she sat.

Tiffany looked up toward JW, the incredibly handsome bartender with fire-red hair. His shirt sleeves were rolled to his forearms, which flexed as he lifted a case of beer. The sleeves of his shirt stretched across his biceps. He smiled easily as he worked, talking to customers. She remembered the day of the grand opening, when they'd baked cookies together. She'd expected to spend the day working alone, but he came in, tied on an apron, and helped her until every last mess was cleaned up. Her stomach had fluttered when he'd wiped a smudge of flour from her nose.

When JW's eyes met hers, she looked down at her drink, caught in the familiar spiral, wondering whether she should stay or leave. The longer she stayed, the more she risked rejection or cruel remarks about her body. She longed for a man to love her and want to be with her for who she was, not how she looked. As she looked out onto the dance floor, she watched Jon dancing with Kati. The way he looked at her made her feel as if she were the only person in the room. Tiffany had longed for that kind of love for years, but she was sure she'd never get it. The health condition that kept her from losing weight, mixed with eating binges brought on by anxiety or depression, made it feel like a cycle that never ended.

Lost in thought, she didn't notice JW approaching.

He took a seat beside her and smiled. "You look beautiful tonight," he said.

Heat crept up Tiffany's neck into her face. *He's just being nice to me. He doesn't really think that.* "Thanks," she murmured.

"I need to rest my feet," she said lightly. "These heels are killing me."

She huffed a quiet laugh despite herself.

JW smiled, his green eyes crinkling at the corners. "I'd like to dance with you when I get a break. I want to spend more time with you. I really enjoyed baking together."

Tiffany bit her bottom lip, unsure what to say. When she looked up, Liz, Deborah, Sissy, and Peggy Sue were giving her a thumbs up. "I don't know...I don't dance very well."

JW leaned in and whispered, "Darlin', I used to ride bulls. You stepping on my toes won't hurt a bit. Besides, I'm a good leader."

The heat from his breath raised the hair on her neck. She bit her bottom lip and gave a noncommittal nod.

He walked back to the bar, his swagger confident. She sat there, berating herself for even considering it. They were too different. She looked at Deborah and Luke, their foreheads touching as they slow danced. She remembered the hurdles they crossed to find love.

When a slow song began, JW approached Tiffany and held out his hand. "Do you feel like stepping out there? I want to be the one you dance with."

Tiffany's heart skipped a beat. She stared at him wide-eyed, wanting to say yes but afraid it would lead to ridicule for her large hips and thighs. After a moment, she said, "Maybe."

She stood, placing her hand in JW's, silencing her ex-husband's voice with a single fragile thought: *I am worthy of love.* JW's fingers curled around hers, and her breath caught. She glanced toward the Quiltin' Bees, who smiled and clapped as she stepped onto the dance floor.

Maybe my story isn't over yet either.

ACKNOWLEDGMENTS

This book would not exist without my husband, who never lets me quit, even in the face of a storm. Thank you for reminding me why the story matters when writing gets hard.

To my five children, my life is better because you are in it. Thank you for your love and support before, during, and after each story. I am proud to be your mom.

To Evelyn Dodson, who pulled out all the stops to get this book edited. Thank you from the bottom of my heart. To my work besties Deborah and Tootsie Pop, thank you.

And to the women whose stories of courage and resilience inspired Deborah's journey—this book was written with you in mind.

RESOURCES

If You or Someone You Love Needs Help

If you are experiencing domestic violence or feel unsafe in your home, you are not alone. Help is available.

National Domestic Violence Hotline

Call: 1-800-799-7233 (SAFE)

Text: START to 88788

Online Chat: www.thehotline.org

If you are in immediate danger, please call 911.

Local Support

If you are in South Texas, confidential help is available through:

The Purple Door

24-Hour Hotline: 361-881-8888

Website: www.purpledoortx.org

ABOUT THE AUTHOR

I am a romance author who writes emotionally rich, small-town love stories rooted in resilience, community, and second chances.

Raised in Missouri, I spent weekends on my grandparents' farm in Southeast Missouri, where I developed a deep love for small-town life. I now live and write in South Texas, where my work is shaped by family history rooted in farming, close-knit communities, and the quiet strength found in everyday life. I grew up surrounded by books and by my grandfather's stories of growing up during the Depression, his time in the service, and how he fell in love with my grandmother. From those stories, I learned that love isn't always loud, but it is lasting—lessons passed down by an extraordinary storyteller.

Quilting is at the heart of both my life and my writing. As the owner of Cardinal Creek Quilting in Orange Grove, Texas, I see quilting as a form of storytelling—taking pieces of the past and stitching them into something meaningful, warm, and enduring. That same belief threads through my novels, where love is hard-won, healing, and always worth the risk. It's creating family heirlooms one stitch at a time.

ALSO BY ANGIE COLE

Their Shattered Hearts

Their Mended Hearts